THE DO-OVER

Also by
Lynn Painter

Better Than the Movies

THE DO-OVER

LYNN PAINTER

SIMON & SCHUSTER BFYR
NEW YORK LONDON TORONTO SYDNEY NEW DELHI

SIMON & SCHUSTER BFYR
An imprint of Simon & Schuster Children's Publishing Division
1230 Avenue of the Americas, New York, New York 10020

For information about special discounts for bulk purchases, please contact Simon & Schuster
Special Sales at 1-866-506-1949 or business@simonandschuster.com.
The Simon & Schuster Speakers Bureau can bring authors to your live event.
For more information or to book an event, contact the Simon & Schuster Speakers Bureau
at 1-866-248-3049 or visit our website at www.simonspeakers.com.
Interior design by Tom Daly
The text for this book was set in EB Garamond.
Printed and bound in the UK using 100% renewable electricity at CPI Group (UK) Ltd
First Edition
2 4 6 8 10 9 7 5 3 1
Library of Congress Cataloging-in-Publication Data
Names: Painter, Lynn, author.
Title: The do-over / Lynn Painter.
Description: First edition. | New York : Simon & Schuster BFYR, [2022] |
Summary: Sixteen-year-old Emilie, stuck in a cosmic Groundhog/Valentine's Day
nightmare where she discovers her family is splitting up and her boyfriend is cheating
on her, decides to embark upon The Day of No Consequences, but when her repetitive
day suddenly ends, she must face the consequences of her actions.
Identifiers: LCCN 2022002446 (print) | LCCN 2022002447 (ebook) |
ISBN 9781534478862 (hardcover) | ISBN 9781534478886 (ebook)
Subjects: CYAC: Dating (Social customs) Fiction. | Family problems—Fiction. |
Valentine's Day—Fiction. | LCGFT: Romance fiction. | Novels.
Classification: LCC PZ7.1.P352 Do 2022 (print) | LCC PZ7.1.P352 (ebook) |
DDC [Fic]—dc23
LC record available at https://lccn.loc.gov/2022002446
LC ebook record available at https://lccn.loc.gov/2022002447

For
The Lonely,
The Daydreamers,
The ones who find their friends
between the pages of books—

YOU MATTER, and your happy ending WILL come.
Sometimes the wait is just longer in real life than in fiction.

THE DO-OVER

PROLOGUE

Valentine's Day Eve

When Valentine's Day rears its sugary-sweet, heart-shaped head, there are two types of people who receive it.

First, you have the full-on lovers of the holiday, hopeless romantics obsessed with the idea of love itself. These individuals believe in fate and soul mates and the notion that the universe sends out winged, mostly naked babies to shoot arrows into select single people, thus infecting them with true love that may cause drowsiness and a massive happily-ever-after.

Then you have the cynics, those curmudgeonly souls who call it a "Hallmark holiday" and complain that if true love exists, its proclamations should be expressed spontaneously on any random day and without the expectation of gifts.

Well, I am neither—and both—of these people.

I *do* believe that Valentine's Day is an overcommercialized Hallmark holiday, but I also think there's nothing wrong with enjoying the materialistic side effects of the celebration. Bring on the chocolates and flowers, and throw in a gift card to the local bookstore while you're at it.

And yes, I believe in the existence of true love. But I strongly suspect that fate and soul mates and love at first sight are concepts created by the same people still waiting for Santa to show up with that puppy they asked for when they were seven years old.

In other words, I *absolutely* expect love in my life, but there is no way I'm going to sit around and wait for fate to make it happen.

Fate is for suckers.

Love is for planners.

My parents got married on Valentine's Day after a month of dating. They fell passionately, wildly in love when they were eighteen. Immediately, and with zero consideration of real-world facts like compatibility and differing temperaments.

While this foolish behavior led to, well, *me,* it also led to years of disagreements and shouting matches that were the soundtrack of my childhood before their relationship devolved into a screaming breakup next to the tiny cherub fountain on our front lawn.

But their inability to use logic in the face of feelings gave me the gift of clarity, of learning from their mistakes. Instead of dating boys who make me swoon but are totally wrong for me, I only date boys who hit their marks on my pros-and-cons sheet. I only date boys who on paper (or an Excel spreadsheet) share at least five common interests with me, have a broad outline of their ten-year plan, and dress like they aren't prone to random outbursts of basketball.

Which was why Josh was boyfriend perfection.

He X'd every single box on my pre-boyfriend checklist the very first time we met, and he'd been overperforming every day for the entire three months we'd been together.

So, as I stood in front of my closet on that Valentine's Eve, selecting the perfect outfit for the following day, I was excited. Not about nude, armed infants or epic cosmic surprises, but about my plans. I had the entire day plotted out—the gift, the words I would say, the appropriate timing of both—and it was going to be exactly what I wanted it to be.

Perfection.

Why would I wait for fate to lend a hand, when I had two perfectly capable hands of my own?

CONFESSION #1

When I was ten, I started putting confession strips into a box in my closet so that if anything happened to me, people would know that I was more than just the quiet girl who followed the rules.

THE FIRST VALENTINE'S DAY

When my alarm went off on Valentine's Day, I was smiling. To start with, I actually had a boyfriend, and he wasn't just a *meh* boyfriend, either. Josh was smart and handsome and arguably the most likely student at Hazelwood High to succeed in a big way. Every time we studied together and he put on his Ivy League tortoiseshell glasses, I swore that my heart actually folded over on itself, causing the sweet pinching feeling that shot warmth through each and every one of my nerve endings.

In hindsight, that feeling was probably some sort of atrial defect caused by my steady diet of black coffee and energy drinks. But I didn't know that yet.

I pushed back the covers and climbed out of bed, ignoring the sound of Logan's open-mouthed sleep-breathing from the other side of the mattress. My three-year-old stepbrother liked to sneak into my room and sleep with me because he pretty much thought I was amazing.

And he was right. Because as I walked over to where my planner sat open on my desk, I *felt* amazing. I hummed "Lover" as I put on my glasses and consulted the day's list.

To-Do List—February 14
Reorganize scholarship planning binder
Study for Lit test
Remind Mom to email copy of insurance card to office
Remind Dad of parent-teacher conferences and make sure he puts it on his calendar
Send email to internship adviser
Exchange gifts with Josh
Say "I love you" to Josh!!!!!!!!!!!

I lingered on the last one, picking up my pen and doodling hearts around it. I'd never said *those* words romantically before, and since our three-month anniversary happened to fall on THE day, it was almost as if the universe had scheduled it *for* me.

Filled with buzzy excitement, I went into the bathroom and turned on the shower. As I stuck my hand under the stream of water to test the temperature, I heard:

"Em, are you almost done in there?"

Ugh. I rolled my eyes and stepped under the water. "I just got in here."

"Joel needs to go potty." Lisa, my dad's wife, sounded like her mouth was planted on the door. "Bad."

"Can't he go upstairs?" I poured shampoo into my hand and rubbed it on my head. I adored the twins, but living with toddlers sucked sometimes.

"Your dad's in there."

Sighing, I said, "Give me two minutes." I rushed through the rest of the shower, refusing to let the disruption ruin my mood. After toweling off and throwing on my robe, I ran past Lisa and a squirmy Joel, back to my basement bedroom. I breezed through blowing out my too-curly hair—still humming love songs—before plugging in the iron and steaming out the pesky crease on the right sleeve of my dress. I knew my best friend, Chris, would roll his eyes and tell me I was being hyper-anal, but why leave the crease when it takes a mere two minutes to get it out?

I got dressed and ran upstairs to scarf a protein bar before leaving for school. As I ripped open the wrapper, my eyes wandered over to the pie pan that was sitting beside the microwave like temptation incarnate. Yes, the leftover piece of French silk pie would taste amazing, I thought as a took a big bite of peanut butter and whey, but a slice of sugar and carbs was no way to start the day.

I looked away from the chocolate dessert and focused on chewing the dry protein bar.

"Good Lord, slow down." My dad was sitting at the table, reading the paper and drinking coffee like he had every single day of my life. His hair was flame-red, the potent original to my watered-down coppery-brown version. He gave me a smart-ass smile and said, "No one here knows the Heimlich."

"Isn't that, like, a parental requirement or something? How do you and Lisa have kids and no Heimlich-ing skills?"

He stared directly at my overfilled mouth. "We foolishly assumed our offspring wouldn't suck down food like sows."

"You know what happens when you assume, right?"

"Yeah." He winked and went back to the paper. "Someone's an ass."

"Oh, come on, you guys." Lisa came into the kitchen with Logan on one hip, Joel on the other. "Can we please not swear around the babies?"

"They weren't in here," I said through a mouthful of bar, "when he said it."

"And technically," my dad said, throwing me another wink, "'ass' isn't a bad word. It's a donkey." I grinned while Lisa looked at me as if she wished I would disappear.

I'd been splitting time between my mom's and my dad's since they divorced when I was in elementary school, but I was still just a nomad in the way. At both of their houses. To be fair, Lisa wasn't the stereotypical evil stepmother. She taught kindergarten, made my dad happy, and she was a really good mom to the boys. I just always felt like I was in her way.

I grabbed my backpack and my car keys, threw out a goodbye, and ran for the door.

The sun was bright even though the air was freezing, and we'd gotten a dusting of snow overnight, but it looked like my dad had already scraped my windows. I heard my phone from the depths of my bag, and pulled it out just in time to see that Chris was FaceTiming me.

I answered and there were my two closest friends, smiling at me from in front of the red lockers of the junior hallway. I smiled at my phone's cracked screen, at my favorite faces in the whole world.

Roxane had dark brown skin, cheekbones for days, and the kind of eyelashes that suburban moms tried to emulate with extensions, and Chris had heavy-lidded brown eyes, flawless porcelain skin, and curly black hair that stuck up in the most perfect way. If they weren't genuinely amazing humans, it'd be hard not to hate them for their good looks.

"You're at school already?" I asked.

"Yes, and guess what we just saw?" Chris asked, waggling his eyebrows.

"I want to tell," Rox said, moving in front of him on the screen.

"I saw, so I tell." Chris nudged her out of the way. "Josh is already here and I saw him put a gift bag in his locker."

I screeched and tiny-clapped before hopping into the old Astro van that my dad insisted "had character." "Big or small?"

"Medium," Chris said, and then Rox chimed in with, "Which is good because too big just means a crappy stuffed animal, and too small means a coupon for free hugs. Medium is good. Medium is the dream."

I laughed. Their enthusiasm made me happy because up until lately, they'd been anti-Josh. They said he acted like he was better than everyone else, but I knew it was only because they didn't really *know* know him. He was just so smart and confident that it was sometimes *misconstrued* as arrogance.

Hopefully this meant that they were reconsidering their opinions.

Rox's boyfriend, Trey, popped up in the background and waved. I waved back before I ended the call, dropped the phone, started the van, and sped toward school. Finneas crooned sweetly out of the speakers, and I sang along at full volume to every single word of "Let's Fall in Love for the Night."

I couldn't wait to see Josh. He'd refused to give me a hint as to what my present was, so I had no idea what to expect. Flowers? Jewelry? Even though it'd taken two full coffee shop paychecks, I bought him the Coach band he wanted for his watch. Yes, I was broke now, but seeing his face light up when he opened it would make it worth it.

My phone buzzed on the passenger seat and at the first red light I glanced over.

Josh: Happy VD. Are you here yet? And what do you want first—poem or gift?

Poem, definitely.

I smiled, and the light turned to green. As I cruised through our suburban neighborhood, the song on the radio (my antiquated van didn't even have Bluetooth capability) switched to something screamy and metal, so I started scanning for a tune worthy of the momentous day.

Billy Joel? Nope.

Green Day? Negative.

Adele? Hmmm . . . that might just work—

I glanced down at the dashboard to turn up the volume, then looked up just in time to see that the truck in front of me had stopped suddenly. I stood on the brake, but instead of stopping, my tires locked and I began sliding. *Shit, shit, shit!*

There was nothing I could do. I slammed into the back of the truck. Hard. I braced myself for the car behind me to hit, but it thankfully stopped in time.

Barely breathing, I looked through the windshield to see my hood was totally crumpled. But the person driving the truck was stepping out, which hopefully meant they were okay. I grabbed my phone, opened the door, and got out to see the damage.

"You were texting, weren't you?"

"What?" I looked up, and there was Nick Stark, my Chemistry lab partner. "Of course not!"

His eyes dipped down to my hand, to my phone, and he raised an eyebrow.

What were the odds that I would've hit someone I knew? And not just someone I knew, but someone who'd never really seemed to like me. I mean, technically he'd never been a jerk to me, but he hadn't ever been friendly, either.

On the first day of Chem, when I'd introduced myself, instead of saying *Nice to meet you* or *I'm Nick,* he'd just looked at me for a few seconds before saying "Okay" and going back to looking at his phone. When I'd accidentally spilled my energy drink on our lab table a few months ago, instead of saying *It's okay* like a normal human when I'd apologized, Nick Stark had stared right at me and, without smiling, said, "Maybe you should lay off the caffeine."

The guy was kind of an enigma. I'd never seen him around outside of school, and he didn't really have a clique or friend group that I was aware of. Even though we were juniors, I still didn't have enough information to figure out how to classify him.

And I hated that.

"You were the one who was stopped in the middle of a busy street," I said.

"There was a squirrel crossing," he replied in a near-growl.

"Listen, Nick." I took a deep breath, found my mental mantra—*You are on top of this, you are on top of this*—and managed, "Don't blame—"

His eyes narrowed. "I'm sorry. You are . . . ?"

I crossed my arms and squinted *my* eyes. "Are you serious?"

"You go to Hazelwood?"

"I'm your *lab partner.*" Was he messing with me? The guy never really spoke other than the occasional one-syllable response, but still. "We've shared a table in Chem the entire year . . . ? Ringing any bells here?"

"That's you?" His eyes roamed over my face like he wasn't sure if he believed me or not.

"Yes, that's me!" I was losing my cool because I had very big plans for the day, and this surly boy was holding me up from making my perfect Valentine's Day happen.

And also not remembering me, which . . . what the hell?

He said, "You have insurance, right?"

"This is unbelievable," I muttered, looking at his old red truck that didn't appear to look any worse in the back than it did all over. "It doesn't look like there's any damage. From this end, at least."

"Insurance information, please." He held out his palm and waited. I kind of wanted to push him for his attitude of driverly superiority, but he was a lot taller than me and had broad shoulders that didn't look like they'd budge easily.

So instead, I leaned into the van and snatched my backpack from the seat before opening the glove box and pulling out the small binder I put together the day I got the van. I flipped to the yellow divider—the "In Case of Accident" section—and slid the insurance card out of its protective sleeve.

He took it and his eyes narrowed. "You keep it in a notebook?"

"It's not a notebook, it's an emergency binder."

"And the difference is . . . ?"

"It's just a way to keep everything protected and organized."

"Everything?" He looked at the binder and said, "What else is in there?"

"A list of mechanics, tow truck companies, first aid instructions . . ." I rolled my eyes and said, "Do you really want me to continue?"

Nick stared at me for a solid five seconds before muttering what sounded like *Hell no* as he pulled out his phone and snapped a photo of the insurance card. After that, he insisted on calling the police when my van started smoking. I tried to insist that it was drivable—I needed to get to school and hear my poem, dammit—until the engine went up in flames and the firemen had to put it out.

Ugh, my dad was going to kill me.

And then my mom was going to pick apart my corpse until there was nothing left.

And I wasn't going to have time for Josh's poem until after first block.

"Here." Nick came over from his truck and held out a coat. "I know it doesn't match your outfit, but it's warm."

I wanted to say no because I blamed him for this disaster, but I *was* chilled. My classic pink Ralph Lauren oxford dress had been too cute to cover with a coat, but that'd been before I was standing out in the cold, watching my vehicle become a bonfire.

"Thanks," I said as I slid into the army-green jacket that nearly went down to my knees.

Nick crossed his arms and surveyed the scene of emergency responders cleaning up the wreckage. "At least you already had a clunker."

"I think you mean 'classic,'" I said, even though I hated my creeper van. There was just something about Nick's attitude—and the fact that he didn't recognize me—that made me want to argue with him.

He crossed his arms and said, "You doing okay here?"

I fake-smiled and bit out, "Wonderful."

I glanced down at my phone. No notifications. Neither of my parents answered when I tried calling them, which wasn't surprising. I desperately wanted to text Josh, but the last thing I needed to do was remind Nick that I might've been distracted when I hit him.

The police officer got there quickly after the firemen and was relatively nice as he wrote me the citation that was sure to get me grounded.

Ugh.

Nick looked at me as the tow truck disappeared with my van. "You want a ride? I mean, we're going to the same place and you're dressed like *that*."

I looked down at my bare legs and brown leather booties, clenching my teeth to keep them from chattering. "Like what?"

"Ridiculously."

"Hey."

He actually grinned at my expression. "I wasn't impugning your fashion choices—you look very, um, *polo player's girlfriend,* don't worry. I was merely referring to your bare legs and the fact that it's, like, twenty degrees outside. Ride? Yes?"

I swallowed and buried my frozen nose in the coat collar. It smelled like cold and motor oil. "Um, yeah. I guess."

"You mean *thank you?*"

That actually made me smile a little. "Thank you so much, my amazing savior."

"That's more like it."

I climbed into his truck, slammed the heavy door, and buckled my seat belt. It rumbled to a loud start before he turned off his flashers and headed in the direction of the school. Whatever angry band he had blaring from that antiquated stereo system was atrocious and way too loud.

"What *is* this?" I turned down the garbage music and held my frozen fingers in front of the vents that were haltingly blowing out warm air.

"If you're referring to the music, it's Metallica. How do you not know that?"

"Um, because I have taste and I'm not a hundred?"

That made his mouth slide into a smirk. "What is *your* go-to driving album, then, lab partner?"

I was currently super into Fleetwood Mac's *Rumours* album but I shrugged and said, "I kind of just listen to the radio."

"You poor, quality-music-starved girl."

"In this instance it would be poor, unintelligible-barking-starved girl."

"Just listen." He cranked it back up and smiled over at me. "Their rage feels good, doesn't it? Feel it, Bunson Burner—breathe it in."

"I'm good." *Bunson Burner.* I shook my head but couldn't hold in the smile as the word "blackened" was grunted out by Metallica all over his truck. "I'll just snort my own rage, thank you."

After a minute he turned the music back down and hit his blinker as the high school approached. He moved the shifter next to the steering wheel, popping it into second gear for the turn, and I think I sounded a little too excited when I said, "This truck is three-on-the-tree?"

He crinkled his brows together. "How do *you* know about three-on-the-tree?"

I crossed my arms and felt kind of cool. "I know lots of things."

His mouth went into a filthy smile. "Well, that is certainly nice to know."

Did he think I was flirting? "I didn't mean it like *that.*"

He chuckled a little *huh-huh-huh* laugh that was deep and rumbly.

My cheeks were burning and I said, "My dad had a car with that. Forget it."

He pulled around to the junior parking lot. "Did he teach you how to drive it?"

"What?" I reached down and pulled my lip gloss out of my backpack.

"The car with standard transmission on the column. Did your dad teach you to drive it?"

"Nope." I pulled down his visor and ran the wand over my mouth, remembering all the times my dad had promised to teach me but ended up getting too busy with work and the twins to actually follow through on his word.

"That's a shame." His truck fishtailed as he turned at the end of the first row. "Everyone should know how to drive a manual transmission."

Yeah, they should. I flipped the visor back up and pictured the stick shift in my dad's Porsche, the decades-old project car he'd always said would be mine when he finished it.

He'd finished it three years ago.

"By the way, did you tell your parents that your machine burned down?" He gave my phone a sideways glance, like he was waiting for me to start texting.

I looked out the window. The fact that neither of my parents had called back was nice in a way, as it postponed the immense amount of trouble I was about to be in. But it also stung a bit that they weren't concerned about why I was contacting them when I should have been at school. Instead of explaining all those complicated emotions, I said, "No, I thought I'd save it as a surprise."

"Good call." He slid into a snow-packed spot, and I reminded myself that it was still Valentine's Day. I may have lost my car and would soon be destroyed by my parents, but in a few minutes I'd be with Josh. He'd read me poetry, give me my present, I would say those magical three words, and everything else would melt away.

"Well," I said, opening the door after he pulled to a stop and cut the engine. "Have a happy Valentine's Day."

"Fuck that," Nick said, biting out the words as if I'd wished him a happy castration as he got out and slammed his door. "I fucking hate this day."

I stepped out of the truck, took off his coat, and held it out to him when he came around. "Well, then, just have a day, I guess."

"Sure," he said, tossing the coat into the back of the vehicle. "Thanks."

CONFESSION #2

I once pulled a hotel's fire alarm because my parents were sleeping in and I wanted to get to Disneyland before there was a line to see Belle.

"Emilie, I have a note here that says you need to go to the office." Mr. Seward, my second-hour teacher, waved a hall pass in front of his face.

"Oh." I put down the book I wasn't supposed to be reading, stood and grabbed my bag from the floor beside me. I'd been in the middle of a fairly intense sex scene, so my cheeks instantly got hot as I felt porn-busted.

"Oooh—Emmie's in trouble."

I smiled at Noah, Josh's best friend. He was a tennis player who'd never said a single word to me until I started dating Josh. Who, coincidentally, I missed this morning because Nick and I got into school just in time for first hour. So far, this day was not going how it was supposed to.

"You know me," I said to Noah as I shoved my book in my bag, grabbed the pass, and exited the classroom. I missed Nick Stark's oversized jacket as I walked down the empty hallway. I'd been frozen solid since the minute I'd handed it back to him in the parking lot. I knew Josh wouldn't have anything that utilitarian in his locker—his light-knit navy cardigan was as warm as it'd get—but I was so cold that I'd probably swing by to pick it up.

I looked down at my phone, but the only message I had was from my awful boss at work, trying to get me to come in when I wasn't scheduled.

Not on Valentine's Day, sir. Or *Stankbreath*, which is what I referred to him in my head.

Which sounded mean, but he really *was* awful. He'd been known to clip his fingernails in the break room, scroll through Tinder while working even though he was married, and he'd never heard of the term "personal space." How else would I know so much about his breath?

I put the phone in my dress pocket and wondered what the office summoning was about, but I wasn't worried. I'd just been notified the previous week that I'd won the Alice P. Hardy Excellence in Journalism High School Fellowship, so it was probably about that.

I still had to pinch myself over that one. Not only had I been accepted into the prestigious summer journalism program, where I'd get to stay in an apartment in Chicago and work alongside fifty other high school students for an entire month, but it was going to be 100 percent paid for.

I was beyond excited for the work, but even more thrilled about how good it would look on my college applications. Most of my friends didn't care about that yet, but I was going to make sure I got into the college of my choice if it killed me.

"Hi, Emilie." Mrs. Svoboda, the school secretary, smiled and gestured for me to go to the counseling office. "Go on back to Mr. Kessler's office. He's waiting for you."

"Thanks." I went back and lifted my hand to knock on the counselor's half-closed office door when he bellowed, "Here she is now. Come in, Emilie."

I walked into his office and saw the woman who'd interviewed me for the fellowship. She was sitting in a chair, holding a cup of coffee and giving me hard-core eye contact.

"Oh. Um, hi." I hadn't expected to see her, but I quickly recovered and went in for a firm handshake. "Nice to see you again."

The woman—Mrs. Bowen—fumbled for my hand and looked shocked by the shake. "You too, though I wish we were meeting under better circumstances."

Even with that warning, I didn't expect something *bad* bad. I expected her to say I needed one more reference, or perhaps that it was imperative they get a headshot from me stat.

I perched on the edge of the chair in the corner. "Oh?"

"Unfortunately there was an error in the scoring of fellowship applications. It has come to our attention that some numbers were added incorrectly."

My heartbeat picked up a little. "Which means . . . ?"

"Which means that you actually *didn't* win a fellowship."

It sounds cliché, but I felt the blood drain from my face. Like, I *felt* it. I saw sparkly stars in front of my eyes and my hearing turned furry as the ramifications of her statement sunk in.

No getting far away for the summer.

No prestigious program to list on my college applications.

Being left behind while Josh attended *his* prestigious summer program.

No Northwestern.

"Emilie?" Mr. Kessler narrowed his eyes and looked like he was afraid I was going to faint. *As if.* There were a hundred things I felt like doing at that moment—most of them violent—and fainting wasn't one of them.

I tucked my hair behind my ears and worked for a polite smile. "So that's the final and confirmed tally, then?"

Mrs. Bowen's lips turned down and she nodded. "We are so terribly sorry."

"Well." I shrugged and smiled. "What can you do, right? These things happen. I appreciate the opportunity."

The woman tilted her head, like she couldn't believe I wasn't freaking out. *Trust me, lady, I've learned that freaking out never changes a thing.* She added, "I just cannot apologize enough, Emilie."

"I understand." I cleared my throat and stood. "Thank you for letting me know."

I left with my head held high and went straight to the bathroom. I hated crying, but there was a huge ball of devastation sitting right on top of my sternum that threatened to knock me over if I didn't take a minute.

I texted both of my parents and neither of them responded.

It was so undignified, sitting fully clothed on a toilet and crying, but it was just such a blow. Everything I'd been working toward might've just been ripped out of my hands.

Because when the topic of college was first broached after the divorce, my parents were very clear that if I planned on going away to school, I was going to have to find scholarships. The dissolution of their marriage had apparently wreaked havoc on their savings, what with all the fighting through lawyers and such, so there was nothing set aside for my education.

I'd taken that to heart and dedicated myself to educational excellence. Since that fateful conversation, I'd earned all As, thrown myself into writing for the school newspaper, and I'd taken the ACT five times even though my score had been exemplary the first time.

Every little point counted, after all.

But in order to go somewhere like Northwestern—my dream school—without my parents bankrolling the excursion, I needed perfection. Impeccable extracurriculars, letters of recommendation, a plethora of volunteer hours. I needed everything.

And even *with* those, I might still fall short.

The other thing that I didn't like to admit to myself was that I didn't want Josh to beat me. We had the same GPA—the same weighted 4.4 GPA—and it irked me when he pulled ahead. I couldn't stand the smug look that crossed his face when he was winning, and if Josh was doing better than me, affection was *not* the feels coming over me.

I spent a few more minutes getting control of my emotions

before I wiped at my eyes and stood. It was Valentine's Day, dammit. I was going to soak up every glorious minute of *that* and not think about the rest until tomorrow.

There were two more written-in-red events left on my to-do list—gift exchange and saying those three big words. I was going to throw myself into checking off those boxes and forgetting the rest.

CONFESSION #3

I have a perfect fake ID.

Between classes, I stopped at Josh's friend Blake's locker to ask if he'd seen my boyfriend. I'd yet to connect with him in person on Valentine's Day, and I desperately needed to see his face. There was no way for us to have the perfect day I'd planned if we weren't together.

Blake was leaning against the wall and texting when I said, "Have you seen Josh? He's usually hanging out in the commons between classes but I don't see him anywhere."

"Nah." He looked over my head, appearing—as always—like he didn't even see me. I'd never figured out if Blake hated me or if I scared him, and it drove me to distraction. Chris always said I had serious issues with needing people to like me, and I always considered him to be wrong except for when I was in the presence of Blake.

He said, "No idea where he is."

"Oh. Well, thanks." I turned away and felt silly just for existing. Blake was one of those guys that made you feel that way.

I first met Josh when we were both selected to be tutors for the Math Lab. We showed up in the counselors' office at the exact same minute, and I almost swallowed my tongue when he smiled and held the door for me. I knew who he was, but then again, who didn't?

Josh was the It boy of the educational excellence crowd.

Not only was he a ringer for that swoony actor whose name was spelled Timothee with two Es, but he had his life together. Debate, DECA, Mock Trial—he wasn't just *in* those activities, he was the best at them.

And he knew it.

Josh had the confident swagger of one who was wholly positive that he knew more than everyone else in the room. He casually referenced Shakespeare and Steinbeck while discussing daily nothings, he could often be found conversing with teachers in empty classrooms during passing periods, and he dressed like he was already a college professor, right down to the good leather accessories.

I'd been sucked in by his smile, but it was his ability to thoroughly analyze *Titus Andronicus* that made me fall for him. Most people hadn't read my favorite (and most brutal) Shakespearian play, but it was his favorite as well. We bantered for a solid twenty minutes about Titus and Tamorah and the hellscape that'd been patriarchal Rome, and he'd been so perfectly perfect for me that I'd gone for it. I'd smiled and asked him if he wanted to study with me after school at Starbucks.

I'd had to call in sick to work in order to make it happen for us, but I'd known it would be worth it. Because, in every way, Josh was the perfect guy for me.

I was moping my way to my locker when I had an idea. What if I left Josh's gift on the front seat of his car? Mr. Carson usually let him ditch study hall to go on a coffee run next period, so this way I wouldn't have to stand there feeling awkward while he opened it because I wouldn't be there. And once he saw my amazing present for him, he would rush to find me and give me mine.

I snuck out the side door and headed for his car, a 1959 MG coupe that he'd restored with his dad and loved more than life itself. Made him feel very James Bond. Only when I got close, close enough to touch the hood ornament, I saw—

What? I squinted into the bright February sun and looked through his windshield. Josh was in his car, sitting behind the steering wheel. But he wasn't alone.

He was facing someone on the passenger seat. All I could see through the windowed reflection was long blond hair. Which happened to be the defining feature of Macy Goldman, the stunningly beautiful girl he'd gone out with before me. The engine turned on and made me literally jump as I stood there staring.

My stomach felt heavy, even as I told myself they were just friends. He was going on a coffee run, and she probably wanted coffee too, and was riding along to help him bring it all back.

I was about to walk over and knock on the window when it happened. I was standing there with that box in my hand, that box wrapped up in bright red heart wrapping paper, when she leaned closer to him and brought her hands up to his face.

Frozen, I watched as she held his cheeks in her palms, and then kissed him. My breath stopped in my chest as the moment held—*Push her away, push her away, please, Josh*—and then.

Then.

As I stood there in the freezing parking lot, gripping Josh's present, he kissed Macy back.

"NO!"

I hadn't realized I'd said it out loud until their heads jerked apart and they both looked at me. Josh immediately threw open his door, but I wasn't sticking around to talk. I turned and headed back toward the building.

"Em, wait!"

I could hear his footsteps, and then his hand was on my arm, stopping me. He turned me around, and I blinked back tears and managed to say, "*What?*"

Josh ran a hand through his hair, looking confused. "*She* kissed *me*, Em!" His breath puffed in front of his face as he spoke quickly. "I'm sure it looked awful, but I swear on my life. *She* kissed *me*."

He had tears in his eyes, too, and I wanted to punch him in the mouth. I was supposed to be saying I love you, yet *her* lip gloss was on *his* mouth.

"You have to believe me, Em."

"Get away from me," I said through gritted teeth, turning and leaving him behind in the parking lot.

CONFESSION #4

I once stuck a flyswatter into a neighbor's oscillating fan, just to see what would happen. It blew apart.

It wasn't until after I pretended I was about to vomit—complete with the covering of the mouth and the running for the bathroom—that I convinced the nurse to sign a pass to let me go home.

And it wasn't until after I had the pass that I remembered I no longer had a car.

So on top of everything else, I had to walk home. It was twenty-three degrees outside and there was snow on the ground, yet I was going to be trudging through drifts in ankle booties and a shirtdress.

Nick Stark had been right. I was dressed ridiculously.

I shoved the pass into my backpack and was about to exit the building when I heard, "Emilie!"

I turned around and there was Macy Goldman, walking toward me. I wanted to just ignore her, or maybe pull her hair, but a twisted part of me wanted to hear what she had to say.

"Listen." She ran up to me, breathless, and said, "I just want you to know that Josh isn't lying. We were about to get coffee, just talking in his car, and I was the one who leaned in and kissed him. There is nothing going on between us."

I regretted listening to her, because up close, she was even prettier than she was from a distance.

"It was all me," she said. "He did nothing wrong."

"So." I felt surprisingly numb as she looked up at me with a nervous expression. "You still like him, then?"

That made her look super uncomfortable. She pressed her lips together before saying, "Well, I mean—"

"Forget it." I shook my head, suddenly exhausted with everything. "It doesn't matter."

"Yes, it does, because Josh—"

"I can't talk to you right now." I turned and exited the building.

I'd wanted love that was better than my parents' love, something that was built to last. That wouldn't end with the neighbors calling the cops when my mom broke off statue-Cupid's head and threw it at my dad. But now, I felt as heartbroken as I did on that terrible day.

I started trudging home, trying to hold it together as the winter wind whipped at my face. Thank God my dad lived in the next subdivision; any farther and frostbite might've been yet another surprise I could've added to that momentous Valentine's Day.

My phone buzzed, and I wanted to scream when I saw it was my boss again. I *always* helped him out when no one else would, so he *always* called me because he knew I couldn't say no. I put my phone away without answering.

When I finally got home, I was surprised to see my dad's car in the driveway. He was usually at work that time of day.

I unlocked the front door and went into the living room. "Hello? Dad?"

He peeked around the wall of the den. "Hey, squirt; why are you home?"

"Um. I got sick."

"You okay?"

I nodded, although I wasn't at all okay. It was the day where it was all supposed to happen for me. For once, instead of sadly commemorating the anniversary of my family splitting off into two separate units, I was supposed to feel the rush and say the words. I'd done my homework, I'd found the perfect guy, and today had been earmarked for *love*.

Now, however, it appeared as though I'd finish the day without saying or hearing those three words. I'd probably finish it with a stomachache, buried under a pile of Snickers wrappers.

Maybe I needed to grab my planner and add that to my to-do list.

"Well, I'm actually glad you're here, because I want to talk to you about something before the boys get home."

"Okay . . . ?"

"Sit down." He gestured for me to go into the den, and when I did, he plopped down onto the love seat and patted the spot beside him. "I don't even really know how to say this."

How many times could one person hear that in a day?

"Just say it." I plopped down next to him, closed my eyes, and pictured Josh kissing her. Macy Goldman. "How bad can it be?"

He let out a breath. "I've been offered a promotion, but it requires we move to Houston."

My eyes opened. "Texas?"

"Texas."

"Oh. Wow." That was like fifteen hours away from Omaha. Before I could say anything else, he said—

"After a lot of soul-searching, I've decided to take the job."

His words were a punch to the gut. How was his fifty-fifty custody supposed to work from the other side of the country? I took a shaky breath and said, "You have?"

"Yep." He gave me a wide, genuine smile, like he was thrilled about the news and not at all worried about me not sharing his wild enthusiasm. "It's a great opportunity, and you know Lisa's whole family is from Galveston so it'd be nice for the boys to be closer to their grandparents. You're going away to college soon, so really, it won't affect you that much."

"In a year and a half. I'm going to college in a year and a half." I cleared my throat and burrowed a little deeper into the sofa, trying not to sound emotional as I asked, "When would you be moving?"

"Next month. But your mother and I talked about it, and we both think that since you're sixteen, you're old enough to decide what you want to do."

My head was spinning. "What do you mean?"

"Well, since you're graduating next year, I'm sure you don't want to move and start a new school. We discussed it, and without fighting—I know, surprising, right?—came to the decision that you can stay here with her until you go to college if that's what you want."

"What's my other option?"

He looked surprised by my question, probably because he knew how into Josh and my friends and school I was. "Well," he started, running a hand over the top of his head, "you can certainly move south with us. I just assumed that wouldn't be your choice."

I blinked fast and felt a little suffocated, like waves were washing over my nose and I couldn't catch my breath. My dad and his perfect new family were moving to Texas. And he had no qualms about leaving me behind.

How could he even consider moving across the country without me? In his defense, the dynamics between my parents and me were so dysfunctional that he probably had no idea how much he meant to me.

I had always been a "good" kid, the kind of kid that parents didn't have to worry about. My homework was always done, I never talked back, I always followed the rules, and I happily went along with what everyone else wanted. In a normal nuclear family, that kind of stuff made parents proud, right?

But in a family such as mine, it made me forgettable.

My post-divorce dad had a new house, a new wife, and two shiny new little munchkins; a fuller-than-full life. And my post-divorce mom had a new house, a new husband, a puggle that she treated like a baby, and a shiny new career that was more time-consuming than an actual human child. So that left me to play the unfortunate role of the leftovers from their previous marriage who just schlepped back and forth between residences, showing up on my court-assigned days and somehow surprising them with my presence.

I cannot count the number of times I'd entered one of their houses only to hear someone say, *Oh, I thought you were at your dad's/mom's today.* I also cannot count how many parent-teacher conferences and dentist appointments were missed because they each assumed the other was taking me. Or the times I crashed at my grandma's without telling either of them and no one ever called to see where I was.

I was so good that my parents didn't have to worry about me.

So they didn't.

At all.

That being said, the two of them were far from equal. My mom was Driven with a capital *D*. She was all work, all the time, and she seemed to think her primary role as a parent was to ensure I behaved the exact same way. My dad, on the other hand, was funny, chill, and sweetly concerned about me when he wasn't distracted by his lovely new life. When we were together, we were still the same close-knit father-daughter duo that we'd always been. I *adored* my dad.

He just sometimes forgot about me if I wasn't standing right in front of him.

He was looking at me intently, clearly waiting for my answer. *Did a tiny part of him want me to go with him? Or—did a tiny part of him want me to NOT go with him?* I shrugged and worked for a smile. "I'm going to need to think on this one a little."

He nodded in agreement and shifted the conversation to my wrecked car. He'd seen my text at lunch, but by then it'd been too late for him to call me. I listened to his lecture about paying attention and following too closely, but all I could think about was the fact that I was going to have to memorize what it sounded like when my dad got home every day so I wouldn't forget.

All I could think about was the fact that he was absolutely fine with leaving me behind. With the woman he'd divorced and called "impossible to live with."

I went up to my room and called my grandma.

"Hellooo?"

"Hey, Grandma." I sniffled and tried to keep everything inside. I felt like if I let go for a second, I'd never be able to stop crying. "I, um, I need to come over. Can you come get me?"

"Are you at school?"

"No." I looked out the window and noticed the sun had disappeared behind the clouds and the sky was just dark gray. "The nurse sent me home early. I'm at Dad's."

She made a noise. "Are you sick?"

I wrapped my arms around my body. "No. I saw Josh kissing someone else so I fake-barfed. I had to get out of there."

"That little prick. I'm on my way."

Twelve minutes later, my grandma pulled into the driveway in her '69 Mustang. I knew it was her without looking because her beloved murdered-out muscle car rumbled like a motor beast. I ran down the stairs.

"I'm going to Grandma Max's."

My dad looked at my face and he knew I was upset. "When will you be home?"

I grabbed my backpack from the floor. "She said I can crash there."

Lisa came out of the kitchen looking irritated—I hadn't even heard her come home. "But I just put chicken in the oven."

"Um, thanks. I'll heat it up tomorrow."

She frowned and gave my dad a look before I escaped out the door.

CONFESSION #5

My grandma taught me to do burnouts
in her car when I was fourteen.

"The soup will be ready in twenty minutes."

"Sounds good." I lay on the crushed-velvet sofa, wrapped up in sadness and the smell of soup, and stared at the television. "Thanks."

"You do know, darling," my grandmother said, carrying an afghan across the room and laying it over my legs, "that your worth is greater than what Josh or any other boy thinks."

"I know." But I didn't. I didn't want to listen to her be kind when the reality was that I wasn't enough for Josh.

He'd texted me five times since I'd left school:

Can we talk?

Did you leave?

Meet me by my locker after school—please?

Going to go to the library now, but I did nothing wrong, Em. This isn't fair.

Now I'm pissed. Call me.

I was just too broken to formulate words and sentences in

response to his inquiries. Every time I tried—and I tried every five minutes or so—I ended up crying and picturing him kissing Macy.

"Sometimes I don't understand why you don't open your mouth and say the words that are on your tongue," my grandma said, walking over to the kitchen and turning down the stove. "*I* get the privilege of hearing you let loose with your anger. Others should, too. You are not the people-pleasing mouse you purport yourself to be. Burn some cities down with your rage!" Her speech was punctuated with her aggressive stirring of the soup.

"What do you want me to do, Grandma? Just unload on people?"

"A little bit, yes." She glanced over her shoulder at me and said, "Quit worrying about making everyone else happy."

"I'm not good at it like you." Grandma Max was fierce and absolutely incapable of losing an argument. "It's easier to just say what the people want."

She grabbed two bowls out of the cupboard and started filling them with soup. "But doesn't that eat you up inside?"

I shrugged. My insides were shredded, regardless of how they got that way. I pictured Josh and felt my heart literally get heavier in my body. Because if he wasn't a match for me, what did I know about love . . . or anything? It'd been hours since I'd left school, and I felt like I should be finding some perspective, but instead I just felt empty.

I dropped the throw on the sofa, went over to the table, and sat beside my grandma, thinking about the newest awful decision

I had to make. I'd sat at this table with her hundreds of times. Could I really leave her and go to Texas? She said she'd be fine if I decided to go, but would *I*? My grandma was one of my best friends, and the only one I was ready to tell about Texas yet. I'd like to say I was worried about how my widowed grandmother would survive without my presence, but it really was the other way around.

She took a bite of her soup. "Pepper!"

"What?"

She went over to the stove and started messing with the stockpot. "I was distracted and forgot to add pepper. Grab some and sprinkle it in your bowl before you take a bite."

"I'm sure it's—"

"Don't be lazy. Go get the pepper shaker in the china cabinet and properly season your soup."

I went over to the armoire and pulled out the tabby-cat pepper shaker. "I doubt pepper will make that big of a difference."

"Hush and shake."

I shook pepper into my bowl, sat down, and lifted my spoon to my mouth. But instead of tasting grandmotherly deliciousness, my mouth was instantly on fire. In a very bad way.

"Gah!" I felt a shock go through my entire body. My spoon fell to the floor and I grabbed the glass of milk she'd set beside my bowl. I gulped down every drop, but my mouth was still burning. I ran over to the kitchen sink and put my lips under the faucet, turning it on and sucking down every wet, extinguishing drop I could get.

"Dear Lord, Emilie, what has gotten into you? Did you over-pepper your soup?"

I wiped my lips with the back of my hand. My mouth was still simmering, but it no longer felt like my saliva was going to eat away at my teeth. "I don't know what's in that shaker, Grandma, but it isn't pepper. My mouth still tastes like fire and I barely used any."

"Oh, my." Grandma Max's eyes narrowed. "You used the tabby shaker?"

"It has a 'P' on it."

Her eyes got a little twinkle, even though she didn't smile. "That atrocious pepper shaker was a wedding gift from my mother-in-law. It has lived in my cabinet since I received it fifty years ago. I didn't even know it had anything in it."

"Are you telling me that I just ate whatever was inside of the shaker when Great-Gram Leona bought it? A half-century ago?"

She coughed around a laugh.

"What if it was those 'Do Not Eat' silica pellets?"

My grandma walked over to the table and shook some into her palm. "No." She lifted her hand and sniffed. "It appears to be pepper, just very old pepper."

"Fifty-year-old pepper. Perfect." My mouth tasted like the bottom of a dumpster. "That's it. I'm going to bed."

"But it's only seven o'clock."

"I know, but I feel like every minute I'm awake on this nightmarish day is a danger to my life. So far, this Valentine's Day has wrecked my car, revoked my fellowship, stolen my boyfriend, moved my dad far away, and possibly poisoned me. I'm going to read myself to sleep before things get any worse."

"I find it unlikely that things could get any worse."

"Right?" I walked over to the linen closet and grabbed the clear bag of bedding that Grandma always kept clean for my sleepovers. "But I'm erring on the side of caution, just in case."

CONFESSION #6

I've left my initials somewhere inside of every library book I've checked out since the second grade.

THE SECOND VALENTINE'S DAY

When my phone started playing "Walking on Sunshine" at six o'clock, I blinked and squinted to see my phone in the dark. Six? I felt like I hadn't slept at all. Like I'd *just* gone to—

Wait, what?

I stared at the glow-in-the-dark stickers I'd put on my ceiling in middle school. When had I come home? I pushed back the covers and got out of bed, looking at Logan's wide-open little mouth as he lay sprawled across my mattress. I remembered going to bed at Grandma's the night before, but I couldn't remember leaving her house.

I'd been wiped out, though. The day from hell had sucked every bit of life from me, so it was entirely possible I'd been so out of it that I didn't remember Grandma bringing me home.

I glanced at my planner, lying open to February 14 on my desk, just like it'd been the day before.

To-Do List—February 14

Reorganize scholarship planning binder

Study for Lit test

Remind Mom to email copy of insurance card to office

Remind Dad of parent-teacher conferences and make sure he puts it on his calendar

Send email to internship adviser

Exchange gifts with Josh

Say "I love you" to Josh!!!!!!!!!!!

I blinked fast as everything from Valentine's Day rushed back. Josh and Macy, the summer program, my dad—every single part of my life was demolished in just one day.

I quickly flipped the page and jotted a new—and suckier—to-do list. The items that hadn't been decimated the day before actually hadn't been completed, which never happened. I was usually a stickler about checking those boxes, but the Valentine's Day shit show had made me forget my planner entirely.

To-Do List—February 15

Talk to Josh about the kiss

Make decision on Texas move

Reorganize scholarship planning binder

Study for Lit test

Remind Mom to email copy of insurance card to office

Remind Dad of parent-teacher conferences and make sure he puts it on his calendar

I grabbed my robe and went into the bathroom to shower. I started the water and stepped in, letting it pour over my head, scalding and sliding down my neck as tears involuntarily started up again.

"Em, are you almost done in there?"

Seriously? "I just got in here."

"Joel needs to go potty." Lisa sounded like her mouth was once again planted on the door. "Bad."

"There is a bathroom upstairs." I forcefully squirted shampoo into my hand. I wasn't in the mood for a battle. Not after yesterday.

"Your dad's in there."

I was going to strangle someone with my bath sponge. "Just this once, can you maybe ask my dad to get out? I didn't get much sleep last night and I really need this shower."

"You know how your dad is in the morning."

Holy. Balls. "Give me two minutes!" I rushed through the rest of the shower, muttering through gritted teeth like a grumpy old man while slamming bottles down as hard as I possibly could.

Back in my room, I blow-dried my hair before sliding into comfy pants and my favorite Northwestern hoodie, a wardrobe selection made wholly out of poutiness. I wanted absolutely zero human interaction, so I put on headphones as I entered the kitchen. No way was I going to discuss the whole Texas thing without a little more sleep.

Luckily no one was in the kitchen, so I wolfed down a bar as fast as I could while reading the next chapter of the Christina Lauren book that I'd promised to return to Rox when I got to school. Maybe if I finished quickly, I wouldn't have to see another per—

"Good Lord, slow down." My dad walked in with the newspaper in his hand. "No one here knows the Heimlich."

I pulled the headphones down to my neck. "Ha, ha." *Yesterday was hilarious. Funny, funny stuff, Dad.*

"So." He grabbed a mug from the cupboard and put it under the Keurig. "Did you wrap up the way-too-expensive present you bought for ol' Josh? Lots of cheesy red hearts and 'I love you's?"

"What?" I swallowed and the bar felt stuck in my throat. "You want to know if I wrapped his present? Yesterday?"

He raised an eyebrow and pushed the middle button. "I just assumed you'd be all amped for Valentine's Day, but I see you're wearing sweats and looking grouchy, so maybe not. Did I miss something?"

What was he even talking about? I had no idea so I just went with—"You know what happens when you assume, right?"

"Yeah, someone's an ass."

"Oh, come on, you guys." Lisa came into the kitchen with Logan on one hip, Joel on the other. "Can we please not swear around the babies?"

Were they kidding me?

"They weren't in here when he said it, remember?"

"And technically," my dad said, throwing me a wink exactly the way he'd done the day before, "'ass' isn't a bad word. It's a donkey."

I felt my eyes squinch up as I looked at my dad and then at Lisa. Were they trying to be funny, or something? Yeah, no—she still looked at me as if she wished I would disappear.

I grabbed my backpack and my car keys before remembering the van. "Aw, jeez, I forgot about the wreck. Can either of you give me a ride to school?"

"What wreck?" Lisa set Joel down and shifted Logan to her other hip, looking at my dad. "She wrecked the van?"

Before I could answer, my dad said, "No, she didn't wreck the van. I just went out and scraped the windows, remember?"

"Well, then, what did she mean about the wreck?" Lisa looked at him, and he looked at me and said, "No idea. What did you mean, Em?"

I looked around him and out the kitchen window. There, in the driveway, was my Astro van with the windows scraped. I pointed. "Where did that come from?"

"What, your car?" My dad looked at me like I was being a goof. He didn't look—at all—like someone who was pranking me. "I'd say Detroit. You know, because GM . . . ?"

I glanced at Lisa and she tilted her head a little and crinkled her eyebrows. "Em?"

"Um, I, uh, I was just messing." I tried for a smile and pushed toward the door. "I've got to go."

The sun was bright when I stepped outside and I squinted as I carefully walked in the fresh snow by the front of my car. Not only was it not smashed, but it didn't even have a single, solitary scratch on it.

How?

I climbed inside and started it up, my mind scrambling to figure out what the deal was. My phone buzzed and I pulled it out of my pocket. Chris and Rox were FaceTiming me.

I pressed the button to answer and there they were, looking exactly as they had the day before, faces squished together in the junior hallway.

"Guess what I just saw?" Chris asked.

"I want to tell," Rox whined, pushing at him while grinning.

"I can't talk right now—I'll call you back." I disconnected as my mind flipped over like a T-shirt in a dryer. Things were bonkers all of a sudden. I backed out of FaceTime, and my eyes landed on the calendar on my phone.

FEB 14.

My phone said it was "FEB 14." But . . . it wasn't. It was the fifteenth.

Right?

Out loud, I said, "Hey, Siri, what is today's date?" and her little robotic voice confirmed—it was the fourteenth.

Huh?

I started driving toward school, confused, until it hit me.

I *dreamed* about the very terrible Valentine's Day. I *had* been excitedly looking forward to the big day; it made sense I would dream about it, right? It was like when little kids dream about Christmas.

So I hadn't already had a terrible Valentine's Day; it had all been just a bad and slightly psychic dream.

I let out a big breath and smiled.

I floored it, because I couldn't wait to see Josh. I wished I'd opted for better than a baggy sweatshirt, but that didn't seem important anymore because I still had *him*. I could already picture him, looking all cute in one of his plaid button-downs, hanging out in the commons, and I couldn't wait to be by his side and shake off the wildly bad dream.

My phone buzzed on the passenger seat and I glanced over. *Josh.*

Happy VD, baby. Are you here yet?

Ha! That's exactly what he'd typed in my dr—

I looked up and the truck in front of me had stopped. *Noooooo!* I slammed my foot on the brake, but it didn't help.

I hit Nick's ugly truck—again.

Just like in my dream.

I got out.

"You were texting, weren't you?"

"Please, not again."

"You were texting. Admit it."

"Nick Stark, so help me God, I might throat-punch you if you say that again."

This time he raised his eyebrows. "Come again?"

My brain tried to wrap around what was happening. I pointed at myself and said, "Emilie Hornby, your lab partner. And I wasn't texting."

He actually grinned when I said that, the corners of his mouth turning up as his eyes moved over my face. "You doing okay here?"

"Wonderful." I rolled my eyes and went through the motions, everything eerily the same as the day before. It was obvious he didn't think he'd ever met me before, and I felt cloudy as I struggled to figure it out. My hand shook as I handed over my insurance card. Was this déjà vu? Had I dreamed about Valentine's Day?

Was I actually psychic?

I didn't even attempt to call my parents when the cops and the tow truck arrived. I silently accepted his proffered coat and rode to school with Nick, who must've sensed my inner turmoil because he didn't say a word. I listened to Metallica barking out the lyrics to "Blackened," and this time the music seemed a bit more fitting. It perfectly accentuated my WTF morning.

As Nick drove, I studied his profile. His dark hair, prominent Adam's apple, hard jawline, tall body—all the same as in my dream.

Just for fun, I looked out the window and said, "I love Metallica so much."

His eyebrows went straight up. "Seriously?"

Not at all seriously. But I had to test the upside-down, repetitive-day universe, didn't I? "Sure. I like their rage—it's almost like you can *feel* it, y'know?"

His mouth turned all the way up and he looked at me like we were soul mates. "Well said, Hornby."

I looked back at him and wondered how I would ever get out of the dream sequence. Was it my fate to crash into him every morning for all of eternity? I knew that couldn't be right and there had to be *some* explanation, but I was really starting to get freaked out. *I'll pretend that I'm all right and everything will be fine*—it'd always worked for me in the past. When we got to school, I stood on shaky legs after getting out of his truck. I don't know why, but as I handed back his coat, I asked him, "Everything is going to be okay, right?"

He looked down at the coat for a minute, like he was trying to interpret my question. "Sure. Why wouldn't it?"

CONFESSION #7

I failed swimming lessons seven times before my mom finally gave up on me.

Everything at school was the same as the day before. I got called to the office and lost the summer program. Then I went outside and saw Josh and Macy. Honestly, I don't know why I even went to his car—maybe I somehow thought I'd seen it wrong the first time. Maybe I thought I'd see something that would explain it all away. I don't know what I was hoping for, but all I ended up with was an even greater sense of rejection.

Because this time I noticed how into her he looked as he watched her talking to him in the front seat. This time I noticed just how beautiful she was, sitting there in her white sweater with her blond hair framing her face like a Barbie halo.

I turned and went back inside before the kiss could happen, a little surprised that it was no less painful. I might've thought it'd be easier with a warning, but it wasn't. It still felt like my entire solar plexus was being crushed by a car. Because I'd done everything right, and it still wasn't enough.

I kept my eyes down and headed for the nurse's office. I didn't want to talk to anyone, or worse, have anyone see the tears that were blurring my vision. I almost made it out of the blue hallway when I heard, "Em. Wait up!"

I stopped but didn't raise my eyes. I couldn't.

Chris grabbed my elbow. "So tell us what he got you!"

"Em?" Roxane's knees bent and then her face was lower than mine. I must've looked pretty pathetic because she said, "Oh, honey, what happened?"

I blinked fast and shook my head. She grabbed my arm and yanked me into the girls' bathroom. Chris followed, as he had many times before, grabbing a paper towel and dampening it before wiping at my smeared makeup.

"We don't cry tears of mascara in the bathroom, remember?" he said, giving me an empathetic pout.

I just nodded. Suddenly, I was incapable of words.

"I *knew* he was going to turn out to be an asshole." Chris tossed the paper towel and put his arms around me. "He's too cute and charming to be that cute and charming. Who was it?"

I just shook my head. "It doesn't matter, does it? Macy Goldman, but I think—"

They both groaned.

"What?" I pulled away and crossed my arms. "It isn't about the *who,* it's about the fact that he did it at all. Macy is irrelevant."

Chris's right eyebrow went up. "Yeah, okay."

I looked at Rox. "Seriously."

Roxane gave Chris a matching eyebrow-raise. "She's in shock and doesn't know what she's saying."

"Yes, I do!"

"Then be honest, here. Being cheated on sucks, period." Chris put his hands in the pockets of his trendy leather jacket. "But being cheated on with the most perfect girl in school is, like, a whole 'nother level."

"''Nother.'" Rox pulled a piece of gum out of her purse and put it in her mouth. "Is not. A word."

"It is too."

Rox crossed her arms. "I've showed you the dictionary page that is not-shockingly absent of a ''nother' entry, and I've dragged you into Ms. Brand's Honors English class and garnered her professional opinion. Which, of course, was in my favor. Because it is not a word. It is what confused rednecks say when they aren't sure whether they should say 'other' or 'another.'"

Somehow their bickering dried up my tears. It was normal. Routine. It was how the three of us behaved on a daily basis when Valentine's Days weren't being left on repeat. I said, "Hey, I'm going to take off. Thanks for making me feel better."

"Did we do that?" Chris tilted his head and lowered his eyebrows.

"I did." Rox pushed him out of the way and gave me a quick hug.

I looked at them both and was so freaking grateful they were my friends.

Chris said, "My mom is making BBQ tonight—you should come over."

His mom's barbecue was delicious. I'd always considered myself picky until I started hanging out at his house. His mother was

Korean, and her food smelled so good that before I'd even had a chance to be picky, I was eating kimchi, bibimbap, and mandoo—while begging for more dinner invites. "Maybe I will, I don't know."

Rox said, "Go home and binge-watch that filthy show I was telling you about. It'll make you feel better."

I felt marginally better when I went to the nurse's office, and walking to my dad's was less frigid than it'd been the day before because I wasn't in a dress. The entire time way home, I went over and over the questionable events of the past twenty-four or forty-eight or *whatever* hours.

"What in the hell is going on?" I shouted to the snowy, frozen houses that were quiet in the way that suburban neighborhoods were quiet on weekdays as I walked down the street. "How is this happening?"

The only explanation was that I was having a dream that very second. I was having a vivid, realistic dream—about having a vivid, realistic dream—and I just needed to wake up from it.

I pinched myself, and—

Ow. Shit.

I got home and listened to my dad tell me about Texas, and I went to my grandma's and let her take care of me again, just like the day before.

As soon as it got dark, I went out on her porch and wished on every single star I could see that when I woke up in the morning, things would be fixed. Once I went inside, she told me to pepper my soup and I had an idea.

It was pretty *out there*, but so was everything else.

I went over to the armoire and pulled out the tabby-cat pepper shaker. "Hmm."

"Hush and shake."

"No way." I looked at that bitchy-looking, badly-painted feline and wondered. "What if it was the half-century pepper?"

"Pardon?"

"The pepper might have caused this. In movies, it's always weird exposures to random things like perfume or old snowballs that cause time loops to happen."

"I think the tragedies of the day have taken a toll on your logic. Perhaps you should—"

"Listen. Grandma. If I tell you something that seems impossible, do you promise not to judge me?"

She nodded, sat back down at the table, and patted the chair beside her. I plopped down and scooted closer, but didn't even know where to start. "I know this sounds impossible."

"Just tell me, dear."

"Um, okay. You know how today is Valentine's Day?"

"Yes?"

"Well, what if I told you that yesterday was Valentine's Day for me, and today was a total repeat?"

She crossed her arms. "Is it possible that it's just déjà vu?"

I shook my head. "I thought the same thing at first, but I know that things are going to happen before they do."

"Like . . . ?"

"Like I knew Josh was going to cheat today because I already watched him do it yesterday. I knew I was losing the summer scholarship because I already did yesterday. I know that Great-Gram Leona gave you that ugly cat pepper shaker as a wedding gift because you told me that yesterday, and I also know that if you check my phone there will be a new message from Josh that says 'Call me. Now I'm pissed.'"

That made her eyebrows go up.

"My phone has been in my backpack out in your car since you picked me up; I haven't looked at it since I called you. Go get it and let's see if I'm right."

Her eyes traveled all over my face before she stood and went out into the garage. I was sure she probably thought I was delusional and was humoring me, but it felt good to tell someone about my upside-down life. When she came back in, she was holding my phone and staring at it in disbelief.

"So . . . ?"

"Dear Lord, Emilie, we'd better go get a lottery ticket, don't you think?"

CONFESSION #8

When I was ten, I used to sneak into my next-door neighbor's backyard on summer days and swim in their hot tub when they were at work. No one ever knew.

YET ANOTHER VALENTINE'S DAY

The minute my alarm went off, I knew for certain that the whole thing was real.

I lay there in my bed, cocooned in the heaviness of my down comforter and staring up at the ceiling, not wanting to leave my pillow-soft bed and face it. Because even though I didn't have a clue about the how or why, I was definitely living in a day-on-repeat loop. I'd gone to sleep at Grandma Max's, yet here I was again, waking up in my own room to that annoying song Josh had programmed into my iPhone to wake me up.

I glanced over at Logan, sound asleep with his mouth wide-open.

Yep—been here, done this.

I sat up and reached for my phone. And I thought, *What if the universe wants me to fix something?*

I didn't believe in fate and karma and that sort of nonsense, but I also didn't know how to explain what was happening.

Somehow I was reliving the same day for a third time.

What if these repeating Valentine's Days weren't karmic punishment for something I did in a past life or some other horrible reason? What if they're a *gift*, an opportunity to right a day that went so very wrong?

It was worth a shot, right?

Yes. That was what I was going to do.

I worked through it all in my mind while I took a shower (fast because of Joel's potty needs, of course), ticking off all the things I needed to correct from the previous day. Then I created a *new* to-do list.

To-Do List—February 14 (again)
Avoid wrecking car
Avoid scholarship meeting in counselor's office
Ensure Josh and Macy cannot kiss
Convince Dad that he doesn't want to move to Texas

How hard could all of that be, right?

After I showered, I slid into my lucky plaid dress. It wasn't new and adorable like the shirtdress from the original Valentine's Day, but if ever I needed the luck of the dress that had scored me my highest ACT score, it was today. I paired it with tights and my suede boots—warmer than the day before, but still cute—and headed for the door.

As I drove toward the school, I was hyperfocused on the snow-slushed road. My phone was nestled deep in my bag, my hands carefully placed at ten and two. I was traveling in the left-hand lane, whereas I'd been in the right on the other days, so I was all set up to *not* crash into Nick Stark.

Taylor Swift was singing about Coney Island while I drove as carefully as a student driver on test day. It was imperative, in my opinion, that I rectify this easiest of complications. I left two car-lengths between my creeper van and the silver minivan in front of me, confident I was going to miss Nick entirely and start the day right.

Did I paint your bluest skies the darkest gray?

Traffic was moving pretty well in spite of the snow, and I started to relax once I passed the intersection where I'd hit him the day before. Step one of my plan—not totaling my car—was complete. I could almost feel the tension draining out of me when all of a sudden, a huge semi-truck blasted past on my right, shooting slush all over my windshield.

Totally blinding me.

"Dammit!"

I hit the brakes as I flipped on the wipers, but my tires locked on the packed snow and I couldn't stop. In an instant, I saw everything as my window cleared. My car, sliding into the right lane because I had to jerk the wheel to avoid oncoming traffic.

Sliding directly toward the pickup truck in the other lane.

"Shit, shit, shit!"

I mashed my foot on the brake, but it was no use. I slammed into that vehicle—harder than I'd hit the day before—actually moving it as I rammed the side of the truck bed.

"No, no, no, no!" As my car jerked to a stop, I was staring directly at a truck that looked exactly like Nick Stark's truck. *What the hell, universe?*

My hood appeared to be just as crumpled as the day before, maybe more. I unbuckled my seat belt, my shaking hands making the task trickier than usual. I was just grabbing the door handle when it was yanked open from the other side.

"Hey—you okay?" Nick looked down at me, but instead of being a jerk, he looked concerned. "You hit pretty hard."

"I think so." I nodded and he stepped back so I could get out of the car. I could smell his soap or shampoo as I stood and closed the door. "Oh no—it's smoking."

He and I both looked at my smashed hood as smoke started billowing out. Nick said, "We should probably get out of the road."

His voice sounded sleep-gravelly as he pulled his phone out of his pocket and walked toward the side of the road. I followed, a little shaken up by the violence of the crash and also by the undeniable fact that I'd been unable to avoid the Nick collision.

I thought my plan had been foolproof, but the universe apparently had something else in mind.

Nick spoke to 911, and then he must've been on hold because he looked at me and whispered, "Aren't you cold in that?"

And he said "*that*" while looking down at my legs in the same way he would've eyeballed me if I'd been dressed like a Teletubby.

And honestly, I *was* freezing. It felt like the air was ice, stabbing me through my tights and on my cheeks, but I said, "Nah—I'm good."

While simultaneously fantasizing about the jacket that I knew was in his back seat.

But I just couldn't let him win.

He gave me a smirk that called me a liar before he went back to talking into his phone. I clenched my teeth to keep them from chattering and wondered—again—how he looked like such an adult. I mean, he was my age, but there was something so . . . *over twenty-one* about the guy.

"They're on their way," he said, shoving his phone back into the pocket of his jeans.

"Thanks." I had to force myself to look not frozen when I said, "I'm Emilie Hornby, by the way. We sit at the same table in Mr. Bong's class."

His eyebrows crinkled together. "We do?"

Yeah—it was just as irritating on repeat. "Yes, we do. Since the beginning of the year."

"Hmm." He looked at me. "You sure?"

"*Yes*," I said through a groan, rolling my eyes.

"Um . . . ," he started, watching me like I was a lunatic. "Are you doing okay here?"

"I. Am. Wonderful." The sirens showed up at that point, and everything was on repeat. Car caught fire, I got ticketed, Nick brought me his jacket, which I begrudgingly accepted, and gave me a ride to school.

I realized as I buckled my seat belt that I needed to be more adaptive during this day of fixing things. Because I didn't have the exact recipe for what exactly needed to be fixed. I might not have been able to avoid the wreck, but perhaps I was supposed to fix our interaction instead.

I didn't know the exactitudes, so I needed to try to fix every little thing.

"Thank you so much for the ride," I said politely, turning my lips up into what I hoped was a pleasant smile. "It's very nice of you."

"It's not really nice," he said, putting the car into first and letting out the emergency brake, "so much as it is practical. If I let you walk to school and you freeze to death, surely that would put a crimp in my karma. But by giving you a ride somewhere that I'm already going—no sacrifice on my part at all—I'm actually *earning* good karma."

I sighed. "Lovely."

He smirked but didn't look at me. "It *is* lovely."

I looked out the window and tried again. "I love this song, by the way. Metallica's awesome." That made him give me the side-eye.

"*You* like Metallica."

I nodded and pursed my lips. "Sure."

His eyes narrowed. "Name three songs."

I crossed my arms and squinted back at him as he looked at me like I was a liar. Why was he insisting on sabotaging me? "I don't have to name three songs to prove I like them."

"Then I'm just going to assume you're a poser." His eyes were back on the road again.

"Posing at what, exactly? Someone who likes the sound of angry old guys barking out words?"

That made his lips turn up into an actual smile and he glanced over. "See? I knew you didn't like them."

I rolled my eyes, which made him chuckle, and I told myself that it didn't matter. My interaction with Nick Stark was surely irrelevant in the whole fixing-the-day plan. So I said what was actually on my mind.

"Do you always come at people when they're just making small talk?"

"I wouldn't call it 'coming at people.' I just think if your *small talk* is about a band, you should probably know about said band."

I scoffed. "I was being polite—ever heard of it?"

"I wouldn't really call pointless lying 'polite.'"

"Come on—it wasn't lying." I gave my head a shake. "I was mentioning it for the sake of conversation. It's what strangers do when they're attempting to be nice."

"But we aren't strangers." He looked at me with a smirk. Again. "You said you're my lab partner."

"I *am* your lab partner!"

Bigger smirk. "So then why did you say we're strangers?"

I sighed. "I have no idea."

It was horribly quiet for a few minutes as his old truck drove in the direction of our school. It was awkward and uncomfortable, but better than when he was talking. So—of course—he ruined it when he said, "Wait a second—now I know where I've seen you. Aren't you the girl—"

"Who sits by you in Chem? Yes," I interrupted.

"—who choked in the cafeteria?"

Man, I would never live that down.

"I didn't choke." I cleared my throat. "It just got stuck in my throat."

That made him look away from the road to give me a cocked eyebrow. "Wouldn't that be the literal definition of choking?"

"No, it would not," I huffed, knowing I was huffing but unable to stop. "Choking is when food gets stuck in your windpipe and you cannot breathe. I could breathe; I just had food stuck in my esophagus."

He rolled in his lips and narrowed his eyes. "You sure that's right?"

"*Of course* I'm sure—it happened to me."

He made a noise. "I've just never heard of that—I don't know if it's a thing."

"I am *telling* you that it happened so you actually *do* know that it's a thing." I could hear my voice getting high-pitched, but the boy was beyond frustrating. "Some people have a condition where food can get stuck in their throat. I have to take omeprazole every morning to ensure it doesn't happen again. So it is definitely a thing."

He pulled up to a stoplight, and when the truck came to a complete stop, Nick turned his head and looked at me.

His mouth wasn't smiling, but there was something teasing in his eyes when he said, "Are you sure you're my lab partner?"

I groaned. "*Of course* I'm sure."

"That girl is super quiet, whereas you seem pretty chatty."

"I'm not chatty."

"You seem excessively chatty, actually."

"Well, I'm not." I was actually a quiet person. *Shit.*

"Yeah, okay."

We didn't speak again until we got to school, where I thanked him for the ride and very nearly threw his coat at him. He caught it gracefully, and as I turned away, I could have sworn he was smiling.

I had to force myself to take a deep breath and focus. It didn't matter that Nick Stark was intent on ruining my chances of fixing this day—I had work to do.

When the office sent a pass for me, I grabbed my bag and started in that direction. But instead of turning toward the administration area, I walked all the way back to the farthest restroom in the building, the one that was past the library.

I didn't really have a good plan on how to keep my spot in the summer program, but part of me wondered: If they couldn't find me, might they consider just letting me in to save us all the awkward embarrassment of their mistake?

I mean, what was one more spot, really?

It was the best I could come up with at that moment, so hiding in the bathroom was what I was going to do. I glanced behind me before pushing in the bathroom door and going inside. It smelled like cherry—a wafting reminder of the in-between-class vapers—but I was alone.

Whew.

I set my bag next to the sink and pulled out my makeup pouch. I spent a few minutes touching up my cheeks and lips. I had complicated feelings about Josh after seeing him kiss-but-not-really-in-real-life Macy, but I was forcing myself to forget about that.

She had kissed *him*, after all, and if I'd stuck around, would I have seen him pull away? I was going with yes.

Presents, poetry, and *I love you*—those boxes were getting checked. I had total confidence in my theories about relationships and love, and I wasn't going to let a tiny little peck screw it all up. Today was going to go perfectly, and tomorrow would be February 15.

Unfortunately, the makeup freshening didn't take long, and after that I didn't know what to do with myself. I could scroll through my phone to pass the time, but there was a whole nervous-awkwardness thing that made me tense as I stood by the sink.

Did I hear someone coming? Who was it? Teacher or student? Nice or mean? Was I supposed to pretend to be doing my makeup if they came in or . . . what? The minutes were ticking by like they were in slow motion.

Finally, I decided to go into a stall. It seemed disgusting, sitting on a toilet—once again—while fully clothed, but at least I could relax. I took my bag into the first slot, locked the door, and started laying down a two-layer-deep covering of toilet paper across the seat. When it was finally thick enough where I could no longer see the black seat, I sat down.

I pulled my phone out of my front pocket and texted Josh.

Me: I cannot believe it's V-Day and I haven't seen you yet today.

Josh was quick to respond, my phone making the familiar horse's *neigh* sound that he'd programmed as his own personal ringtone. Right?! Your present is burning a hole in my locker. Where were you this morning?

That made me relax a little. I smiled and texted: Wrecked my car on the way to school—I'll tell you about it later.

Josh: Oh, shit.

Me: Right? Now, regarding my present, is it burning a big hole or a little hole?

Josh: That's for me to know and you to find out. But I have to go take a quiz now, babe.

Me: Fine. Xoxo.

I backed out of messages, feeling relieved. Regardless of what'd occurred on the other Valentine's Days, there was no way Josh would be kissing Macy that day.

Take that, Mace.

Since I wasn't going anywhere soon, I leaned down, unzipped my bag, and started digging for my book. If I was stuck hiding in the restroom, why not make use of the time and read, right? I had to take out the bottle of Diet Coke in order to grab the paperback, so I set it on the floor and pulled out the novel.

My toes were already killing me because my adorable new boots were a half size too small, so I slid my feet out and rested them on top of the soft suede as I settled in to read.

I shoved my phone into my pocket with one hand as I gripped the book with the other, but as I pulled my hand out of my pocket, my cuff bracelet caught the edge of my phone. I grappled for it as it started falling, but it was like I was watching in slo-mo as the phone tumbled and went through the tiny gap that existed between my outer thigh and the edge of the toilet seat.

"Gah!" I jumped up, but it was too late. I looked down into the TP-decorated toilet. My beautiful rose-gold phone with the adorable floral case had immediately sunk to the bottom of the germ-infested porcelain bowl. "No, no, no—shit, shit, shit."

As my ears started pounding, I realized that my stockinged feet were now directly on the disgusting floor.

Ignoring that for now, I rolled in my lips, took a deep breath, and plunged my hand into the freezing-cold bacteria-laden water.

"Dear Lord." I pulled it out, holding the dripping device—which was surely destroyed—out in front of me.

I opened the stall with my dry hand and moved through the opening, leaving my bag in the stall. I needed to scrub the skin off of my hands and sanitize my phone. Feeling the cold bathroom floor under my feet, I clenched my teeth. How had this happened?

I'd taken one step out of the stall in my stockinged feet when the bathroom door opened. I froze as three girls filed in, talking loudly among themselves.

No, no, please, no.

It wasn't just any three girls; it was *them*.

There were a lot of popular people at school who seemed nice enough, but Lauren, Nicole, and Lallie were the ones who enunciated like Kardashians and actually told people they couldn't sit with them at lunch.

On any given day, they could randomly decide your hair was ridiculous and start a school-wide joke of a nickname that followed you all the way though graduation and still existed at your ten-year reunion.

I'd felt marginally less vulnerable around them since I started dating Josh, only because they liked him. They still didn't talk to me, which was fine, but their threat was neutralized by their friendly relationship with my boyfriend.

But it was like time stopped and for a split second, I was able to see myself through their eyes. A bookish non-popular, coming out of a bathroom stall with a dripping phone in her hand and her shoes off. That led their eyes to the floor of stall number one, where my boots, a book, and a half-consumed bottle of Diet Coke all sat together as if I'd just been having a toilet picnic.

They kept talking to each other and didn't say anything to or about me—thank goodness—but as I turned on the faucet and started lathering my hands and my phone, I definitely saw the eyebrow-raises.

Perfectly arched eyebrows, mind you, but eyebrows that said they'd definitely be talking about me after they left.

Which, thankfully, was only moments later. Once they were gone, I ran to gather my stuff, re-boot myself (after wiping hand sanitizer on the bottom of my tights), and wrap my tainted phone in a hundred paper towels before zipping it into my bag's outside pocket.

Okay. So. The bathroom ordeal made total perfection unachievable. But I still had hope that achieving romantic perfection could potentially save the day.

I sat anxiously through my next class because (a) I didn't have a phone so I had no way of knowing if Josh was texting, (b) I was worried the office was going to try again, (c) I was stressed that rumors of my potty picnic were already circulating, and (d) I was paranoid my boots were going to start smelling like Fritos since I'd zipped my feet into them while they were still slick with sanitizer.

I was trying to avoid thinking by taking extensive notes on my laptop, when an email notification popped up.

I clicked into my in-box and my stomach dropped when I saw who it was from.

Mrs. Bowen, from the summer program.

I'd hoped to discuss this in person, but since we weren't able to locate you, email will have to suffice.

"Dammit," I muttered under my breath as I read my rejection in a cold, professional email message.

"Ms. Hornby?" My World Civ teacher, Mrs. Wunderlich, looked at me as if I'd just spoken in tongues. "What was that?"

"Nothing. Sorry."

She went on to do the requisite ten-second teacher stare, a gaze that informed me I had done wrong and she hoped I was dying of mortification, before going back to her lecture.

Perfecting this day was looking more and more challenging.

When the bell rang, I gathered my things and very nearly

sprinted through the halls in order to get to the west entrance earlier than on the other days. I bumped and *excuse-me*'d through the congested hallways, and once I reached the double doors, I moved to stand behind the huge arrangement of indoor plants.

I wasn't hiding—really. I was . . . lurking. Maybe. I knew Josh wouldn't kiss Macy, but I was curious to see them arrive and get a sense of their vibe when they were together.

"What are you doing?"

I jumped at the sound of the voice, and when I turned around, it was Nick Stark, smirking at me like he knew exactly what I was up to. I glanced behind him before quietly saying, "Shhh. Go away."

"Um." He gestured to the mini jungle I was protected by. "Are you stalking someone from back here?"

"No, I'm waiting for my boyfriend. Can you—"

My head swiveled around and my words stopped when I heard Josh's voice. I felt Nick's gaze follow my own as Josh and Macy walked in our direction, and I grabbed Nick's sleeve and pulled him behind the plants with me. I couldn't have him drawing their attention to my lurking. Josh was talking and Macy was smiling—beaming, actually—and Josh was walking a little sideways so he could face her better.

I mean, no big deal. They were friends, right?

"Come on, Josh." Macy's eyes were animated as she said, "If you let me come along, not only do you get the joy of having me ride shotgun in your James Bond–mobile, but I will allow you to make the call on what we do with all that time."

They stopped in front of the doors and he smiled down at her. I could tell he was enjoying the attention. "That sounds like a *lot* of power—I'm not sure I can handle it."

"Oh, I *know* you can't." My heart was pounding in my chest and my stomach dropped out of my body as she leaned closer to him and said, "But you should try."

He said, "I guess I *could* use someone to hold the drinks."

"Told you."

"And all your help will cost me is a tall vanilla latte?"

"I can't believe you remember my order," she said, and laughed.

Why couldn't she believe that? It was everyone's Starbucks order, for the love of God. Every girl at this school probably had the same drink at least once. It didn't make him freaking Einstein.

He looked charming, and sexy, and I kind of wanted to punch his pretty nose as he said, "I remember everything, Mace."

"Uh, you sure he's your boyfriend?" Nick whispered, and I kind of wanted to punch him, too.

Josh pushed the doors open and he and Macy started walking outside, and I don't know what came over me.

"Wait!" I yelled as I grabbed Nick's sleeve, pulling him with me as I ran after them, pushing through the doors and jogging as they both stopped and turned around. I saw Macy glance nervously at Josh but my boyfriend slid into a confident smile as he said, "Em!"

I realized as I stumbled to a stop—with Nick at my heels—that I had no idea what I was doing. No plan, other than to yell and scream and stop them, with Nick as some kind of a buffer. Now that I was in front of them, I was clueless. I cleared my throat and said, "Are you going on a coffee run?"

Macy's face relaxed and Josh said, "Yeah. You know Mr. Carson—needs it every day."

"Awesome." I nodded. "Nick and I are dying for coffee and need to get out of here. Care if we come with?"

I glanced at Nick, waiting for him to ruin it for me, but he just frowned, which wasn't too different from his usual expression, actually. Josh looked at Nick, clearly confused about what the guy was doing there, and Macy said, "Of course."

Josh, still squinting at Nick, said, "You know how big my car is, Em. You up for riding in the middle?"

"Sure," I muttered, regretting all of my terrible decisions as the four of us silently walked to his car. I shot Nick a look, raising my eyebrows as if to say, *Pretty please just go along with this.* Surprisingly, he rolled his eyes and walked beside me, which didn't even make sense because there was no way he actually wanted to ditch school to go to Starbucks with us.

We weren't even friends.

But despite his attitude that morning, I found his presence comforting. Something about his I-don't-give-a-shit hotness and the way he said whatever he was actually feeling made me feel like I had an ally.

Weird, right?

Josh's car was a tiny little two-seater, so when he unlocked the door, I had to climb—in a dress—across the passenger seat and into the tiny spot in front of the gear shift. Macy got in beside me, Nick had to squish in beside her, and the four of us jammed together in the world's most awkward sandwich.

I turned and put my legs on Macy's side of the floorboards, so as to not be straddling the stick shift, making our legs touch and upping the embarrassing horror of the outing. *And* I had to put my arms over the backs of the seats so I wouldn't flop around on top of them every time we turned a corner. I accidentally touched Nick's shoulder, making him look over at me. Leaning back so Macy couldn't see, I looked at him and he mouthed, *What. The. Fuck.*

In the midst of the awkwardness, a tiny part of me wanted to laugh. Instead, I mouthed, *Please help me,* which made him sigh in a way that I hoped meant he found me ridiculous but would help me.

Josh flipped on the heater and left the parking lot, and it was the worst kind of quiet in the car.

What was I even doing?

"How many coffees are you getting today?" I tried to sound utterly unaware of the dynamic as we drove toward Starbucks. "Big order?"

Josh turned the corner, making me dig my fingers into their headrests in order to not fly out the window, as he said, "Just five. Ours and his."

"Got it."

More quiet.

"You don't have a class this hour, Macy?" Nick asked, looking at me as if to point out how sketchy this seemed.

"I'm in Carson's class with Josh, so I just told him that Josh needed help carrying the drinks."

"Ah." Nick, still looking at me, said, "That's convenient."

"I texted you earlier to see if you wanted something," Josh said to me, turning on his blinker and switching lanes.

"Oh, yeah—my phone is dead."

"I always forget to charge mine, too," Macy said.

"I actually dropped it in the toilet," I said, instantly regretting sharing that little gem. "I mean, not a dirty toilet—it wasn't dirty. I mean, yes, all toilets are dirty, but I mean there was nothing in it."

Shut up, shut up, shut up!

"Holy Christ," Nick muttered at the same time Macy said, "Oh my God."

Yes, we were all calling out to the Lord in response to my phone's disgusting swim.

"Right?" was all I could manage.

Josh pulled into Starbucks, put the car in neutral, flipped his sunglasses up on his head, and looked at Nick, who was looking out the window. Josh had that debate-captain-superiority look on his face as he asked, "Okay, so I know what the girls want. What about you, dude?"

Nick didn't even look over. "I'm good, but thanks. Dude."

Josh glanced at me, like he was looking for an explanation as to why Nick Stark was with us and being a jerk, and I smiled and shrugged. As if I had any clue what was going on in life anymore.

After Josh came back with the drinks, we sped back to school, with Josh cranking up the radio so conversation was impossible, which I appreciated.

As we pulled into the parking lot, Macy turned down the radio and said, "What is that smell?"

And she put her perfect little nose in the air and started sniffing.

I sniffed, but didn't really smell anything other than coffee.

"You're right, it smells like feet in here." Josh put the car in first, pulled up the emergency brake, and turned off the engine while wrinkling his nose.

Oh no. I scrunched up my face and pretended to be disgusted, too. "*Josh*. Did you maybe leave some socks in here or something?"

That made Josh glare at me. We both knew that he spent countless hours—every weekend—buffing and loving up on that tiny little car, before he said, "There are no socks in my car."

"You sure?" Nick asked. "Because it really smells like dirty socks."

Josh looked like he wanted to kill Nick. "Why would I have dirty socks in my car?"

"I have no fucking idea."

Before their noses could hone in on my booties I said, "Can you guys let me out? My legs are *beyond* cramped."

We filed out of the car, and the four of us went back into the school. Josh gave me a little peck—the obligatory goodbye kiss—when we had to go our separate ways. I held my coffee and watched him and Macy walk away.

I may have successfully kept them from kissing, but that coffee run definitely didn't feel like a win. The bell rang at that moment, destroying my train of thought.

"Thank you for inviting me," Nick drawled, startling me from my thoughts as he gave me an amused smirk. "Witnessing that level of awkwardness was downright entertaining."

"Shut up," I said, unable to hold back a tiny smile.

"Seriously." He turned and started walking away from me, yelling over his shoulder as the passing period crowds swallowed him, "You've really made this an amazing day, Emilie."

I rolled my eyes and headed in the direction of my locker. I was so lost in my thoughts that I didn't hear the giggles at first. Then something in my peripheral vision caught my eye. I glanced to my right and there were Lauren, Nicole, and Lallie, with four other girls, standing in front of a bank of lockers.

Giggling, whispering to each other, and looking directly at me.

I walked faster and breathed a sigh of relief when I walked through Mr. Bong's door. Suddenly finding myself on those three's radar was not something I'd anticipated, and it surely wasn't something I wanted.

The relief was fleeting, though, when I reached my table and Nick was smirking up at me with his chin resting on his hand.

I sat on my stool and unzipped my bag, pulling out my textbook and my binder, ignoring him completely.

He said, "So that was weird, right?"

I rolled my eyes and opened the book, flipping toward our current chapter.

"One minute you were telling me to go away, and the next you were dragging me along on the world's most awkward trip to Starbucks."

I didn't answer, and his voice got a little quieter when he said, "You do know he's cheating with her, right?"

I looked at him out of the corner of my eye, continuing to flip the pages of my textbook. "Can we go back to not talking?"

"I don't think we can." He reached his hand over and stopped me from turning another page. "Because we're no longer strangers."

This was the cherry, wasn't it? The cherry on top of the god-awful attempt at perfecting the day. Looking from his hand to his face, I sighed and said, "But we can be. I'm chatty—and you *hate* that—and you're surly, which *I* hate. So let's just pretend we never ran into each other this morning and you can go back to not knowing who I am."

That made him smile, a smile that was—to be honest—potent as hell. He was such a scowly introvert that it almost made you miss how unbelievably handsome he was.

But when he was present—and smiling—he was club-you-in-the-gut-with-a-board attractive.

Such a waste on an asshole.

"I don't think I can do that," he said, crossing his arms and really *looking* at me. "And you didn't invite me to coffee—technically, you dragged me."

Mr. Bong came in and started talking, which foolishly made me think Nick would shut up and leave me alone. But there was no such thing as good luck on this day.

"Guess what I read last period?"

I said, "Shhh."

"Dysphagia." He leaned closer and said, "That's what it's called when food gets stuck in your throat but you aren't choking."

I coughed out a laugh. "What is your deal?"

"No deal."

"You never talk to me in Chem, and now you have information on the weird health thing that happened to me last year in the cafeteria. What are you up to?"

He gave a little chuckle and straightened as Mr. Bong glanced in our direction. "I just wanted you to know that I looked it up, and it *is* actually a thing."

"I know it's a thing—it's *my* thing! It happened to me."

"Emilie?" Mr. Bong—and the entire class—was looking at me. Because yeah—I might've said it a little loudly.

I murmured, "Sorry."

Mr. Bong went back to his lecture, and when I glanced at Nick, he was shaking his head and clearly trying to hold in a laugh. I shook my head, but the mischief in his face made it impossible not to smile a little.

"Long story short—my car got towed."

I looked at Chris in disbelief as he put on his coat and slammed his locker. On top of everything, of all the tragedies of that god-awful day, Chris had no car with which to drive us home? I said, "So . . . ?"

"So we're walking home, I guess, because Rox is already gone and my parents are both in meetings."

"Ugh," I groaned. "I cannot believe this day."

"I checked and the wind chill is just south of ten degrees, so yeah—this is gonna blow."

"You guys need a ride?"

I closed my eyes when I heard the voice. *Of course* Nick Stark was there. Why wouldn't he be? He was every-fucking-where that day. I opened my mouth to give him a big old *No thanks* when Chris said over my shoulder in a near-squeal, "For real?"

I turned in time to see Nick shrug and say to Chris, "Sure. You ready now or—"

"I have to do something first," I interrupted, giving Chris a look. "I have to, um, run something to the north hall meeting room really fast."

Chris rolled his eyes, catching on to what I was up to. "I just want to go home, Em."

"I need to find Josh first. I'll be quick." I held up a finger at them, turned, and started speed-walking down the hall toward the meeting room, but they followed me. Over my shoulder, I said, "You don't have to go with me—I can meet you at the car."

"Nah—we want to," Nick said, giving me a smart-ass look as they kept walking with me.

"Can't you go over to his house later?" Chris sighed dramatically and added, "Like a normal human being on Valentine's Day?"

"I just have to give him his gift before I go." We reached the meeting room, which was where Mock Trial did their thing, and I took a deep breath. "One minute and I'll be ready."

Chris rolled his eyes. I knew I was acting desperate, but really—I was desperate. I gestured for them to move and give me a little space, but they weren't budging.

Fine.

I pulled open the door and popped my head inside. People were sitting at multiple tables, talking, and I squinted as I scanned the room for Josh. I was almost ready to give up when I noticed the back of his head, sitting at a table on the other side of the room.

I was a little surprised by the bubble of rage that blurbled inside of me at the sight of his curly hair—the outing with Macy was too fresh—but we were going to do the damn love thing if it killed me.

"Josh!" I whisper-yelled. "Pssst! Josh!"

He didn't hear me, but Owen Collins—one of Josh's I-purport-myself-to-be-a-college-professor friends—did. He stood and said, "Joshua, you are being paged by your girlfriend."

Which made every single head swing around in my direction.

"Can we go, please?" Chris muttered from behind me.

"One sec," I said as Josh walked across the room and toward me.

"This is so romantic," I heard Nick mutter, sounding like he thought anything but.

Chris giggled.

"Hey. Em." Josh looked at me. "What's up?"

"I, um, I have your present." I held up the wrapped box and smiled. "I thought maybe we could do our exchange really quick before I go."

"I don't have your present with me." Josh glanced behind him and then said to me, "And I really have to go."

"But don't you have to work after this?" I tucked my hair behind my ears, anxious to convince him because I desperately needed to turn the day around so February 15 was a possibility. "I really want to give you my gift *today*."

"Desperate much?" Chris said, and I knew he was right, even as

I kicked out my leg and struck his shin. I knew he was right, but I still had to try.

Maybe my "*I love you*" utterance would change everything.

"Listen, Em," Josh said, not even bothering to hide his annoyance this time. "I don't know what this is, but I'll talk to you later. I *have* to go."

"Okay. Well, um, I just wanted to tell you that I love—"

"Chicken." Nick pulled open the door, making me stumble backward, and he popped up beside me. "She loves chicken and thought you, her boyfriend, should probably know that."

Josh looked back and forth between Nick and me before saying, "Who even are you?"

Nick smiled. "I'm Nick."

I pushed Nick out of the doorway. "I don't *love chicken*, I love—"

"Look, I have to go, Em. We'll talk later."

He walked away, and I saw Owen looking at me like I was a pathetic, clingy loser. Which I was. I turned around and Nick was leaning against the wall and shaking his head, and Chris was staring at me with his mouth wide-open.

"I cannot decide whether to hug you after you humiliated yourself so badly, or kick your ass."

"Please," I said, turning away from the Mock Trial door and walking into his chest. "Kick my ass."

Chris wrapped his arms around me and I buried my face in his hoodie. He said, "There, there, Em," and patted my back for five seconds before saying, "Now get off and let's go before our ride ditches us."

"I *do* need to go," Nick said, and Chris gave him directions to our houses as we walked down the hall and exited the building.

I *had* humiliated myself. I knew I was forcing things, but I was right. I was right about Josh and about love, and how to break out of this time loop.

The only upside was that I'd probably be waking up to the same day again tomorrow, as every attempt to change the day had resulted in a trainwreck, so at least it would be forgotten, and I'd get my do-over.

As we buckled up—Chris in the middle this time—he asked, "Is everything okay, Em?"

I shrugged and clicked my belt in place. "I, um, I just *really* wanted us to have a big Valentine's moment."

"I'd say you succeeded," Nick said, putting his truck in first before pulling out of the parking spot.

"Shut it," I replied.

"I'm not going to say anything bad about Joshua because I respect that you like him, but don't you think he was kind of . . . prickish to you just now?" Chris glanced over at me and said, "I mean, yes, you were acting . . . oddly, but he was a bit of a tool."

I glanced over at Nick as I quietly said to Chris, "Maybe we can talk about this later . . . ?"

"Oh, come on, Emmer." Chris gestured toward Nick and said, "After he witnessed that pathetic display of lovesick tomfoolery, I'd say he's fine to be grandfathered into this discussion."

"Did you talk to Alex today?" I asked.

"Nice subject change," Chris said to Nick, and then he said to me, "And of course I did—I'm not a wishy-washy little baby bitch."

Chris had had a crush on Alex Lopez for months now. They were friends—they both ran cross country so they knew each other pretty well—but Chris was afraid of ruining their friendship by asking Alex out. He'd decided that on Valentine's Day he was going to see if Alex wanted to hang out. The plan was to pull one of those "Valentine's Day is lame when you're single so since we're both single and alone, do you want to get a pizza and watch old movies?" kind of things.

I gasped. "You seriously did it?"

He smiled a little secret smile and said, "I stumbled into it. At first I totally choked, but then he said he felt like a loser for having no plans, so he left me the perfect opening."

"That's amazing!" I laughed as his face transformed into happy sunlight. Chris liked to act too-cool, like, all the time, but he was one of the more vulnerable people I knew underneath it all. "So what are you going to wear?"

"No." He held up a hand and shook his head. "I'm not ready for the stress yet. Can we just take a moment and picture his adorable face? Like, when Alex is all serious about a topic and goes off, the combo of intensity and boyish cuteness is just too much."

I nodded; he was so right. "I know *exactly* what you're talking about. Last year I had him in Halleck's American Government class, and after he popped off on Ellie Green because, well, she was being so super Ellie-ish, I was obsessed with him for days. Adorable plus intense equals holy crap."

"Right?" He was beaming again, and I was so, so happy for him.

Chris had been my best friend since we'd both gotten fake notes to miss swimming our freshman year. We assumed we'd be able to just sit out, but Coach Stroud made us stand on the side of the pool and do the strokes with our hands. On dry land.

I would've died of mortification by myself, but Chris made it into choreography. I'd laughed so hard at his ludicrous dances that we'd both earned detentions.

We spent the rest of the drive to Chris's discussing Alex Lopez's greatness, and Nick was quiet. I was making all sorts of internal judgments about his silence until he said to Chris as he pulled onto his street, "Just make sure you let him see the real you; then the guy doesn't stand a chance."

"Who are you, Nick Stark?" Chris teased. "I haven't talked to you since second grade Cub Scouts, and now here you are, acting like some kind of hot, grumpy Cupid."

"You shut the fuck up right now."

Chris started laughing, and so did I. "I can't believe either of you were in Cub Scouts."

"I'll have you know I was the best knotter in the squad," Chris said, unzipping the outside pouch of his backpack and pulling out his keys.

"Pack," Nick corrected, slowing as Chris's house approached.

"Pack," Chris repeated, rolling his eyes and shaking his head at me.

"Thanks for the ride, Nick," Chris said when we pulled into his driveway. I opened the door and got out so he could get past me, and I wondered why Nick hadn't dropped me off first. It seemed like he'd have to backtrack now, but maybe Nick had to go somewhere in the direction of my house or something. Maybe he had a hot older girlfriend who lived by me and he was heading over to pick her up. Despite his being witness to the most mortifying moments of my life today, he was still practically a stranger.

When I got back in and closed the door, Chris gestured for me to roll down my window.

"You sure you're okay?" he asked, turning his lips down like he was worried. "That stunt with Josh was very *not* like you."

"I just . . . I don't know. I really had my heart set on a perfect Valentine's Day this year so I might've forced things."

"You think?" Chris said.

"I wanted to tell him that I love him, but then Nick—"

"NO," Chris snapped.

"—ruined it."

"I don't think *I* was what ruined it," Nick said from behind the wheel.

Chris said, "You're joking, right? You were going to say the L-word?"

Why was he saying it like I was out of my mind? "I'm totally serious."

His eyes got huge and he shook his head back and forth. "No, no, no. Em, you don't love him."

"Yes, I do—"

"How long have you even been going out with him? Isn't it a little soon?"

"Three months today, actually."

"Three months." His eyes shot over to Nick and then back to me. "Today?"

"Yep."

His eyebrows went all the way up. "Don't you think this is a little convenient?"

"What do you mean?"

He said, "Okay. Here you are, Little Miss Planner. Little Miss To-Do List. As long as I've known you, you've been obsessed with everything fitting into neat little boxes that you can check off."

"What's wrong with that?"

"Nothing." He gave me a sweet face and said, "I think your compulsive need for control is adorable. But don't you think saying I love you on your three-month anniversary that happens to be on a love holiday is just a little too penciled-in-the-date?"

I felt myself blush. I didn't want to talk about it anymore. "Don't you need to go in your house now?"

"Fine, I'll shut up," he said. "If you want to 'I-love' the shit out of him, just call him later."

I rolled my eyes and waved before he turned and ran up the steps and into his house. Nick put the truck in reverse and backed out, and just as he put it in first, he said, "You know you don't love him, right?"

"What?" I looked at his profile and said, "How would *you* know?"

"How would you *not* know?" he said.

"I'm not having this conversation with you," I said, annoyed. Thank God I lived close to Chris and was almost home already.

"Well, you should have it with *someone*." He glanced over at me. "You're saying the L-word, but a few hours ago you were hiding behind plants to see if he was cheating on you."

"That's not what I was doing—"

"Bullshit," he said.

"It's not," I lied. "I was just waiting for him."

Nick braked in front of my house, pulling the car over to the curb. He shoved it in neutral, pulled up the parking brake, and turned to face me. "Even if that were true—and we both know it's not—the vibe between you and your 'boyfriend' was awkward and polite. It was tense and weird. For fuck's sake, it wasn't love."

"Why do you care?" I said, almost crying now. I was tired of the repeating days, of thinking about Josh and Macy, of Nick acting like he knew anything about me or my relationship.

His face was unreadable. "I don't."

But . . . did he? He looked so serious that it made my stomach feel flittery. I grabbed my bag and said, "Good. Um, thanks for the ride."

"Anytime."

Inside, I went straight to my room, hoping to maybe just avoid the promotion discussion with my father entirely. Unfortunately, he came up right after me and told me the "good news" while tousling with Joel on my bed, tickling the kid and putting on a glorious display of fatherly love that I found to be terribly depressing.

As if that wasn't bad enough, he and Lisa talked about Texas all through dinner. The things they could do there, the suburbs where they hoped to find a house, the restaurants they hoped to frequent, the touristy things the boys would love. Valentine's dinner that night was apparently sponsored by the Texas travel commission.

By the time I was ready to go to sleep, I was totally dejected. Josh hadn't called or texted, so I stood in front of my bedroom window and made a wish upon a star, just like I was seven and wishing for my parents to stay married.

"Star light, star bright, first star I see tonight. I wish I may, I wish I might, have this wish I wish tonight." I stared out at the brightest star I could find, narrowed my eyes, and said, "I wish that I could have the perfect Valentine's Day and make this loop end."

I climbed into bed, hopeful but realistic.

I hadn't made it the perfect day—not even close.

But perhaps I only needed to fix, like, one thing. I mean, technically, I'd prevented Josh from cheating on me, so that had to count, right?

As I climbed under my covers, though, an image of me in his front seat, squeezed between him and Macy and Nick while my boots smelled like Fritos, popped into my head.

Yeah, that prevention probably didn't count for much.

CONFESSION #9

In seventh grade, I went through a phase where I took taxis all over the city, just for something to do when I couldn't handle being alone anymore.

ANOTHER VALENTINE'S DAY

When I woke up the next morning to that god-awful song, I realized that I had no idea what to do next. I still thought I needed to change things, to fix things, but I couldn't figure out what, exactly. I made a new list.

To-Do List—February 14 (again)
Take different route to school
Convince Mrs. Bowen that she must honor scholarship
Ensure Josh and Macy cannot kiss
Convince Dad that he doesn't want to move to Texas

I tried taking a different way to school. I stuck to the neighborhoods all the way there, but still managed to collide with Nick. This time he pulled out right in front of me on Edgewood Boulevard.

He came to my door again and pulled it open. "Hey—you okay?"

I got out of the car. "You pulled out right in front of me."

Nick's eyebrows went up. "I'm sorry?"

"You should be—this whole thing could've been avoided." I was thoroughly enjoying playing the hard-ass for once. "Insurance information, please."

His eyes narrowed. "You first, since *you* hit *me.*"

"Fine." I went back in my car and grabbed the info while he grabbed his. Once we exchanged, I looked at his insurance card and said, "Stark. Nick Stark?"

He didn't answer, but just looked at me like he was already annoyed by what I was about to say. I said, "Do you have Mr. Bong for Chemistry?"

His eyes narrowed the tiniest bit. "Yeah . . . ?"

"Huh—I recognize your name from attendance. Fourth block?"

"Yup."

"Hmm—small world." I pointed to my engine and said, "That's a lot of smoke—I bet this thing catches fire. Let's move."

This time I called 911 while he looked at his phone, and this time I was wearing jeans, boots, my wool peacoat, and a hat, so he didn't fetch me that old jacket. He did offer me a ride to school, but this time I had a perfect plan for peace.

As I buckled up, I said, "Thank you so much for the ride."

To which he responded, "No problem."

And then I took my new book out of my bag, opened it to the folded page, and started reading. Surely I'd be his dream passenger if I read my book and didn't say a word, right? His truck started moving and I started reading, but I only made it two sentences before he said, "Are you seriously reading Rebecca DeVos in my car?"

I looked over at him, torn between surprise that he'd heard of the author and annoyance that he sounded disgusted. "Yeah . . . ?"

"She is one of the most overrated authors in American literature. She puffed up her prose with so many flowery, fluffy descriptions that it's hard to even find the plot." He gestured to my book and said, "That story is one of the worst. I'm not sure if I ever figured out what the main character looks like because I had to use a dictionary and a thesaurus to decipher the freaking colors."

"Let me guess." I looked at the antiquey dashboard of his old truck and thought again what a mystery Nick was. Even after a couple of days of knowing him, he didn't make sense to me. I said, "You're a big Raymond Carver fan."

"I appreciate his work," he said, turning down the music, "but there's quite an expanse between DeVos and Carver. I could name twenty writers who are more purple than Carver but less . . . overblown than DeVos."

So could I. I actually wasn't loving the book and absolutely agreed with him. Which still shocked me. "Dina Marbury is a redhead, by the way, with pale, flawless skin and blue eyes."

Technically they were "eyes the color of the brightest summer sky, cloudless and cerulean and shimmering with the flawlessness of the jewels worn by kings, queens, and the smattering of mistresses who dappled the land," but *blue* was close enough.

"I knew I was supposed to root for her, but between you and me, I was happy when Dina walked into the ocean."

"Nick." I shut the book and said, "I wasn't there yet—did you seriously just tell me the ending?"

He gave a little laugh. "Oh, shit—sorry."

"It's actually okay." I reached down and shoved the book into my bag. "To be honest, I probably wasn't going to finish."

"Now, see?" He hit the turn signal and slowed for the corner. "I did you a favor."

I rolled my eyes. "She actually walked into the ocean? Wow, that sounds stolen from—"

"*The Awakening*?" He glanced over at me as the truck came to a complete stop.

"Yes! I mean, that seems like a once-in-a-lifetime book ending, doesn't it?"

"Exactly." Nick gave me something close to a smile with his eyes before turning back to the road and accelerating as the light turned green. "Like we wouldn't notice that she stole Edna Pontellier's big finish."

We talked about books for the rest of the drive to school, and it occurred to me as we walked into the building that we'd actually gotten along on Valentine's Day. For the first time. It felt like the start of a brand-new day until he said, "Why are you smiling like that?"

I glanced over at him, his nose wrinkled up and his eyebrows low over squinted eyes. I said, "What?"

"I don't know. We were walking like normal humans, and then you just started scary-grinning."

"I wasn't scary-grinning."

"You seriously were." He shook his head. "Like some creeper who enjoys televised parades and dressing cats in sweaters."

I narrowed my eyes. "Everybody likes cats in sweaters."

"Whatever you say. I gotta go." He said it like I wanted him to stay or something. And I didn't. So I said, "*I* have to go, actually."

"That's what I said," he said.

"No, you said *you* have to go, like I wanted you to walk with me when in all actuality *I* have to go."

He raised his eyebrows. "Are you okay here?"

I just shook my head and muttered, "Wonderful."

After that, I tried changing things with the counselor by showing up when they sent a pass and maturely making my case. I explained all the reasons why they should make a spot for me in their summer program, and they smiled and politely told me that it wasn't possible to add more space.

Then I tried waiting for Josh at his car with his present. A big part of me wondered why I was even trying at this point. If he and Macy had feelings for each other, did I even *want* to salvage our relationship? But another part of me knew I was right about everything and this was my chance to jump into the gears of time and ensure Macy couldn't ruin us.

I perched myself on his car's teensy hood, gift in hand, and waited. Froze to death and waited. When the two of them finally walked out the side door, Macy must've seen me because she stopped and said something to Josh. Before he could spot me, she grabbed his sleeve and steered him back inside.

Excuse me?

When I got up to follow them, my tights got stuck on the corner of his hood and got a huge hole, so I kind of wanted to shank Macy by the time I got back inside. I was still freezing as I walked down the hallway, overcome with a frustrated sadness as I realized that things might never be normal again.

What if I stayed stuck in this day forever?

Meanwhile, in Chemistry, Nick decided it was a good time to discuss the fact that I'd worn a red sweater on Valentine's Day.

"Aren't you just adorable."

"What?"

He gestured to my shirt with his pencil. "Your whole matchy-matchy, Hallmark-holiday outfit—super cute."

"That's not what this is." I looked down at my shirt and said, "It's just a red sweater."

"Really?"

"Yes, really."

He gave me a knowing look and said, "How do you explain the heart bracelet and matching earrings, then?"

I rolled my eyes and shook my head. I'd been going for a terse brush-off, but for some reason, tears filled my eyes as I said, "Don't you have anything better to do than analyze my fashion choices?"

He leaned a little closer, his eyes all over my face. "Are you crying?"

"NO," I said loudly, but the tears betrayed me by falling from my eyes.

"Oh, fuck—no." He swallowed and said, "No, no—I'm sorry—I was just messing with you."

"It's fine," I said, sniffling. "I'm not crying."

"Yes, you are," he said quietly, his eyes serious for once as they stayed focused on my face. "Please, please, stop."

"Fine, I *am* crying." I sniffled again, trying to keep it together. "But not because of you."

"Promise?"

I rolled my eyes and swiped at them. *"Yes."*

I took a deep breath, trying to calm myself. I *never* cried. But the idea that I could be stuck in this terrible Valentine's Day purgatory, forever, was really sinking in. Would I never get any older? Have a shot at a journalism career? See the twins grow up? It was all too much.

"How can I make it stop?" he asked, looking so uncomfortable that it was almost funny. "Seriously."

"I'm fine." I sniffled and ran my index fingers under my lower lashes. I took a deep breath and told myself I could fix this. "All better."

"But—" He gave me the sweetest closed-mouth smile and said, "You sure?"

I nodded and couldn't help but smile back. "I'm good."

"Hallelujah." He exhaled, like he was letting out a huge sigh of relief, and said, "Because the thought of being nice to you for the rest of Chem is a little exhausting."

I half laughed as I shook my head. "It's that hard?"

He shrugged. "It's not that it's hard, it's just that I prefer watching you blink fast and get all offended at everything I say."

Another repeating day, another eye lost to over-rolling in the presence of Nick Stark.

I closed out the day with another failed attempt to convince my father to stay.

This time, I pointed out that he couldn't leave my grandmother—widowed and living by herself—and move across the country. What would she do? She'd be so alone, right? I knew he adored his mother, so surely my argument would shake his moving resolve.

But he smiled when I said that. He said, "She wants to go with us, Emmie—ask her. She's *thrilled* about warm weather and cowboys."

"She is?"

"You're surprised?" he asked, still smiling.

"Well, not about the cowboys."

So not only did I fail to convince him, but I learned the worst news ever: I'd be losing Grandma Max as well. She hadn't even mentioned that possibility when we'd talked about it on the first Valentine's Day, but I'd also been a bawling mess, so I didn't blame her.

I wished upon a star—again—before going to bed, but I was starting to lose hope that a freaking glowing orb in the sky had any interest in helping me at all.

After that, I became obsessed with changing the results. In any way that I could. Regarding the lost scholarship, I tried:

-Not showing up when the office called

-Showing up and begging for their mercy

-Fake-crying with an absurdly detailed fabricated story about my grandfather's dying wish to see me in that program

-Fake-crying with an absurdly detailed fabricated story about my elderly—and dying—grandmother's love of journalism

-Offering Mrs. Bowen a small bribe

None of those attempts provided me a changed result. With Macy and Josh, I tried:

-Lying in wait in my car and frantically honking the horn every time their faces got close together in his lame-ass tiny vehicle

-Texting Josh that I heard a rumor about Macy and herpes and mouth-rot (not my finest moment)

-Throwing a baseball at Josh's windshield once he and *Mace* were ensconced in his ridiculous car. The ball actually made contact and cracked the window, but my throw was too slow and their lips touched before the resultant balling so it was all for naught. And I had to duck behind a car and slink back toward the doors like a Marine under siege.

Nothing was working.

As far as the car situation, I tried:

-Driving my dad's car to school, but I still hit Nick.

-Riding to school with Chris, but he crashed into Nick instead of me. Ironically, I still ended up catching a ride with the surly one when Chris had to go to the hospital to get his neck checked.

I tried walking to school, but even *then* I ended up with Nick. I couldn't believe my eyes, but his truck was parked on the side of the Hickory Oaks subdivision street that led to our school—I was assuming he lived in the house beside it. The hood was up, and he was doing something underneath it. I tried quietly walking by, but just when I thought I was past I heard him say, "Excuse me—hey. Can you help me for like one second?"

I glanced in his direction and put my hand on my chest. "Me?"

"Yeah."

I said, "Um, no offense, but I'm a sixteen-year-old girl—it's not really safe for me to help strangers. Can I call someone for—"

"I'm not a stranger—we're in the same Chemistry class."

What?

So he actually knew I was his lab partner? Had he been messing with me every single time we'd met? I said, "Are you sure? I mean, you kind of look a little familiar, but—"

"Yes, I'm sure—we sit at the same table. So will you help me?"

I stepped off the curb and approached him, trying not to smile as I felt some sort of a win by his recognition. "What do you need me to do?"

His hair was a little windblown, but his eyes were like the deepest blue in contrast to the black of his zipped-up jacket. I'd always thought they were brown, but they actually made me think of DeVos's flowery prose; she'd kind of nailed his color with the whole cloudless-summer-sky thing.

He said, "I just need you to start my truck while I hoosh this frozen thing with starter fluid," interrupting my distracted thoughts about his pretty corneas. "Have you ever driven a stick?"

I put my hands in my pockets and buried my neck a little deeper in my wool coat. "No, but I know how to start a car with a clutch."

"Perfect. Would you mind?"

The smell of him—soap, cologne, I didn't know what it was—hit me hard, but I pushed all of that aside. I said, "Sure."

I went around his truck and got in, having to move the seat forward in order for my foot to be able to push in the clutch all the way. I left the door open so I could wait for his command, and when he said "Now," I turned the key.

That old truck didn't want to turn over, but Nick must've known what he was doing because all of a sudden, it roared to life. I revved it a little before he yelled, "Can you put it in neutral and leave it running?"

"Sure." It felt familiar—comforting—to be in this position. I used to help my dad when he worked on the Porsche by doing this exact thing, only I'd been twelve at the time. I threw the truck into neutral and got out.

Nick slammed the hood down and came around to the driver's side. He said, "Thanks a lot. She hates the cold."

"She?"

"The truck."

I rolled my eyes and my Nick-warmth went away. "I hate that so much."

"What?" He looked interested, but not offended. "What do you hate?"

"When men feel the need to refer to their beloved vehicle as female."

That made him give me the smart-ass smile that I'd grown

accustomed to over the course of our repeating-days relationship. "Why is that?"

"It's just so sexist. It rings of the patriarchy and of men objectifying women. Like, *I love this beautiful piece of metal so much that it very nearly turns me on. Like woman.*"

His smile held as he said, "It was my brother's truck, for the record, and he nicknamed it 'Betty' because it used to belong to our great-aunt Betty. And we also have a dog named Betty."

"So, fine." I shrugged and said, "I'm a raging feminist lunatic, I guess."

"You guess."

"Yeah, I guess." I rolled my eyes and just felt . . . out of sorts all of a sudden. "Technically, I'm starting to think I'm just a straight-up lunatic across the board."

He crossed his arms over his chest. "You doing okay here?"

"No, I'm not doing okay here!" I sighed and groaned and wondered how many more times he was going to ask me that before my premature death from time-loop frustration. I shook out my hands and tried my mantra—*You are on top of this*—but it didn't work and I groaned again and yelled, "I'm actually fucking TERRIBLE and something WEIRD is happening to me, but it is SO WEIRD that I can't even talk about it!"

"Wow." Nick's mouth kicked up a little at the corners, and then he actually laughed. "It must be *very* weird to make someone like *you* have a meltdown like *that*."

I sighed and said, "You have no fucking idea."

That made him laugh again—*sweet Lord* he was a handsome boy when he wasn't being an ass—and he said, "Do you want a ride? To school? I mean, I'm going there and if you're walking there—this is probably faster. And warmer."

Who was this nice and charming person? I tucked my hair behind my ears and said, "That would be great. Thank you."

I picked up my bag and got in the truck, suddenly nervous. Which was bizarre because it felt like I'd been in that truck twenty times, and I hadn't been nervous any of those times. Of course, he'd been a jerk all of those times; Nice Nick was new.

"Do you always walk to school?" Nick got behind the wheel and pushed in the clutch. "I'm surprised I've never seen you before."

"No," I said, buckling my seat belt. "Today was, um, kind of like an experiment."

"And the findings were . . . ?"

I straightened and dared to glance at Nick, who was waiting for my answer with an amused expression on his face. I said, "The findings were inconclusive because I was pulled off the experiment to be a Good Samaritan to this guy with a broken-down car."

"Bummer on the experiment, but the guy sure sounds cool."

I did laugh, then, unable to resist. "He might be cool, but I have it on good authority that he's actually a grouchy hermit who won't even speak to his lab partner in Chemistry."

"I *knew* you recognized me." He pointed when he said it, grinning, and I couldn't believe the irony. "Miss I-don't-talk-to-strangers."

I laughed a little more and said, "You can never be too careful."

"Of course," he said, turning his eyes back to the road.

"Did you finish the reading for today?" I asked, wondering how someone could smell so good but also so subtle. It wasn't like the expensive cologne Josh wore—which I enjoyed—but more like fresh body wash or dryer sheets. I could hyperventilate on his cleanliness. "I totally forgot, so I'm going to have to cram next hour."

"I didn't do the reading, but I never do." He hit his turn signal and made a left into the junior parking lot. "I wait until the night before a test, like all normal high school students."

"You're calling me abnormal?"

He pulled into the shockingly open spot in the first row before saying, "I'm calling you unique."

I must've made a face because he gave me a little smile as he turned off the truck and said, "What? I meant it as a compliment."

I unbuckled my seat belt and opened the door. "I know—that's what's weird."

He set the emergency brake, pocketed his keys, and grabbed his backpack from where it sat between us. "Why is that weird? I've never insulted you."

Now, he'd insulted me handfuls of times in that very truck, but so far, that day, he was a freaking delight. So I said, "Well, no," and got out.

He came around to my side and we walked into school together. He didn't say anything else, nor did I, but his scent was in my nose and I was feeling warm and tingly as the snow squeaked under our shoes.

When we got inside, and I pointed south because I had to turn down the first hallway to go find Chris, he stopped. He looked down into my eyes with his *ridiculously* blue ones and said, "I don't know what the terrible thing is that you're dealing with and can't talk about, but when all else fails, I say fuck 'em."

I swallowed and forgot how to talk, because blue eyes were pointed directly at me in a shivery way, and I noticed how nice his mouth was. I fumbled for words and managed, "I, um, really don't—"

He reached out a hand, tugged lightly on the piece of hair that had come out of my ponytail, and he said, "Fuck 'em, Emilie."

And then he walked away.

I went through the motions, and when they called me down to the office like they did every day, I actually showed up and spoke the truth. I looked at Mrs. Bowen and said, "Can I be honest? This is devastating to my plans; I was counting on this for scholarship applications. Is there an alternate program that might have an opening?"

I expected my daily rejection, but she tilted her head and pursed her lips instead. She started talking to Mr. Kessler about a program I was unaware of, and then she left the room to make a call.

I asked Mr. Kessler, "Do you know this program?"

He nodded. "I do. It's very, very good and would look great on an application."

"Do you think I have a shot?" A feeling that was something like hope bubbled up inside of me.

He shrugged and gave me an encouraging dad-smile. "Anything's possible."

Mrs. Bowen came back then, but she hadn't been able to reach the person she'd hoped to speak with. She said she would "do some checking" and get back to me, and I could tell she meant it.

When she was leaving, she apologized again, only this time she added, "We will find a way to make this right, Emilie. You have my word."

Things were lining up in a way that had me optimistic about my February 15 chances.

After class, I made the adult decision to not even go near the hallway-exit parking lot where I'd repeatedly seen Josh step out with Macy. Hopefully the universe that was working for me so far that day would keep them from kissing, but at least this way, I wouldn't have to see it if they did.

It'd be the whole tree-falling-in-the-forest thing; if I wasn't there to see it, did it really ever happen?

I mean, yes, when I let myself picture it—picture them—my stomach still hurt and I felt like a fool, but I needed to put that out of my mind and nail my perfect day if I ever wanted life to return to normal.

I was meticulous with my intentions, doing my best to be extra nice to everyone and extra attentive in class. I even smiled when I passed Lauren, Lallie, and Nicole in the hallway.

When I got to Chemistry, Nick was already at our table. I took a deep breath, nervous for some reason that I didn't choose to explore, and walked over to my spot.

He glanced up when I set my bag on the floor and said, "Hey." Smiled. "It's you."

I sat down and said, "It *is* me."

My cheeks were hot as we exchanged some kind of a hey-I-know-you-from-this-morning look. His eyes trailed over my face before he said, "Thanks again for helping me this morning."

I shrugged. "Thanks again for the ride."

"Listen up," Mr. Bong said as he walked into the classroom, his eyes on the phone in his hand as he walked over to his desk. "It's pop-quiz time, so I need everyone who sits on the right side of their lab table to move to the seat directly behind them."

Bong always made us switch seats for exams because he seemed to think we were cheating collusionists with our lab partners. Since I was on the right side, I grabbed my bag.

"Wait." Nick picked up his phone from where it was resting on top of the table and said, "Give me your number and I'll text you."

I felt my mouth drop open and I tried being cool, but Nick was asking me for my phone number. *What was happening?* Nick Stark was asking for my number, and I kind of wanted to give it to him. I gave a half-laugh, suddenly nervous, and said, "Why would I do that, exactly?"

He just said, "You'll find out when I text you. Number, please."

I told him, and he punched the numbers into his phone.

My phone lit up. Nick: Guess who?

I smiled and moved to the seat at the other table before responding. Me: My surly lab partner . . . ?

Nick: It's the cool guy who gave you a ride to school.

That made me smile. Me: Ah—THAT guy.

Nick: Do you want a ride home?

I gasped. Like, literally gasped. Because—dear Lord: Was Nick Stark asking me out–ish? What was this day? Who was this boy?

What was happening?

Me: I've got a ride, but thank you SO much!

When I pressed send, an unexpected feeling settled in my chest. It was something like . . . regret.

But I was on the verge of possibly escaping the fourteenth of February, and I couldn't risk it. I needed to perfect the rest of the day, and that included Valentine's Day with my boyfriend.

Nick: So if Betty doesn't start, you're unavailable for turnover duty?

Why was I disappointed that I was unavailable for turnover duty?

Me: Unfortunately yes. But I'm sure there are lots of strangers you could summon who can start your truck.

Nick: We aren't strangers, remember?

I glanced over at him, and he was looking directly at me with one eyebrow raised and a smirk on his lips. I felt a little light-headed as I texted: Oh, yes—that's right.

Mr. Bong started handing out quizzes, and we weren't able to talk or text for the rest of the hour. Which was good; I needed to stay focused. The second I turned in my quiz, I left the room without even daring to glance in Nick's direction.

I stayed happy and nice and positive through the rest of the day, and when I rushed to meet Josh at his locker after school, he turned and smiled at me with a huge grin.

"Thank God—thank *God*." He leaned forward and pressed his

forehead against mine. "It's Valentine's Day and I haven't even seen the Emmie of my heart yet. Where in God's name have you been hiding all day?"

I smiled up at him, but a tiny part of me was wondering if he'd kissed Macy. And if he hadn't, had he wanted to? Had they talked and flirted as they'd gone on the coffee run? He looked the same as always, but something inside of me felt different when I looked at him.

I pushed that nonsense away and said, "Nowhere. Do you have time to open my present before Mock Trial?"

He turned away from me and reached into his locker while saying, "Only if you have time to open mine."

That made me tease, "I *guess* I can find a moment."

The first package he gave me was a rectangular box—obviously chocolates. I ripped off the paper, then smiled at him. "My favorite dinner—thank you."

"Of course," he said, covering his heart with both of his hands. "Sweets for the sweet."

"And *from* the sweet," I added, grinning because it was romantic and also the perfect words to be said on the perfect Valentine's Day. I didn't want to get ahead of myself, but it felt like I might just be getting it right.

"Now this, my sweet," he said, holding out a small square box.

I exhaled on a laugh, caught up in his smile and the festivity of the gifts. I pulled open the white gift box, and nestled inside was a silver bracelet. I raised my eyes to his, and he was grinning expectantly.

I waited for an explanation, but after two seconds of smiling blankly at him, I squealed, "Omigosh, Josh, I love it so much—thank you!"

As he insisted on putting it on me, I said nothing, dreading the rash that would cover my skin within hours. Because I'd told Josh an entire story—last week—about how silver made me break out. Yes, people sometimes forgot things, but it had been a long story that included a trip to the ER and he'd commented on how if we'd been dating at that time, he would've smuggled in a pizza for me to eat.

So now he was buying me silver?

I pushed that down, though, for the sake of a perfect day, and watched him open the watchband. He loved it—I knew he would—and it made him wrap his arms around me and kiss me big on the lips, school hallway be damned.

When he pulled back and looked down at me, I grinned. Cleared my throat. Then I took the deepest of breaths, looked at his brown eyes, and said, "I love—"

"Not yet!" He held up a finger and said, "Not another word until you hear my poem."

I closed my mouth, a little shaken. Had he known what I was about to say? He was giving me a huge smile, so I didn't think so.

He read me the poem he'd written, saying I fit into his poems like the perfect rhyme, and he wrapped me up in a big hug. It was beautiful, like all his poetry, and afterward I smiled through the hallways as I headed for Chris's car. *Love is not what is, but what isn't. My ears aren't happy when she isn't speaking; my fingers bereft when her skin is absent.*

I hadn't had a chance to say it—*I love you*—but I was okay with that. He'd used the word "love" in his poem about me, so that was almost like he'd said it first, and I could still tell him when he called me later that night.

When I got outside and the cold hit me in the face, I heard the horn before I saw Chris. That goofy smart-ass was honking to the tune of "We Will Rock You," and I was crying from laughter by the time I reached his car.

"Could you *be* any slower?" he yelled out the window.

"I'm sure I could," I yelled back, laughing even harder when I reached for the door handle and it was locked. "Let me in!"

"Fine." He hit unlock and said, "But only because I need ten bucks for gas."

"Typical." I got in his car and closed the door, and as I slammed it shut, I saw Nick Stark one row over, messing with his truck's engine. I rolled down the window and yelled in his direction, "Do you need help?"

His eyes raised from the motor of his car to my face and I was instantly warm. He was doing that sarcastic half-smile thing when he yelled, "No offense, but I'm a sixteen-year-old guy. It isn't really safe for me to talk to strangers."

I laughed and yelled, "We're not strangers, Nick Stark."

His half-smile went wide and whole. "That's right—we're partners."

I laughed again and I heard Chris make a noise. I ignored it and said, "Seriously, though—do you need help? Or a ride?"

"What am I—your Uber now?" Chris muttered.

"No, but thanks," Nick said. "She's actually running now so I'm good."

"Well, okay, then." Why was I disappointed? "See you."

He gave me a look that was suspended—frozen—before life went back to full speed.

"Hey, hon." My dad came out of the kitchen with a dish towel over his shoulder. "How was school?"

I smiled and set down my bag. I had already taken off Josh's bracelet on the ride home and shoved it deep in a pocket of my backpack so I wouldn't have to think about it. To my dad, I said, "Good. Hey—can I talk to you for a quick second?"

"I have to stir my sauce, but sure."

I followed him into the kitchen and climbed onto one of the counter stools. He was making spaghetti and meatballs—Grandma Max's recipe—and it smelled amazing.

"What's up?"

I reached out and grabbed an apple from the fruit bowl. "Mom told me about the promotion." A lie, of course, but I was getting ahead of this.

"Christ—are you kidding me?" My dad's shoulders dropped and he looked pissed. "I told her I wanted to talk to you first—"

"No—it's okay." I took a bite of the apple and said, "She misunderstood something I said and thought I already knew."

"Oh." He closed his mouth and stirred his sauce, looking deep in thought. My dad was one of those dads who maintained a younger vibe; like, he had all of his hair and hadn't gotten soft yet. That being said, there were a few gray hairs in his temples that hinted at his true age.

"Yeah, so, can I be honest here? I want you guys to be able to move to your dream town or whatever. I really do. But," I said, trying to get the courage to say it in the right way, "I hate the thought of you moving away from me. Like, I love Mom, but *home* is when I'm with you."

My voice cracked at the end and everything inside of me wanted to clarify that it was *fine* and he shouldn't worry about it, but I forced myself not to. I looked down at the red skin of my apple.

"Wow. Um, I'm going to be honest here, Em—I didn't expect this." I looked up in time to see him rub the back of his neck like he was uncomfortable. "I guess I thought it wouldn't matter much to you."

"That you're moving across the country?" I blinked fast because crying never helped anything. I still couldn't believe I'd melted down like a baby in front of Nick in Chem, even if he had no idea it had happened. "How could it not matter? You're my *dad.* The boys are my *brothers.* This is my home."

He stopped stirring. "But you seem so happy with your mom. I guess I just . . ."

"Assumed. You assumed." It felt bitter on my tongue, and there was so much more I could say, but I didn't want to mar the perfect day. "I love Mom, but *you* are my home."

He swallowed and I saw his nostrils flare before he said, "Oh, Em—I'm so sorry."

I shook my head and fought back tears. "Don't be. You didn't know because I never said anything." *I'd never wanted to rock the boat.* "And I don't want to keep you from moving. I just, um, I don't know—I thought maybe we could find some options to make this work."

He came around the counter and sat down on the stool beside me. He told me it'd been killing him, the thought of not being able to see me every day, and he said we—he, Lisa, and me—would sit down tomorrow and find a way to make it work.

When I went up to my room that night, I was buzzing with happiness. I felt closer to my dad than I had in ages, I hadn't wrecked my car, a summer program was still a possibility, and Josh and I had had a perfect Valentine's Day.

I climbed into bed and thought about the silver bracelet. I mean, it *was* very pretty, and it looked expensive. Why was I making a big deal about him forgetting my allergy?

My phone buzzed, and I reached for where it was charging on the nightstand. I thought it would be Josh, but it was Nick Stark.

Nick: Your ChapStick is in my truck.

Me: What?

Nick: I just got home and when I grabbed my backpack, your ChapStick was on the floor underneath it.

He had to be talking about my Burt's Bees, which I hadn't been able to find all day.

Nick: I'll bring it to Chemistry, but I just wanted to let you know.

Me: Thanks. How'd you do on the quiz?

Nick: Aced it.

Me: Wow. Cocky.

Nick: Guilty. I've got hella Chem swagger.

Me: You really ARE a cool guy.

Nick: I know. So did your BF give you Valentine's flowers?

Me: Candy and a bracelet, actually.

Nick: So are you wearing your jewels right now while jamming chocolate into your face hole?

That made me laugh and I texted: I left the candy in my friend's car and the bracelet gave me a rash, so big no.

Nick: Holy shit—he got you a bracelet that turns your arm green??

I sighed and started to text, but, before I even really knew what I was doing, I found myself hitting the call button.

"Hello?"

"The bracelet didn't turn my arm green. I'm allergic to silver."

"First of all, is that really a thing?" he asked. "And second, I bet he wishes you would've told him that little tidbit of personal info before he dropped coin on your baubles."

"It *is* a thing—I am allergic." I grabbed my soda off the nightstand and said, "And I *did* tell him. He must've just forgotten."

"Let me get this straight." His voice was deep and a little gravelly, like he'd just woken up. "You told Josh Sutton, arguably the smartest kid at our school, that you're allergic to silver. And then he bought you a silver necklace for Valentine's Day."

"Bracelet."

"Whatever. He's clearly trying to kill you."

I started laughing, in spite of wanting to choke him for making me doubt Josh. "He is not."

"Are you sure?" I could hear the smile in his low, quiet voice. "I mean, you can never be too careful."

"I've heard that." I cleared my throat and couldn't believe I was talking to Nick Stark on the phone. That *I* had called *him*. "So where were you all night?"

"Whoa—back off, creeper."

"Shut it," I said through another laugh. "Were you working?"

"I was."

"And . . . ? Where do you work?"

"Should I be alarmed by how interested you are in my comings and goings?"

"Absolutely not." I remembered what he thought about small talk, so I said, "I was just hoping you can get me a hefty discount at one of my favorite places. Bookstore, coffee shop, pizza delivery—any of those would work for me. I like having connections."

"So." He sounded a little more awake. "You'd like to use our acquaintance for your personal gain, is that what you're saying?"

"Precisely." I smiled into the quiet of my bedroom and said, "Although you needn't make it sound so mercenary."

"Well, I hate to disappoint you, but I work at 402 Ink. A tattoo shop."

He worked at a tattoo shop?

Everyone knew that he'd gotten tattoos last year—as a sophomore—so that made him seem wildly edgy since the legal age without permission was eighteen. But to work there? That was some straight-up street cred.

"I'm not disappointed," I said, picturing the smirk that would curl his lip when I said, "I'm planning on getting two massive sleeves next week, so this is perfect."

"Sure you are."

"You don't know."

"I think I do."

I gave a nod in agreement, even though he couldn't see it, and asked, "What do you do there?"

"Everything that isn't a tattoo. Answer phones, social media, website, cash register—I'm their bitch, pretty much."

"Oh." I lay back on my pillow and pulled the covers up to my shoulders. "That sounds interesting, actually."

"You'd think." He sounded like he was walking when he said, "What about you? Job?"

"I work at Hex Coffee."

"Really? Huh—I'm surprised I've never seen you there."

"You go there a lot?"

"No. I actually hate coffee."

That made me snort. "Of course you do."

"I'm more of a tea guy."

"Lying again?"

"I seriously drink four to five cups of Sleepytime every day."

"You *have* to be lying."

"Swear to God."

I tried picturing him drinking tea and frankly, it was too

adorable. He gave off strong Jess Mariano vibes when he talked about books, and the tea just made it bigger. I said, "I hate tea."

"You would."

"You aren't going to try to convince me that I'm wrong?" Josh loved tea and was always trying to get me to try his. "Tea drinkers are usually pushers who swear by the fact that if you just try tea the way they drink it, you'll like it."

"Why would I care what you drink?"

"I . . . have no idea."

"Listen, I have to go. I just didn't want you freaking out and losing your ever-loving shit over your ChapStick."

"I was about to, so your call is most appreciated."

"You seem the type."

"I know."

He made a little laugh sound and said, "Sorry about your terrible Valentine's presents, by the way."

"It's fine." That made me laugh again. "What'd you get your girlfriend?"

"Girlfriend—please. I don't have time for that."

"But if you did . . . ?"

I don't know why, but I really wanted to know.

"If I did? I don't know—not chocolates and anaphylaxis, that's for sure."

I laughed again and said, "Come on. Commit already."

"Fine." He made a growly sound and said, "Uh, something that mattered to her, I guess. I mean, if she was a bookish person like you, I'd try to find a special edition of her favorite book or something."

"Oh." I wasn't even going to let my mind go there, to the utter fantastical gift possibilities.

"But someone recently told me that I'm kind of a surly person, so gifts and Hallmark holidays kind of aren't my thing."

"Ah." I thought back to that morning at his truck and said, "Bummer on the surliness, but the girl sure sounds cool."

That made him fall into a charming hoarse laugh that trickled through my veins and dipped all the way down to the tips of my toes. "G'night, Emilie Hornby."

"G'night to you, Nick Stark."

I'd just pressed end when a text came through.

Josh: Salutations, sweet Valentine.

I felt guilty as I responded. Me: Greetings.

Josh: We're swamped so I can't call until break, but I wanted to send a quick hello, in case you fall asleep.

Me: Right back atcha. 😉

Josh: Are you wearing your bracelet?

Me: Nope—in bed.

Josh: I remembered that you love shiny things and it reminded me of your smile.

I didn't particularly like shiny things—I wasn't a bling girl—and how would a silver chain bracelet remind him of my smile, anyway? What—my smile in sixth grade, when I had a mouth full of braces and wore headgear when I slept?

I could still hear Nick Stark: *Something that mattered to her.*

I texted: Awwwww. <3 But the poem was the shiniest gift.

Josh: Sweetie. 😉 Gotta run. Lates, Emmiecakes.

Me: Lates.

I plugged the phone back into the charger, turned off the light, and settled into my pillow. I really *had* had a great Valentine's Day with Josh—poetry and jewelry, what more could a girl ask for, really? It'd been everything I'd wanted out of the day, even before falling into this abyss of repetitive days.

The perfect boyfriend, checking off nearly all of the romance boxes I'd jotted down in my planner.

So why didn't I feel more . . . I don't know . . . *swoon* when I thought about him? The Macy thing, of course, but this was something else. He'd written a poem about me, but somehow the thought of Nick Stark talking about what he'd buy for a hypothetical girlfriend was more sweepy-off-my-feety than poetry.

I quickly shut down that train of thought. I knew nothing about Nick Stark—other than what he liked to read, what he listened to, what he smelled like, where he worked, how his laugh sounded when he was sleepy over the phone—and he was probably the jerk I'd always thought him to be.

Josh was perfect for me, and I was just tired.

I didn't wish on a star that night. The day had been so close to perfect—in such an organic way—that I didn't need the galaxy's help.

I got this, Milky Way.

I fell asleep, not even noticing that, with talking to Nick on the phone, I had forgotten to say "I love you" to Josh.

CONFESSION #10

When I was three, I used to chase Billy Tubbs down the block, and if I caught him, I tackled him to the ground and bit him all over his back. My dad says he cried every time he saw me.

YET ANOTHER GODFORSAKEN VALENTINE'S DAY

My alarm went off and I hurled the phone across the room.

"Nooooooooooooooooooooooo!"

"Walking on Sunshine" kept playing after the phone hit the wall and landed somewhere in the dark, but instead of retrieving it I just buried my face in my pillow and full-on screamed until I was out of breath.

I was in hell.

How could that day not have changed the course of events?

I grabbed my robe and went into the bathroom to shower. *Again.* I started the water and stepped in, knowing what was coming. I counted to five and then—

"Em, are you almost done in there?"

Bingo. Lisa was going to press her mouth against the doorjamb and tell me that my little brother needed to use the bathroom. Just like every other day, I yelled, “I just got in here.”

“Joel needs to go potty. Bad.”

“There is a bathroom upstairs.” I poured shampoo into my hand and rubbed it on my head. I knew what her answer was going to be, but it somehow seemed important to play the game.

“Your dad’s in there.”

This time I yelled, “Douse him with ice water and he’ll jump right out.”

There was a pause before she murmured through the wood, “You’re seriously not going to get out?”

I thought about it for a second and came up with, “I don’t think so. Sorry.”

Whoa. I rubbed my hair harder as one thought suddenly overtook all others in my brain.

I. Had. Immunity.

Yes, being stuck in an eternal Valentine’s Day purgatory was the worst, but what I hadn’t considered until now was that I could do whatever I wanted and not face any of the fallout.

I could absolutely use Nick Stark’s words as my mantra for the day.

Fuck ’em.

I took an extremely long shower in honor of that fact, and by the time I got out and dried myself, I had an epiphany.

I could say whatever I wanted to anyone, and it would be erased the next day. I couldn’t get grounded or suspended or even arrested, because the next morning I’d be back in my bed at my dad's house, walking on freaking sunshine, and no one would remember my transgressions.

Let the games begin.

I got out of the shower and went straight to my planner.

To-Do List—February 14: DAY OF NO CONSEQUENCES
WHATEVER I FUCKING FEEL LIKE

Instead of rushing to free up the bathroom like I usually did, I dragged a stool in front of the vanity. I cranked the volume on my phone and blared the new Volbeat album while I spent far too long making on-point eyeliner tails. I went full-on good makeup and straightened my hair so I could put it in the *perfect* high ponytail.

"Not too shabby, Em." I looked at my reflection. *Interesting.* As it turned out, if you spent an entire hour on your appearance, you looked pretty good. I leaned forward and blotted my red lipstick against the mirror, leaving a perfect mouth print.

Next, I went into my closet and dug, knowing exactly what I was going to wear to school. I had the *cuuuutest* black leather pants, but I'd never had the guts to wear them to school because they were tight with a capital *T-I-G-H-T*.

And *so* not me. Or at least the me that everyone thought I was. But the pants made my butt look killer, so I was going to wear the hell out of those bad boys.

I paired them with my softest cashmere sweater and the suede boots I'd only worn once, and I hopped down the stairs with my backpack, humming in anticipation of what was destined to be a Top Ten day.

I'd heard my dad leave while I flat-ironed my hair, so it was just Lisa and the twins left at home. I walked into the kitchen and went straight for the last leftover slice of French silk pie.

The twins were in their little kiddie seats at the table, jamming pieces of pancakes into their pouty mouths and looking disgustingly adorable. I laughed as Logan pushed his sippy cup off the table and watched it land on the floor.

Little turd.

Lisa picked it up and set it beside him. Her face was tense, so I knew she was pissed about my refusal to get out of the shower for Joel.

But I didn't care—not today.

Normally I bent over backward to be the perfect houseguest. I made a huge effort—all the time—to make my dad and Lisa forget how much tidier their new life would be if it were just the four of them.

Today, however—screw it. Screw the guilt and the bending over. I grabbed a fork and ate the chocolate pie straight from the tin, and when I was finished, I dumped it into the sink without even rinsing it.

"Hey. Lisa." I turned around and gave her my biggest smile. "Does my dad still keep the keys to the Porsche in his workbench in the mudroom?"

"Why?" She crossed her arms over her chest and glanced at the pie pan in the sink. Which, to be honest, was bothering me, too.

The dishwasher was *right* next to the sink; why would anyone leave a dish in the sink?

I forced myself to ignore the pan.

"I'm running late and need something with a little more kick than my car." On the Day of No Consequences—which I would henceforth refer to as the DONC—a Porsche would serve me better than the van.

Without bothering to wait for an answer, I ran into the mudroom and pulled open the drawer. "Sweet—he does."

"Now wait just a minute. Did your father say you could take his car?"

He would never. He loved that car. Adored it. Would tongue-bathe it if that were guaranteed to forever protect the shiny black paint. My dad had bought the crappy old Porsche from a junkyard when I was a kid and spent countless hours fixing it up with my Uncle Mick. It didn't look that cool, but it was fast and sleek.

And also not an Astro van.

"Don't worry about it. You guys have a great day, 'kay?"

"Emilie, you are not taking that car, do you hear me?"

I tilted my head and turned my lips downward. "I hear you, hon, but I'm afraid I *am* taking the car. Toodles."

I left and closed the door behind me, half expecting her to chase me out into the driveway. *Toodles?* I giggled as I realized what I'd just done and said.

I hummed as I went into the unattached garage and got the Porsche before Lisa could stop me. That baby purred to life, and I pushed my aviators up the bridge of my nose and squealed out of the driveway faster than you could say *Bitch got it goin' on.*

Wow. I stomped on the gas and flew down Harrison Street, hugging the road and stretching the legs and doing all those amazing car-things that amazing cars were said to do on TV commercials.

Translation: I hauled ass.

Gone were the Valentine's Days that started with crappy cars and car accidents. Gone were the Valentine's Days that left me crying in the school bathroom. Gone were endless days of borrowing Nick Stark's old jacket, and gone were the days that'd felt important but obviously were not. This new-and-improved Valentine's Day was beginning with fast cars and Metallica on blast, and I *dared* the universe to dump on my parade.

Not this time.

I glanced in my rearview mirror just as the cop turned behind me and flipped on his lights. My stomach clenched for a second until I remembered—no consequences. Technically, I could lead him on a high-speed chase that would make it on all the national news channels if I wanted to, but that seemed like more trouble than I was interested in.

Especially since I *wanted* to get to school. I had a lot to do that day. I pulled over, got out my license and registration, and rolled down my window.

When the cop appeared, he looked grumpy. "License and registration, please."

I handed it to him and said, "I know I was speeding, by the way, and I'm sorry."

"You were going ninety-six miles per hour in a forty-five zone."

Oops. "I'm really sorry."

"You're going to need a lot more than an apology, young lady. I'll be right back."

He went back to his car and I turned up the radio a little. I started singing along to "Blackened," my not-at-all random musical selection for the DONC, and then I amused myself by waving at every person who gawked at me when they drove by.

Was this how it felt to be a rebel? Because I kind of liked the way this felt. I kept cackling to myself, giggling uncontrollably, when I thought about the wild fact that I'd been pulled over in the car I'd stolen from my dad without permission for going thirty miles over the speed limit.

Who even was I?

I started to get nervous when it was taking so long, and especially when the tow truck showed up, but then I had to remind myself that it didn't matter. Nothing mattered. Whatever happened, I would wake up tomorrow, free and clear.

The officer finally came back to my window. He handed me the registration and insurance card, but he kept my license. "You're getting a citation for reckless driving. You'll have to go to court for this. Because you were going so far above the posted limit, this is not a ticket you can pay without seeing a judge. Do you understand?"

I nodded and squinted up into the sun that was shining behind his big head.

"Your car is being impounded because of the high rate of speed.

Here is a pamphlet listing all of the information about how long it will be impounded for and how you can get it back at that time."

"My car is going to jail?"

"Better it than you, don't you think?"

"Of course." Jail would totally mess up my plans for the day.

"Your license is also being revoked until your court date. At that time, the judge can make the decision on whether or not it's possible for you to get it back."

"Wow—you guys aren't playing out here today, are you?"

He took off his glasses and looked at me with his eyebrows all screwed together, like he couldn't believe my nerve. "Young lady, this is a big deal."

"I know. I was just joking, you know, to try to lighten the mood."

"Do you have someone who can come pick you up?"

Since my parents sucked at taking my calls and I wasn't in the mood for their buzzkill lectures anyway, I said, "My parents are both in meetings this morning so I know they can't answer their phones. I have a really important assignment due in first block that I don't want to miss, either. Would there be any way that you could maybe just drop me off at Hazelwood whenever you're done here?"

CONFESSION #11

I've daydreamed for years about getting in a fistfight with Khloe Kardashian. I'm positive I could take her.

The officer dropped me off with a look that was half impressed and half disgusted. As soon as I got into the school, I went straight to Josh's locker. If I couldn't find a way to end the repeating days, at least I could dump him for kissing Macy and feel like I had some kind of control over my romantic life. I'd missed all of first period, but happened to get lucky enough to show up during passing period, which meant the odds were good that he'd be there.

My phone vibrated. Dad: Call me NOW.

So Lisa had told him about the car.

Or the cops had.

I turned down the north hall and—wow. There he was.

Josh was standing beside his locker, laughing with Noah, and it kind of took my breath away. He was just so *Josh* in that moment. Pretty and funny and the guy who should've been perfect for me.

He'd read Sylvia Plath to me on a blanket in the grass, for the love of God. How could it be that he wasn't the one?

"Emmie!" His eyes landed on me and my face got hot, just like it always did. He grinned the smile that told me he knew what he did to me and he said, "Get over here!"

I walked over to his locker and before I had a chance to publicly *buh-bye* him like I'd planned, he wrapped his long-fingered hands around my waist and pulled me against him.

His friends walked away, the friends that I'd planned on impressing with my epic dumping abilities.

"There you are." He set his forehead against mine, and I got sucked into his deep, quiet voice. "The prettiest girl in school."

"I, um—"

"You want your Valentine's present now?" He pulled back a little and tucked my hair behind my ear. "You look incredible today, by the way."

Instead of opening my mouth and saying dumping words, I said, "Thanks."

"Ms. Hornby. Mr. Sutton. Please get to class." Ms. Radke, the Lit teacher, crossed her arms and gave us the stink eye from behind her wire glasses.

Josh grinned at me. "Missed your chance. Lunch?"

I nodded, and he dropped a peck on my lips before turning and walking in the other direction.

"Get moving, Ms. Hornby."

"Emilie, I have a note here that says you need to go to the counselor's office."

"Okay." I stood up from my desk and walked toward Mr. Smith, my Calculus teacher. The man was a walking nose hair, so I looked at the smartboard behind him when I said, "Thanks."

The DONC had lost a little of its excitement after seeing Josh, mainly because he'd behaved the same way he always had, which was perfect.

Ugh. So, so perfect. Like, the way he'd smiled when he'd seen me by his locker; that didn't look like the smile of someone who was done with me and moving on to Macy. Maybe I *hadn't* been wrong about everything.

Right?

I was grabbing the handle of the office door when I heard laughing in the direction of the snack store. I glanced over my shoulder and—of course—the melodically tinkling giggle came from Macy Goldman. She was laughing in the hallway, tossing her hair like a supermodel, and looking down at—

Oh.

Even after the repetitive days of witnessing them kissing, my chest felt like it was caving in as I saw Josh sitting on the floor with Noah, smiling up at Macy. He was smiling up at her in *that* way. The exact same enamored way he'd looked at me.

For the first time since I'd seen them kiss, I wasn't hurt or sad—I was pissed. Livid, actually. So angry I wanted to kick things over or possibly punch something. I gritted my teeth and went into the office. I didn't even bother with Mrs. Svoboda, but instead just went straight back to Kessler's office.

"Here she is now."

I walked into his office but I didn't sit. I didn't look at him, either. I just crossed my arms and seethed, glaring at the woman who was about to yank away my summer as if she was responsible for everything that had gone wrong in my life. She wasn't, but she was unfortunate enough to be there when it hit the fan.

"If you're here to tell me there was a mistake and I didn't win the spot in the summer program, don't bother. I need that for scholarship and college applications—and I'm not misusing the word 'need' here—and you are *not* going to yank it away from me." I gritted my teeth and the lady looked at me as if she was a little scared. "Just because you have someone on staff who can't count doesn't mean I should lose my only shot at a Pulitzer."

"Emilie." Mr. Kessler tilted his head. "Why don't you sit down?"

"Can't." I held up a hand. "I have someplace I have to be, but you guys are going to have to go back to the drawing board and find a way to make this right."

The woman cleared her throat and looked confused. "How on earth did you know what I was going to say?"

I shrugged. "Intuitive, I guess. Probably what will make me such a stellar journalist, don't you think?"

On that note, I left. What more was there to say?

And it felt good, *doing* something. Instead of being dragged along by my life, I was leading the charge with my fingers wrapped around its scrawny neck. For good or bad, this day was all about me proactivating the shit out of my life.

Because nothing mattered.

Mrs. Svoboda wasn't at her desk anymore. It was empty, her chair vacant, and the microphone for the overhead speakers entirely unattended.

Um.

I glanced around. Nick Stark was sitting on a chair in the office, looking down at his phone. Talk about ironic. I looked at his handsome face and was slapped with a melancholic sadness. Because we'd had an incredible yesterday and had talked on the phone mere hours ago—his had been the last voice I'd heard before falling asleep—yet he knew nothing of it. We were basically strangers again, but I knew what he would buy for a girlfriend if he had one on Valentine's Day.

And I knew he smelled like the cleanest bar of soap.

Focus, Em.

The principals each had their office doors closed, and the nurse was talking on the phone.

I couldn't.

Could I?

I went around the desk, sat in Svoboda's chair, and leaned forward. My heart pounded as I pressed the button.

"A-attention, Hazelwood students. I would like to announce that Josh Sutton is a total ass-bag." I giggled. Seriously. A giggle popped out of my mouth, and my lips curved up into a huge smile as I leaned back a little in the chair. "This is Emilie Hornby, and I am officially dumping you, Josh, because you suck."

Nick's head shot up and he looked over at me like he couldn't believe what he was hearing, and I shrugged because I couldn't believe it either. "You suck so hard, you pompous jag with a stupid car, and I do *not* want you to be my Valentine." I let go of the button, but then pushed it again and said, "Oh, yeah, and it's so pathetic that you refer to your friend group as "the Bards" like you're characters from *Dead Poets Society* or something—you freaking wish. Em *out*."

I heard Nick's deep laugh as I hopped up and went around the desk as fast as I could. I exited the office just as the bell rang, so I was lucky enough to be swallowed by all the students filling the hallway. I was sure they would be sending a pass for me later, but hopefully I could ditch the building by then.

Macy, Noah, and Josh were no longer by the snack store.

I walked to class with my head high, a smile on my face that I couldn't contain. I knew that most of the people I passed didn't even know who I was, but I still greeted my fellow classmates with a supercool chin-nod, like I was starring in my own movie.

In my head, "Sabotage" by the Beastie Boys was playing as I strutted toward Chem.

I was almost to my classroom when I passed Lallie, Lauren, and Nicole.

They were standing around a locker loudly cataloging what was wrong with Isla Keller's outfit while Isla had no idea. She was grabbing a book out of her locker, doing absolutely nothing to deserve their bitchery.

"Seriously, why would anyone wear shoes that atrocious?" Lallie said.

"Oh. My. Gawd." Lauren Dreyer took the lollipop out of her mouth and pointed right at Isla's shoes before shoving it back into that hole in her face. "So ugly."

"What is wrong with you?" I asked, startling them—and myself—with my loud voice.

All three of them turned to look at me. Lallie said, "What?"

"Why are you so petty?" I asked, my heart rate rising as I saw a couple of people stop and look in our direction.

"Um, I'm not the one who was just a total asshole over the intercom," Nicole said, narrowing her eyes at me and looking like an evil queen.

"Yeah, Emilie," Lallie sneered. "Seriously?"

Now, normally I would've been freaking out with an instant stomachache if those girls were getting on me to my face in the hallway. But DONC Em didn't care. I said, "You do realize that you didn't actually ask a question, right, *Lalz*? Or are you too high on bitchiness to piece together more than three words?"

That made Nicole gasp, so I pointed to her and said, "And don't even start on me, Nicole. I've seen you be awful to everyone in the entire world since, like, the second grade, so let's just both assume that you're about to spew some hateful shit on me so you can save your breath and my time."

Lallie and Lauren were puffing up for a comeback—I could see it in their overtanned faces—but I wasn't having it. "Do you realize that everyone—like, for real, *ev-er-y-one*—in this school who doesn't hang out with you hates your guts? Think about that. You are the butt of a million jokes—did you know that? It's on the DL because we're all terrified of you, but you are a laughingstock to eighty percent of this school."

Then I grabbed the stick of Lauren's sucker and pulled it out of her mouth. I almost laughed at the shocked look on her face, but I was able to keep a straight face as I dropped her sucker and walked away, "Sabotage" back to pumping in my head as I floated down that hall.

When I got to Chemistry, I went straight to my table. Nick walked in a minute later but he didn't say a word. He just raised an eyebrow and sat on his stool.

"What kind of car does he have?"

"What?" I unzipped my backpack. "Who?"

"Josh. You said his car was stupid, remember?"

"Ah." That made me smile because Josh thought that thing was the greatest vehicle to ever rumble over the planet. "A 1959 MG."

He rewarded me for knowing with one of his smirks and said, "Ouch."

I watched his Adam's apple move when he swallowed and I was struck by how beautiful he was. Dark hair, ridiculously blue eyes, beautiful cheekbones, and lashes for days. And his body looked hard. I was pretty certain if I ran at him full speed, I would bounce off him instead of knocking him over.

Mr. Bong came in and immediately started lecturing. I didn't have the notes, but I was apparently never going to need them, either. So instead of getting out my notebook, I pulled out my phone.

Dad: Clearly you're not going to call me back, so you're grounded from your phone when you get home. Where is my car?

I knew I should feel a little bad for taking his baby, especially after the nice-but-not-real moment we'd shared last night, but something about his response pissed me off. On most days, he and my mother both took hours and hours to respond to the tiniest of questions. The time I had an allergic reaction to cashews at summer camp and needed to know which urgent care to go to, it took each of them—and they didn't live together—over an hour.

Yet when I waited an hour to respond to my dad about his car, he was losing his shit.

My phone buzzed.

Stankbreath: Can you come in today? Beck called in sick and since I gave you Sat off, you owe me. 😉

Ugh. Work.

I glanced at Nick's profile, remembered the rules of DONC, and responded accordingly.

I'm not coming in AT ALL today because I don't feel like it. Thanks, tho, Paulie.

I put my phone away. Instead of taking notes or paying attention, though, I stared at Nick.

But when he glanced over and caught me, instead of looking away like I usually would have, I just rested my chin on my hand and smiled. *No consequences.* He frowned like he didn't understand, which made me full-on grin.

He looked back at Bong, and I continued drinking him in. After about five seconds, he muttered—without looking at me—*"What are you doing?"*

"Just looking."

"Yeah, I can see that." He wrote something in his notebook and added, "But why?"

I bit down on my lower lip and thought *What the hell* before saying, "You are just really, really attractive."

He still didn't look at me. "You think so?"

Bong stopped lecturing to glare at us. "Mr. Stark, care to enlighten us as to what's so important it can't wait?"

"I can." I raised my hand and said, "I was telling Nick here that I think he's attractive and I was hoping he'd maybe want to hang out since I'm single now."

I knew Nick could be surly, so there was a definite chance he would totally call me out in front of everyone. But it didn't matter because it was the DONC. He turned his head and looked at me with wide eyes.

Bong stuttered, "This is neither the time nor—nor—"

"Absolutely I would," Nick said.

I heard a couple of laughs behind us as Nick gave me the smirk that had become very familiar to me.

"Mr. Star—"

"Do you maybe just want to go now?" I was speaking through a laugh because it was impossible not to.

"That's enough." Mr. Bong's face was getting very red as he stared at us. "I don't know what's come over you today, Emilie, but I will not allow—"

"Let's go," Nick said, grabbing his backpack and standing while hoisting it over his shoulder.

"Sit down, Mr. Stark," Bong said.

"Perfect." I was beaming at Nick as I grabbed my bag and we both turned around to leave. The entire class was gaping at us in shock, and I swear to God I felt an actual electrical current shoot through me, starting at my fingertips, when I felt his hand grab mine and he led me out of the room.

"Stop by the principal's office while you're at it," Bong yelled.

As soon as the door closed behind us, Nick looked at me and said, "Want me to drive?"

Y'know, like ditching school in such a public manner was normal—commonplace—and the biggest concern was who was going to be behind the wheel.

I nodded. "Yes, please."

That made him grin. "Come on."

He pulled me by my hand, his tightening around mine, quickly heading for the side door. "Let's get out before Bong has the resource officer hunting us."

We started jogging down the hall, and I couldn't hold in the laughter. What an absurd, wild thing to be doing at ten thirty in the morning. I breathed in the fresh air as we burst through the exit doors and a frigid, sunshiny breeze rushed at our faces. Nick continued pulling me along behind him in the direction of his car.

And as we ran over the snow-packed pavement, I felt magically, wonderfully not like myself. I was the manic pixie dream girl in a movie, a character created solely to be uncomplicated, unexpected, and utterly unpredictable.

"Here." He stopped beside Betty and unlocked the passenger door. He pulled it open, and then looked down at me. "You still want to do this?"

I met his gaze and wanted to do whatever he wanted when he

looked down at me like that. It was so cliché, but his eyes had a twinkle, a mischievous glint, when he was amused, and I was addicted to that look. I grinned and said, "As long as you have a jacket on the floor of your truck that I can borrow, I am all in."

His eyes crinkled at the corners as he said, "It just so happens you're in luck."

While Nick went around to the driver's side, I got in and reached over the back of the seat to grab the coat. When I shoved my arms into the heavy material, it was so familiar that it was like the jacket belonged to me.

Nick got in and did a double take. Fell into a smile and pointed behind me. "Yeah, um, the jacket is behind the seat. Help yourself."

That made me laugh even more, and as he started the truck, I pulled the hair tie out of my ponytail, shaking my hair and running my fingernails through it while pushing it off my face. I snagged the Ray-Bans from his dashboard and slid them up my nose while propping my feet up on the dash.

"Comfy?" He looked amused and surprised by my actions, so I crossed my ankles and my arms.

I leaned back and said, "Comfier than I've felt in years."

He just looked at me for a second, with that secret smile on his mouth, before giving his head a little shake and saying, "So where are we going?"

"Let's go downtown."

"Downtown it is." He put the truck in gear and pulled away from the school. "Buckle up."

I wanted to squeal as wild energy floated through me,

encompassing me in the thrill of just living for the moment; for my moment. For whatever moment I wanted to be encompassed in, if that made any sense at all. I took over his stereo and switched to FM radio, scanning until I heard the notes of that ridiculous song.

The "Thong Song."

"Oh my gosh—remember this song?" I glanced over at Nick, and he gave me a look that told me he did and he also regretted that remembrance. "Sing it—come on. 'She had dumps like a truck, truck, truck.'"

"God help me," he muttered.

"'Guys like what, what, what,'" I sang.

He said, "Kill me now," but he was smiling against his will as I belted out the entire rest of the song, not caring about anything other than the fact that it felt good.

When it ended, he turned down the volume and calmly asked, "Is there anywhere in particular you want to go once we're downtown?"

"Well, I definitely want to get a tattoo. Other than that, I'm down for just about anything."

His eyes narrowed and he looked at me like I'd just professed myself an alien.

"*What?*"

That didn't change the way he looked at me, so I said, "*What?* Do you know a good place to get a tattoo?"

Obviously, I knew that he did because he'd told me about his job on the phone last night. But he didn't know I knew that, and I didn't want to sound like a creeper.

He said, "Why do you assume *I* know?"

"I've seen your tattoo."

He kept his eyes on the road when he said, "Maybe I did it myself."

"Nope. It's on your right arm, and you're right-handed. That would be impossible. Try again."

"Okay, creeper." His eyes darted over to me. "Maybe I got it in juvie."

"That's a little more believable."

"Nice."

"But still not right. Downtown at Mooshie's?"

He shook his head. "Not."

"What, too cool for you?"

"Too trendy, more like."

"So . . . ? Where *did* you go?"

"402 Ink."

"Okay." I grinned because I already knew that. "So will you take me there?"

"You do know they take appointments, right?" His right hand was relaxed and kind of draped over the steering wheel, his left elbow resting on the window frame while just a few of his fingers actually managed the steering. It was cool confidence, just like him. He said, "All tattoo shops. Odds are not in your favor that anyone can fit you in today."

"Really? Don't you have any connections?" *Any coworkers?* "Any favors you can call in?"

"Just because I have a tattoo doesn't mean I have a contingent of tattoo artists who are available to me for favors."

"'Contingent of Tattoo Artists.' Band name. Called it."

That actually made him smile. "I like it. You'd be the singer, I assume?"

"Are you kidding? I have a terrible voice. Tambourine all the way."

"Weak."

"No, 'weak' is not helping your friend get squeezed into a tattoo appointment."

"Oh, so you're my friend now."

I pulled down the visor, grabbed the lipstick in my bag, and reapplied. "Yes. We're friends, Nick Stark. Deal with it."

Nick turned on his blinker and merged onto the interstate. "If you're my friend, name three things you know about me."

"Um, let's see. Three things." Now, if I had been being honest, I could probably fill a few notebook pages with the things I knew about him from all my repeated days. But I pretended to struggle before I said, "First, I know that you drive a truck."

"Low-hanging fruit, Hornby."

"Okay." I flipped the visor back up and said, "Um. For starters, you don't take notes in Chem but always get a better grade than me."

"You nosy little shit—keep your eyes on your own paper."

I was smiling as I put away my lipstick and said, "Number two, you always smell like soap."

He gave me the side-eye. "It's called showering."

I rolled my eyes. "No, you smell like *soap*, soap. Like you're made of Irish Spring or something."

He made a tiny chuckle sound before saying, "You are such a weirdo."

"Am not. And number three. Hmmm." I looked over at him. "You're less of a jerk than I always thought." It came out more sincere than I intended—a big change from my previous joking tone—and I blushed, looking down at my knees.

"Well I guess that's good," he said, giving me a closed-mouth smile while hitting his turn signal and switching lanes. "Right?"

"Right." I cleared my throat and said, "So will you help me?"

He said, eyes on the road, "Well they aren't open until after lunch, but yes."

"You will?" I squealed it and didn't care. "Yes!"

He just shook his head as he accelerated.

"Okay, Nick," I said, desperate to know every little thing about him, "let's play a game."

"No."

"I will ask a question," I calmly said, trying not to laugh as he didn't look at me but his eyes got crinkly around the corners, "and you will answer."

"Nope."

"Come on—it'll be fun. Like Truth or Dare, only it's all truth and not skanky." I turned the radio off. "I mean, you can ask *me* questions next, if you want."

He gave me the side-eye yet again. "I'm good."

I didn't care about his reticence as I turned toward him, smiled, and said, "Question number one. If the law required you to compete professionally in an athletic event or be killed by a firing squad, which event would you choose?"

He didn't even look at me. "Running."

"Really?" I tilted my head and looked at him in his faded jeans and black jacket. "I just can't picture you running."

"Next question."

"Well, no—the point of the game is that I learn something about you. Do you run?"

"Yes."

"You *do*?" I just couldn't picture it. I mean, he looked like he was in great shape, but he seemed too intense to be a jogger. "You go for runs?"

His eyes squinted a little. "How else would I run if I didn't go for runs?"

"I don't know." I really didn't. But, "Well, what do you listen to when you run?"

"This game sucks," he muttered as he took the St. Mary's Avenue exit.

"Metallica?"

He glanced at me. "Sometimes."

"What else?" I needed to know more about this. "And do you run every day?"

He came to a stop at the traffic light before turning to give me full-on eye contact, the kind that sucked you inside of him so you were aware of nothing but Nick Stark. "I get up at six every day and go for a five-mile run. Is it my turn now?"

I blinked—six in the morning? *Five* miles?

"Not yet." I cleared my throat. "Okay—this one is a hypothetical question. Why would a guy pretend to not recognize a girl he knew from school?"

"What? That's a dumb question."

"To you, but not to me." I giggled in spite of myself, knowing how nonsensical I must've sounded. "I just need a guy's perspective. If a guy was introduced to someone he already knew, but pretended *not* to know her, well . . . what would you say he's up to?"

He looked at me. "I'd say he either doesn't like her and wants to avoid conversation, or else he's got a thing for her and is trying to be cool."

"Okay." Warmth buzzed through me at the thought of Nick *having a thing* for me. Could it be possible? Had Nick Stark noticed . . . and *liked* . . . me before this whole thing started?

Although, it could be just as likely that he *didn't* like me. I thought back to the Em I presented myself as in school, the one Nick saw in class. Would I have liked me if I met me?

Instantly, I decided it didn't matter either way—a very un-Em-like conclusion, I realized. I forged ahead and said, "You've passed the test. One more hypothetical question and you're done."

"Thank God."

"Right?" I smiled and tried to think of the best way to say it—to say it and not sound like a weirdo. "Okay. If you started reliving the same day over and over again—like a time-loop scenario—would you tell anyone?"

"No way."

I was disappointed. "Really?"

"There's no way to not sound like you're out of your mind."

"Oh. That's probably true."

Nick glanced over, his eyes all over my face. "Did I give the wrong answer or something?"

"Nah." I shook my head and added, "No wrong answers on hypotheticals."

"Okay—my turn."

"But I've barely started asking you questions."

"Don't care." He looked down at my sweater and said, "How come you don't dress like this all the time?"

"What?" I crossed my arms back over my chest. "Are you seriously going to talk about the way I dress? Don't be that guy."

"I'm not." He pointed at my body with his chin and said, "But you usually dress like a sorority girl who color-codes her daily planner and secretly hopes to marry a senator. This looks real, like you're not trying to be a Ralph Lauren influencer."

"Okay—two things," I said around a laugh. "First of all, that's totally the look I'm going for. Or *was* going for."

"Shocking."

"And second, you're right about today's outfit—I am feelin' myself." I looked down at the leather pants, slid my finger along the outside seam. "Today is Em-centric, where I am only focusing on what *I* want. And today, I wanted to wear leather pants."

"Well—"

"Nope—my turn. Why are you so antisocial?"

He scowled. "I'm not."

"You've never said a word to me in Chem." Until Valentine's Day started repeating itself, that is.

"You've never said a word to me, either."

"But . . . that's because of your energy."

He scowled harder, saying the two words like I was ludicrous. "My *energy*?"

"You put off a very strong *Don't bug me* vibe. Next question." It was the DONC, so pride didn't matter. I asked, "Are you interested in anyone—romantically—at the moment?"

The scowl disappeared. "Would I be out here committing mayhem in the 402 with you if I was?"

"Probably not but I just needed to clarify."

"Why?" A slow smirk moved his mouth and his eyes got that twinkle as he looked over and asked, "You got plans for me, Hornby?"

That made my cheeks get hot, but I kept my devil-may-care attitude and said, "Today, anything is possible."

"Okay—my turn."

He turned into the Old Market community parking garage, rolled down his window, and grabbed a ticket from the dispenser. "What's your all-time favorite movie? Not the one you tell people is your favorite, but your *actual* favorite."

That made me smile, because he totally saw me in that moment. "I've been known to say it's *Schindler's List*, but it's actually *Titanic*."

"Oh, Emilie." He looked horrified. "You are right to lie about that. Bury that confession deep, deep in your disgusting soul forever."

I asked, "What's *your* favorite movie?"

He put the truck in gear and turned it off. "*Snatch.* Ever seen it?"

"I don't watch porn."

"Get your mind out of the gutter," he said, chastising me while his cerulean (thank you, DeVos) eyes squinted around a grin. "It's Guy Ritchie and Brad Pitt, dumb-ass."

When he came around to my side of the truck, I couldn't help it—I beamed up at him like I was a three-year-old coming face-to-face with Elsa from *Frozen*.

He frowned. "Why are you smiling like that?"

I shrugged. "Because I just kind of like you, I think."

"Oh, you *think*?" he drawled, giving me a teasing smirk that did wild things to my insides. "You drag me out of Chem and you're not sure?"

I shrugged again. "Jury's still out. I'll let you know when I know."

I started walking, pulling him behind me, but his hand tugged me to a stop. His breath clouded around his face as he grinned down at me. "You didn't know to wear gloves or a coat in the middle of February in Nebraska—you don't know shit, Emilie Hornby."

Before I even realized what he was doing, he let go of my hand, pulled off his big gloves, and put them on my hands. They were ginormous on me, but warm inside. Then he reached around my head to yank up the hood of the coat I'd jacked from him.

"You're a damn child," he muttered, still smiling as his face hovered just over mine. "Maybe now you won't freeze to death."

"Y'know, if this was a movie, I would look at your mouth right now. Like this." I let my eyes glance down to his lips. "And you would kiss me."

"Is that right?" His voice was low and I felt his gaze in my stomach as he looked down at my lips.

"Yes," I said, sounding a little breathless.

"Well, thank God we're not in a movie, then."

Ouch. I looked at that face and breathed, "You wouldn't want to kiss me?"

He was quiet for a brief second, and the moment hovered as our collective breaths mingled and shared a cloud in front of our faces. His eyes were solemn, so serious, as he looked at me and said, "I wouldn't want the complications that accompany kissing you."

"Why are you so sad?" I asked.

I hadn't meant to say it, hadn't even realized it was on the tip of my tongue, but I'd never wanted anything more than to know the answer to that question at that moment.

His jaw flexed, unflexed, and his haunted eyes stayed on mine. I felt like he wanted to tell me as his entire being paused in response, but something about the way he swallowed made me want to protect him from his answer.

"Forget it—you don't have to answer." I tugged on his sleeve and we started walking again. "I've got a million other questions."

"Wonderful."

"So tell me your life story." I needed to know every little bit of him that wasn't sad. "Did you grow up here? Who's your best friend? Brothers and sisters? Any pets? Well, other than Betty, that is."

He gave me a weird look. "How do you know my dog's name?"

Shit. "You told me when, um—I don't remember, actually, but I remember you mentioning it sometime."

Nice answer, you imbecile.

Thankfully he just said, "That's our only animal. What about you?"

I pushed his Ray-Bans up my nose. "My mom and her husband have a puggle named Potassium—and I can't even remember where they came up with that ridiculous name. He's cute but we aren't close."

That made him smirk.

"My dad and his wife have a cat—Big Al—who is amazing, but he's been known to pee on the straw rug in the laundry room, so he definitely has issues."

He pushed open the door to Zen Coffee and held it while I walked in. "I also have two little brothers who are my dad's. Man, that sounds utterly dysfunctional, doesn't it?"

"No," he said, but when I raised an eyebrow he amended with, "Maybe a little."

He was giving me another funny look that warmed me, and when we moved into the big line, I said, "The questions were supposed to be for you. Brothers and sisters?"

"Are you always this nosy?"

"Nope—only on the DONC."

"We should talk about this DONC of yours." His eyes flitted down for the briefest of seconds when I unzipped the big coat, and the mere idea of him being interested in my body made my heart pound.

"Why are you doing this?" he asked.

"You wouldn't believe me if I told you." I looked at that face that I knew really well and said, "Let's just say it's a social experiment. What will happen if for an entire day, I do exactly what I feel like, consequences be damned?"

He shrugged. "You'll have a fun day today and a nightmare tomorrow."

"Which is why," I said, lowering my voice a little, "I'm refusing to think about tomorrow."

We moved up in the line, and Nick looked deep in thought. He was probably thinking that I was marginally unstable; I mean, I would think that in the reverse. He didn't even look at me while we waited, which made me worry that he was going to bail on me. That he'd realize my particular flavor of hot messiness wasn't worth detention and he'd make a break for it, leaving me alone downtown.

When we got to the front and the barista looked to me to order, I said, "Could I please have a large Americano? And the gentleman will have a large . . . Sleepytime . . . ?"

I glanced at him and he rolled his eyes before saying, "Large green tea, please."

I laughed at his obvious annoyance in my rightness, and we didn't talk again until we got our drinks and went back outside. We both started walking without even discussing where we might be headed, and I was just starting to feel my cup's heat through Nick's gloves when he said, "For the record, I think your DONC idea is really terrible because you *will* have to face the consequences tomorrow."

I glanced at him and said, "You don't—"

"But I still want to do it."

I stopped lifting my cup toward my mouth and froze. "You *do*?"

"I'm in my own head too much, and I also fucking hate Valentine's Day," he said, looking straight ahead, "so the way I see it, being a dipshit like you for a few hours might be a nice break."

"Awww—so sweet." I finally managed a sip of the deliciously dark caffeinated beverage.

"But you don't want to steal a car or anything, do you?"

That made me snort and choke a little on my coffee. I held up one finger while I coughed, and then I said, "I already did that this morning."

He looked at me with deadpan eyes as a jogger went around us. "Please tell me you're joking."

"Um, sort of . . . ?" I went on to tell him about my dad's car, getting pulled over, and then watching my dad's precious baby get towed away. I managed to make him look scandalized over every word, which felt like some kind of a win. I said, "So I'm not going to get arrested for GTA or anything, but I did, in fact, start my day by taking someone else's vehicle."

He looked at me through narrowed eyes, turning sideways to keep eye contact while we walked. "This is blowing my mind that *you*, the girl I've seen reading in Chem, in the cafeteria, who's always digging in her backpack, which is—of course—*full* of books, is out being a deviant. Before today, I would've guessed you were a candidate for 'Most likely to work in a library.'"

"That's actually my number two career choice," I said, fascinated by the fact that he knew things about me after pretending he didn't on multiple days.

He ignored my words and kept going.

"But here you are, joyriding in Porsches, ditching school, and destroying your ex-boyfriend in a very public way. Was there some sort of a final-straw event that started this thing?"

The image of Josh's lips touching Macy's flashed through my mind but I shoved it away. "Can't a girl just mix up her life a little?"

"An unhinged girl, maybe."

"Well then, I'm that." I might as well be, since the real explanation actually *was* unhinged.

He asked as we went around a food cart, "So is your dad going to kill you?"

"Probably."

His eyebrows furrowed together. "How do you not seem concerned about it?"

I shrugged. "He's just going to yell at me for a while and then it'll be over." He wouldn't, actually, but I couldn't explain that to Nick.

"We clearly have very different parents." He gave his head a shake and said, "My dad is super cool but he would *destroy* me. Like, I am getting scared just thinking about my father's reaction to something like this, and he doesn't even have a nice car for me to steal."

I took another sip of my coffee as we stopped to wait for the light to change. I asked him, "Are your parents still married?"

I was fascinated by people whose parents were still together. It seemed surreal and impossibly beautiful to me, the idea of living out all of your childhood years with both parents, together in the same house.

"Yep," he said, and we both started walking as the signal switched. I waited for him to elaborate and talk about his family, but he didn't say anything else.

"You never answered about brothers and sisters." I leaned a little to my left and bumped him as we crossed. "One? Two? Ten? Do you have any?"

Irritation flashed in his eyes and his jaw was hard when he said, "Do we really have to do the 'Tell me about your family' small-talk thing?"

"Oh. Um, sorry." Coffee splashed onto my glove as I stumbled over a crack in the sidewalk.

"It's fine."

Yeah—sure it was. I looked straight ahead and wondered if it was possible to feel like a bigger dork, because his face had shown exactly how annoying he found me. All of a sudden, I was aware of the biting sting of cold on my cheeks as I struggled to think of something—anything—to say.

"Stop it."

I glanced over at him. "What?"

"Stop feeling like that—I'm not mad."

That made me roll my eyes. "How do *you* know how I'm feeling?"

"Well, your face got all pinched."

"Pinched?"

He shrugged and gestured to my face with his free hand.

"Oh, okay—that explains it."

"Ms. DONC." He grabbed my elbow and led me out of the foot traffic, so we were standing beside a closed storefront. He looked down at me with that handsome face, his soapy scent ribboning around me, and said, "Tell me. What epic Ferris Bueller shit are we doing first?"

CONFESSION #12

I started drinking coffee when I was eleven. My mom left for work when there was one cup left in the pot, every day, and since it seemed like a grown-up thing to do, I did it.

That snapped my attention back to the present. Why had I been worrying about insulting him when it was the DONC? I blinked and said, "I don't really have a plan, per se, but we should check out the First Bank building."

He raised an eyebrow. "Do you have some investing to do?"

"No, I want to sneak up to the fortieth floor." Now I grabbed *his* elbow and we started walking. "Listen to this."

I started telling him what I knew and what I wanted to discover as we walked toward the skyscraper. The First Bank building was the tallest building in the city; forty-five stories, to be exact. My Auntie Ellen used to work there and told me that after it first opened, people made appointments to use the fortieth-floor balcony for marriage proposals.

I also knew this to be true because it was where my young, foolish father had proposed to my equally immature and impulsive mother.

But now, if you Googled it—nothing. No mention of a balcony, no reference to balconied proposals.

It was as if it had never existed.

I'd been obsessed with the missing balcony ever since Ellen had told me about it when I was ten, and I was fixated on the notion that the setting for the beginning of so many people's happily-ever-afters was effectively erased. I'd found it sad, which had made my mother joke that perhaps it was the cosmos trying to right some wrongs. All those couples who'd trekked up there for the big moment could never revisit the spot.

Ever.

Precocious ten-year-old me had even called the building manager, but instead of explaining the closure, he told me I was mistaken. He denied there had ever been such a thing.

I knew better.

So I'd always wanted to sneak up and check it out. I expected Nick to think it was a bad idea, but he listened closely. He nodded and looked up at the towering building as we approached.

And instead of saying no, he said, "I'm sure we need badges to get past the lobby."

My eyes shot to his, surprised that he was matter-of-factly considering going along with this. "Probably."

"So what's our plan?" he asked.

"Hmmm." I bit my lip as we stopped by the fountains that sat in front of the building. *Think, Em—think.* "We could pull a fire alarm."

"Nothing that will get us arrested, you criminal," he said, and laughed, his eyes sweeping over me and making it impossible not to smile.

"Maybe we can bribe a security guard—do you have any money?"

He just looked at me.

"Well? I don't hear *you*—"

"There has to be a side door." He tossed his cup into a green trash can and said, "One of those exit-only doors that nearly every building has."

"And . . . ?"

"And we find it and lurk. As soon as someone comes out, we go in."

I blinked. "That's genius."

"No, it's common sense."

"Fine. No compliment for you, then; I rescind the compliment."

"You can't rescind a compliment."

"Yes, you can."

"Nope. My ego knows you think I'm a genius now, regardless of how hard you might deny it."

That made me laugh. "I do *not* think you're a genius. I said that *idea* was genius."

"Potato, po-tah-toe."

I just rolled my eyes and took a sip of my coffee. Then: "Wait—how did you finish your tea already?"

"I didn't. It sucked and I was sick of carrying it."

"But you *just* bought it."

"Are we going to talk about my tea or are we going to find that door?"

I tossed my coffee into the trash can. "Let's go find that door."

We walked parallel to the building, intentionally behaving like two teenagers casually walking around downtown, just in case of cameras. He told me a ridiculous story as we cased the joint about the time he was working at a driving range and he got stuck inside the golf ball picker.

"I don't even know what a *golf ball picker* is," I said, staring at the building's stone facade.

"A machine that picks up golf balls."

I rolled my eyes. "Well, of course, but I can't picture it."

He said, "You don't have to picture it. Just know I got stuck inside for an hour and almost died of heat exhaustion."

"Couldn't you have broken the window or something?"

Nick shook his head and said, "We were all scared to death of our boss, Matt—he was a total asshole. We never would've considered that."

"You would've rather died in a ball picker?"

Instead of answering me, he said, "Look." Nick pointed to a door that was at the back of the building, painted to match the brick and barely noticeable.

"Do you think people use it?"

"No idea," he said.

The door opened.

I gasped and nearly got trampled by the three women who came out. The lady in the middle apologized while Nick stepped forward and held the door for them like he was a total gentleman.

Not at all like the grumpy, quiet lab partner I'd had all year.

But the minute they turned away from us, he gave me an eyebrow-raise. "After you . . . ?"

"Let's go."

We stepped inside, and the door slammed behind us.

We were in a stairwell. I started for the door to whatever lay beyond when he said, "Wait."

I stopped. "Why?"

"We don't know what it looks like on the other side of that door. But we know we have to go up to forty, so . . ."

And he gave the steps a chin-nod.

"So you want to *climb* forty flights of stairs?" I did *not* want to flex my outta-shapeitude in front of him. Nope. "Not all of us run every morning."

"We can go two flights at a time, and rest in between."

"I don't need your fitness pity."

He raised an eyebrow again. "So you want to . . . ?"

I let out a big sigh. And then I groaned before saying, "Let's do this."

The first two flights were pretty easy, but by the third my quads were starting to cramp and I felt sweat starting to form on my forehead.

"You okay?" Nick asked when we stopped for our first break.

"Are *you*?" I tried to keep myself from panting but sounded pretty out of breath when I said, "This is cake." I noticed that he showed no sign of exertion, other than a slight flush to his cheeks.

"Is it?" He gave me a suspicious look and said, "I'm sorry—have I been holding you up? Do you want to run the next flight?"

OF COURSE NOT. No, thank you. What are you, insane? Those would all be appropriate responses, but my mouth couldn't seem to form the words. Which was weird, because I didn't consider myself to be particularly competitive, especially when it came to athletic endeavors.

But the fact that I could tell he knew I wouldn't do it? It made me say the unspeakable.

"How about the next two?"

His mouth curled into a full-on grin and he took off. I started slow-jogging the stairs behind him, wanting to die in my leather pants, and he immediately slowed and kept pace with me. I looked to my left and there he was, grinning like he could run stairs all day.

I smiled back while my heart pounded and screamed obscenities and tried to remember what its job was.

We ran one flight, then another, but we both kept running after that. My legs started burning, and I was running the steps at a slower pace than if I were walking them, to be honest. My face must've looked pained, because when we reached the next landing, Nick took pity on me.

"Wait." He stopped, and it made me happy to see that he was panting, too. He held up a finger while he caught his breath, which was fine by me because my ears felt too furry to hear out of.

"So," he breathed, "every floor in this building has an elevator."

"Yeah . . . ?" I stacked my hands on top of my head as my lungs screamed.

"So let's get out of the stairwell. Think about it. Odds are good that we can get to an elevator on a random floor of offices before anyone who cares notices us."

"Are you sure?" I didn't want to climb another step, but I didn't want to get busted now that we were getting close, either.

"Positive. Do you trust me?"

I nodded, still trying to un-labor my breath, which made him smile. He said, "Let's stay here for a couple minutes so we don't burst out of the stairwell panting and sweating. People might talk."

An image of Nick and me against the wall of the stairwell flashed in my head.

Whoa.

I was happy when he distracted me and said, "I think it's my turn to ask you a question, anyway."

"No—it's mine." I leaned my backside against the wall and asked, "Let's go big. Have you ever been in love?"

He gave me a look, like he thought it was an absurd question. "That's a hard no."

"Not even close?" I don't know why, but I was shocked by that.

"I've loved, of course, but I haven't been *in* love. Not even close." He looked down and started fidgeting with the zipper on his jacket. "You?"

"Hmmm." I tucked my hair behind my ears and said, "When I woke up on Valentine's Day, I thought I was in love. But here I am, a few hours later, wondering if I ever loved Josh at all."

He raised his eyes. "Maybe that's just because you're mad at him."

"That's what's so weird." I paused to think for a moment, then I said, "Yes, I'm pissed that he kissed his ex-girlfriend, but only a little. Definitely not as much as I should be."

It made me feel . . I don't know . . . regretful. Had my feelings been something less than genuine?

He continued messing with his zipper. "So . . . why . . . ?"

"This is a new realization, so I'm still working it all out."

"Got it." He abandoned his zipper, straightened, then walked over to the door and opened it a crack. His eye was pressed against the opening for a solid twenty seconds before he closed it again.

"All right—the coast is clear." He looked at me over his shoulder. "Are you ready for this?"

"What's our story if we—"

"I got it—no worries." He looked at me with crinkly eyes and said, "You still trust me, right?"

It was weird how much I did. "Right."

"Then let's go. Just pretend we're supposed to be here."

"Got it."

Nick pulled open the door and we walked out. In front of us was a carpeted hallway, with offices on each side of it.

Offices with glass walls.

We started down the corridor and he winked at me, which made me giggle. We hurried past office after office, and a woman in a suit gave us a closed-mouth smile as she came out of her office and walked past us.

After she went by, we grinned at each other because holy crap, it was actually working. We were going to make it to the elevators.

"Excuse me."

Shit. We kept walking, our eyes looking straight ahead as we heard the deep voice of an older man repeat the words from behind us. "Excuse me. You two?"

Nick turned around, and his face transformed itself into that of a sweet, innocent high school boy. I watched in awe, my heart racing, as he said, "Yes?"

"Can I help you with something?"

"Actually, that would be great. Can you point us to the elevator? We're here for an internship orientation and we clearly got off on the wrong floor."

Wow—good one, Nick.

I turned around and the man was looking at both of us through narrowed eyes. I thought Nick was super believable, but the well-dressed old guy still looked suspicious.

I gave him my best good-student smile.

"It's just over there," he said, pointing past us, "but I didn't even see you two get off the elevator the first time."

"That's because we took the stairs," I said, smiling even harder. "I like to move, but my friend here is a little out of shape. I thought he was going to puke on the way up, which is why we ditched the stairs to look for an elevator."

Finally—finally—the guy smiled. "Not everyone can handle those stairs."

I reached out and poked Nick's midsection (which was incredibly hard, for the record) with my finger and said, "Tell me about it. I thought I was going to have to carry this marshmallow."

"Thank you so much for the help, sir." Nick captured my finger in his hand while the guy laughed. Nick said to me, "Come on—we've got to run if we're going to get there on time."

We managed to calmly walk to the elevators, but the second the doors closed behind us, I was cackling. I looked at his wide grin and said, "Nick Stark, you are such a good liar!"

He laughed and moved a little closer. "And you are such an enormous brat with your 'marshmallow' shit."

I felt breathless. He was *right* there, his face just above mine while his body kind of trapped mine between the elevator wall and him, and I realized that I wanted him to kiss me. Something about my stairwell epiphany about my feelings for Josh made me feel wildly free to explore Nick Stark.

"We should go to the thirty-ninth floor," he said, his voice deep and quiet as his eyes stayed on mine, "and then take the stairs from there."

I just nodded as the elevator whooshed us upward. I swore he was leaning closer when—

The elevator dinged.

We both jumped apart and looked up at the numbers. We were apparently on twelve, and more people were getting on. I pushed at my hair as the doors opened and a security guard joined us

What were the odds?

And what had almost happened between me and Nick?

I gave the guard a polite smile and he returned it, stepping inside and pressing the button for floor thirty-six as the doors closed behind him. I gave Nick a sideways glance and he was looking straight ahead, totally unaffected by this interloper's presence.

The car started moving and I watched the illuminated display above the doors dutifully report each and every floor we passed. I cleared my throat and bit down on my lip as the silence very nearly killed me.

When we finally hit thirty-six and the elevator dinged, the tall security guard gave me another polite smile. As the doors opened, I said, "Have a good day."

He gave me a head nod. "You too."

Once the doors closed behind him, I glanced at Nick. He was looking at me with an unreadable expression on his face, and I was begging my brain not to overthink whatever was happening between us. The elevator dinged when we reached the thirty-ninth floor—of course—and he just said, "Ready to do this again?"

I smiled and muttered something in answer, but the truth was that I wasn't capable of actual conversation. I needed a minute to calm my freaking-the-freak-out nerves.

The doors opened, and this floor had a foyer area with a reception desk. It was deathly quiet, and the stern-looking woman sitting behind the desk already looked irritated by our existence.

"Can I help you?"

Nick said, "Can you point us toward the stairwell? The guy in the orientation said we could take them down if we wanted the exercise, but then we got on the elevator and almost forgot. Is it over there?" He pointed toward the other end of the building, and I was in awe of his composure.

She nodded. "I'll show you."

My breath caught in my throat as she stood and came around the desk. Nick smiled at her and they started walking, so I followed.

"What orientation were you here for?" she asked.

"An internship orientation with HR. It's for their new summer program."

"Oh?" She looked at him with her eyebrows down. "I didn't know they had something like that."

"Trust me, we were a surprise to everyone today."

The woman laughed and Nick added, "I'm excited to work in this building, though. Have you worked here long?"

She nodded. "Fifteen years."

"Wow—that is a long time."

"Only to you because you're young." She smiled and glanced back at me. "Trust me, fifteen years flies by."

"So were you here when people used to do proposals upstairs?" He said it so casually, like it was common knowledge to everyone in the world. "Or had that already stopped when you started?"

"Oh, they still did it, but it was usually on evenings and weekends so it didn't really affect those of us who worked here."

"Do you know why it stopped?" Nick asked, sounding so super chill that I was extra impressed by him. "Why the balcony kind of went offline?"

"No idea. I heard a really uptight exec moved into the big office and shut it down, but that was just a rumor." She stopped walking then, and gestured toward the door at the end of the hall. "There is the stairwell, but I warn you. Even though you're going down, it's still a *lot* of steps. Be careful."

"We will." I cleared my throat and said, "Thank you so much."

"Of course."

Nick opened the stairwell door and I walked through; he followed. For a second, when the door slammed behind us, I wondered if he was going to kiss me, but then he said, "We're almost there—let's do this, Hornby."

We walked up the final flight of stairs, and I had no idea what to say. My hands were still a little trembly, and my head was full of a million questions.

When we got to the top, without a word, Nick opened the door. We stepped out and it was another very quiet floor. It seemed to be comprised of ultra-swanky offices—probably the executives—and apparently no one up there made noise.

Like, at all.

"I wonder where the balcony is," I whispered.

"If I had to guess," he whispered back, "I'd say the east side. Wouldn't they want the balcony to look out over the heart of downtown?"

"Ooh—good point."

We walked down the hallway, both of us scanning the area in all directions in an attempt to see something that intimated a balcony was awaiting us. We walked all over the entire floor, but couldn't find anything.

And then Nick saw it.

"Look," he said, and I looked in the direction he'd nodded his head.

"No way."

One of the offices had its blinds open, and the balcony was on the other side. We'd have to go *through* an office to get on the balcony, because the bank of offices had doors which led directly out.

"Let's keep walking—maybe there's a common area."

We started walking farther down the hall, but when we reached the end it was clear; the offices in that row were our only points of access.

"Well, I guess that's it," I said, irrationally sad to give up on the dream. "We should probably go before we get arrested."

The bathroom door to our left opened and another security guard walked out. *Of course.* As he bent at the drinking fountain, I made bug-eyes at Nick. But instead of responding to me, Nick looked over my head. I was about to tell him that we should just forget about it when he said, "Excuse me, sir?"

I turned around to see who he was talking to as Nick walked past me and approached one of the fancy office doorways. The guy behind the desk looked busy and important—like a really cranky exec, with his perfect tie and expensive watch—as he raised his eyes to Nick. "Yes?"

"Can I talk to you for one second?" He glanced back at me, winked, then said to the guy, "I can see you're busy—I swear it'll only take a minute."

I had no idea what was happening as he walked into the guy's office and closed the door behind him. I giggled awkwardly as the security guard straightened and gave me a chin-nod, and I had no idea what I would say if he asked me where I was supposed to be or what I was doing.

"Jerome?" The guy in the office with Nick opened the door and yelled to the security guard. "Hey, can you come in here for a sec?"

We were so busted.

"No problem." The guard went into the office and closed the door behind him. I looked around in the empty hallway and snorted out a little laugh, because life had gotten downright bizarre.

I could see Nick in the fancy office, talking to the two guys. A minute later, the security guard and the executive started laughing. *What in the actual . . . ?* The door opened and Nick—looking like an incorrigible child as he beamed at me—said, "C'mon, Em."

I blinked and walked over to the office, clueless as to what exactly was happening. When I reached his side, Nick grabbed my hand and said, "But now I owe Bill and Jerome a favor."

"Who?"

"Hi, I'm Bill," the executive said, smiling at me like we'd been invited for tea.

"Jerome. Nice to meet you," said the guard, grinning at me like I was adorable.

"Nice to meet you both," I muttered as Nick pulled me forward. He pulled me past Bill's desk, turned the knob, and opened the door that led outside.

"I'm having Jerome lock the door in ten minutes," Bill said as cold air rushed in.

"We'll be done in five," Nick said, linking his fingers tightly between mine and pulling me out on the balcony. The second the door closed behind us I gaped at him.

"Oh my gawwwwwd—how did you do this?" I gasped,

dragging *him* closer toward the edge. "What did you tell them?"

He smirked. "Which one should I answer first?"

"Both of them. Wow." We both walked a little farther out on the balcony, and the city below was breathtaking. It was quiet up there, even though I could hear the distant sounds of the streets, and I totally understood the whole good-place-for-a-proposal thing.

"I simply explained that we'd been on a mission to find the elusive balcony." His face looked a little weird when he said, "I guess they're just nice guys."

I looked out at the view and breathed, "This is incredible."

I tried picturing my parents up there, young and still in love. Had my dad been nervous? Worried my mom might say no? Had she cried tears of joy before shouting "a thousand times yes!"? Had she gritted her teeth, irritated that he'd employed such a big, overdramatic gesture?

It was silly, but I felt a little emotional, standing where it happened.

"Yeah." Nick ran a hand over the top of his hair and said, "I hadn't pictured it being this cool."

"Forty stories is actually way higher than I envisioned," I added, not courageous enough to walk to the edge, even though the railing would be nearly impossible to get over. "Thank you for making this happen."

"It's the DONC, Hornby—no consequences."

Movement behind him caught my eye, and then I gasped. Because there were a bunch of people—like, a small crowd—gathering on that balcony just outside of Bill's office. It looked like everyone and their assistants—and *aw, geez*, the security guard—had stepped out to congregate and . . . stare at us . . . ?

"Nick, what did you tell Bill?" When I looked back at his face, his eyes were on my lips and I almost forgot what was happening, but I asked, "To get him to let us out here?"

He shrugged casually and said, "Don't worry abou—"

"Because we have a crowd watching us."

"What?" Nick glanced behind him. "Oh, shit."

"Oh, shit, what? Is there something—"

"I told him I wanted to come out here for a promposal."

"A promposal?" I couldn't believe he'd said that—of *course* they were out here. Adults loved that sappy crap. *"Nick."*

He looked unfazed as he said, "We'll just tell them I asked and you said yes."

I waited for the rest, but apparently that was it. "That's not a promposal."

He looked surprised. "It's not?"

"No." I rolled my eyes and explained, "That is asking someone to the prom. A *promposal* is when someone does something huge in order to convince someone to say yes. Getting a celebrity to help, making a cake, singing a song, asking in three million rose petals, doing a dance—how do you not know this?"

To be fair, that was just what I knew—perhaps they did it differently elsewhere. But in my town, at our school, that's what it meant. Next-level stuff the likes of an engagement proposal.

"Why would anyone do that for prom?" he asked, looking disgusted. "It's just a dance."

"Do you really want to discuss the merits of a promposal with me at this moment? That crowd—and the security guard—is waiting for a show."

He didn't say a word but got out his phone and started scrolling.

I glanced behind him at the spectators, who were still staring expectantly.

"Um, Nick . . . ?"

"Hang on." He scrolled for another minute, then looked at me and grinned.

"Nick—"

His phone started playing music—loudly. But before I could ask him what the hell he was doing—*was that "Cupid Shuffle"?*—he handed me the phone.

I took it, and then he backed up like five big steps and started doing the *worst* version of the Cupid Shuffle that I'd ever seen. He wore a cheesy smile while doing a rigid, absolutely pathetic rendition of the line dance.

"Seriously?" I yelled.

I started laughing—no, cackling—when he yelled over the music, "Emilie Hornby, will you Cupid Shuffle with me to the prom?"

"Um," I yelled back through the uncontrollable giggles, "are you saying you're my Cupid, shuffling to win my prom favor?"

"Yes!" He nodded while going *to-the-left-to-the-left-to-the-left*. "That is exactly what I'm saying!"

And then he did a spontaneous spin move.

"How do *you* know the Cupid Shuffle?" I asked, knowing

without actually knowing that Nick Stark had never done a line dance in his entire life.

"I've been to a wedding before, and also, the song tells you what to do. Now please say yes."

I couldn't see through the tears, and my stomach hurt from laughing so hard. "First—tell me you love me."

He shook his head. "I love your hair and your sensible shoes, you annoying pain in the ass. Please say you'll prom me."

"Yes!" I screamed dramatically, jumping up and down, making the people behind us burst into applause. "Yes, I will prom you so hard!"

Nick gave me a look and yelled, "Come join me, Emmie!"

"Nah, I'm goo—"

"Get out there," Jerome shouted, giving me a dad-look. "Put that boy out of his misery."

"Aren't there drugs for that?"

Nick grabbed my hand, and I continued cackling for the entire rest of the song as we line-danced like we were at a wedding with a small team of corporate executives joining in behind us.

"This was a great idea, Hornby," Nick teased as he went *to-the-right-to-the-right*.

I laughed, still dancing as I looked at the beautiful skyline and the boy next to me. "I know."

CONFESSION #13

I kissed Chris Baker in the back of an RV in seventh grade, and to this day I can't smell Polo without remembering how noisy his running pants were.

When the elevator doors opened, there were three guys inside, dressed in suits and expensive haircuts. We stepped in front of them, quietly standing side by side as we rode the elevator car down.

"I'm about to smash some waffle fries," one of the guys said from behind us.

"I wish they'd bring back Bernie's Pizza. I like chicken, don't get me wrong, but it's been the only option for too damn long."

"So go get Bernie's."

"Nah, bro—I'm too lazy and the caf is too convenient."

I looked at Nick to see if he also thought the way they were talking was ridiculous, and the way he held his mouth a little too tensely told me he was fighting back a laugh, too.

One of them said "This is us" when the doors opened, and the trio filed out when we scooted out of the way.

Nick let out a big breath, but when the doors started to close he stuck his hand out, and they began opening up again. Quirking one eyebrow in an adorable way, he said, "Hey. You wanna go smash some strips in the caf?"

I squealed. "Ooh—do you think we can?"

He shrugged. "Why not? If they kick us out now, we already got what we wanted."

I started to get excited. "My mom *never* let me eat chicken strips growing up, so they're my secret favorite food now that I only get when I sneak." I knew I was rambling but I couldn't help it. "Y'know, when she's not around."

"Who's not allowed to eat chicken strips?" His eyes did the crinkle thing as he said, "You poor, deprived little book-nerd."

I laughed at that. "Right?"

He gestured toward the elevator doors. "Let's go, then."

As soon as we walked out of the elevator, the sounds and smells of the corporate lunchroom surrounded us. We followed in the direction of the dudes, and boom—just around the corner from the bank of elevators was an enormous cafeteria.

There were tables in the center of the room, and food stations all around the perimeter. Everything looked like generic cafeteria food except for the Chachi's Chicken booth, where a generous line was already forming.

"Chicken?" he asked, his eyes moving around the corners of the cafeteria.

"Chicken," I replied.

While we waited in line, he told me about the time his sister ran over the foot of a Chick-fil-A employee in the drive-thru, and I was tearing up from laughter by the time we sat down with our food.

"I can't believe she went back over it," I said, and laughed.

"She said that when he screamed, it was simple human nature for her to back up to see what was the matter."

"There is a logic there," I said.

"I guess," he said, dipping a chicken strip into his cup of ranch.

"So." I grabbed the table's ketchup bottle and squirted a blob onto my plate. "You said you've never been in love, but . . . like, you *do* believe in it, right?"

"Whoa." He tilted his head and his eyebrows went down. "You are persistent. What're you doing, Hornby?"

"Learning about my DONC partner. Now, if you're shy—I'll start." In real life, I would never broach this topic of conversation because *of course* I would come off as stifling and pathetic. But I wanted to know these things about him, so I was taking advantage of this erasable day. It didn't matter what he thought of this because he'd never remember it.

As soon as I thought that, though, I felt a little ache of sadness. I'd been having so much fun that the fact that tomorrow would be a reset, and Nick would remember nothing—seemed kind of tragic. "Okay. So. Even though you don't see it very often in real life, I absolutely believe in true love. I think it requires work and logic, as opposed to fate, but it's there if you look hard enough."

He gave a nod, like he was accepting my point, and wiped

his hands on his napkin. "But doesn't that sound a little oversimplified to you? It sounds like a kid saying they believe in Santa. Like, yes—of course it sounds great—but if it sounds too good to be true, it probably is."

I dipped a fry in my ketchup. "So cynical."

"It's not cynical at all." He slid a handful of fries through my ketchup blob and said, "I don't grouchily begrudge love—I just don't expect it to come down my chimney with a sack full of presents."

"Love is not the same as Santa Claus."

"How is it not?" he asked, picking up his soda cup. "You hope and wish for it, peeking to see if fate has brought the One to your doorstep, the One who makes you happy forever."

I picked up a strip and pointed it at him. "It's not the same because you're not relying on magic and pretend."

"Have you ever *seen* a first date?" He took a sip of his pop before saying, "Talk about your magic and pretend."

"How are you ever going to get happy," I asked, taking a bite before saying, "when you're thinking that way?"

He looked at me and crossed his arms over his chest. "I'm not looking to 'get happy.'"

I stopped chewing. He didn't appear to be joking. "Are you one of those guys who likes being broody?"

His eyebrows furrowed and he looked offended, like that suggestion was an insult. "No."

"So why wouldn't you want to be happy?"

He shrugged and picked up his soda. "I didn't say that I don't want to be happy. I said that I'm not *looking* to get happy. It's not my goal."

I wiped my mouth with my napkin before setting it down on the tray. "But—"

"I mean, are you *always* happy?" he asked, and I got a little distracted by the sight of his Adam's apple moving as he swallowed his Coke.

"Well, of course not," I said, putting my finger over the top of my straw. "But I'd like to be. I mean, happy kind of *is* the goal. Like, for life, right?"

"Well, sure, but—"

"Because happy is life's default." I pulled the straw from my cup, lifted it to my mouth, and moved my finger, letting the soda drip into my mouth. "Content is the baseline. Sometimes we're not, and sometimes we're freaking ecstatic, but happy is the default."

"You're absolutely wrong." He set down his cup and looked a little bit intense. "Existence is the default. Merely existing, emotionally, is the baseline. *Happy* is, like, this floating, fluid thing that's impossible to hold on to. Elusive as fuck. Sometimes you get lucky and have it, but it's only a matter of time before it slips back out of your hands."

I shook my head, trying to figure out how he could have such a bleak outlook. "That is the most depressing thing I've ever heard."

"No it's not."

"Yes, it totally is." I dropped everything on the tray, done with fidgeting because I needed to find a way to change his ridiculous mind. "According to your theory, anytime you're happy, you have to sleep with one eye open because it's going to implode at any moment."

He gave a surprised little cough of laughter and rubbed his cheek. "That's kind of the truth, though."

"Who hurt you, Stark?" I teased, and regretted it the instant he looked at me. Because—man, oh man—there was a whole lot of sad in his eyes. For just a split second, he looked like a very sad little boy.

Then he smirked, and just as quickly it was gone. "Who shot you up with happy fairy dust is kind of the bigger question."

"It's not happy dust at all. I know that I'm the only one who truly cares about my happiness, so I make it a priority. You should seriously try—like, *really* try, looking at everything in a different light."

Now he smiled. "Is that so?"

"Yes." I smiled back at him and said, "Think about it. On a normal day, you might be thinking, 'It sucks that I have to go to school.'"

He said with a straight face, "I would never think that—education is important."

"You get what I mean. On a normal day when you're feeling less than positive, force yourself to change your thinking. Instead of 'It sucks that I have to go to school,' think 'It's such a nice day that maybe after school I will recline the seat of my truck and read a good book while the breeze smells like springtime.'"

Now he flat-out laughed at me. "Why would I ever think something that ridiculous?"

"How about, 'At least I get to sit next to Emilie Hornby in Chemistry—hubba, hubba.'"

"Really with that?" he said, back to full-on sarcastic teasing with his twinkling eyes.

"Oh, like you've never thought the words 'hubba, hubba.'"

He said, "I can promise you I have not."

"Well, what about your friends, Mr. Existence Is the Default?" I leaned on the table, wanting to learn every single thing about him, and asked, "How is it that you're absolutely free of high school cliques and drama? I see you around school sometimes, and you appear to have friends, but I never hear about you socializing at all. Never see you at any parties, or football games, any other school functions . . ."

"And . . . ?"

"And . . . what's the story? Do you hang with your friends and do activities, or are you an actual hermit?"

He looked over my shoulder, like he was watching someone or thinking about something, and I expected him to give me a smart-ass nonanswer. But then he said, "I used to hang with my friends a lot more. But somewhere along the way, I stopped caring about everything high school. It just feels so . . . pointless. Not the learning, but all of the games."

His eyes landed on mine and he looked . . . intense. "Sometimes

I try to power through so I'm not a 'hermit'—as you so delightfully put it—but it just feels meaningless."

"Oh." I didn't know what to say to that. "Well, maybe if you treat it—"

"Swear to God, Hornby, I will lose it if you tell me to be positive."

That made me smile. "Well, it wouldn't hurt, you know."

One corner of his mouth slid up a smidge. "I think it might, actually."

CONFESSION #14

I once wrote "Beth Mills smells" on a bathroom stall at my junior high after she told everyone that the summer camp I attended was actually asthma camp.

After leaving the First Bank building cafeteria, Nick gave me a piggyback ride to the tattoo shop, letting me bury my cold nose in his neck without complaining, and when he finally stopped, he straightened and I climbed down. The 402 Ink storefront looked cool because it had no markings at all, other than a red neon sign at the bottom of the window.

He pulled open the door, and I followed him inside.

He said over his shoulder, "Getting scared?"

"Not at all. Bring on the needling."

I strolled through the lobby, where there were drawings of tattoos all over the walls and the ceiling. I was nervous, yes, but mostly I was excited. Getting a tattoo was something I'd never considered, something I never would've had the guts to do before this whole repeating-days fiasco.

Now, however, it felt like something I *had* to do while I had a free pass. It would serve, however temporarily, as a printed reminder of the day where—for once—I did what I wanted instead of what I thought I *should* do, instead of doing what everyone else expected.

I barely had a chance to take it all in before I heard Nick say, "Is Dante working today?"

I raised my eyes from the wall and looked at him, standing in front of the reception desk. "So you *do* have a contingent."

He just looked over at me and winked.

I'd always thought winking was cheesy until that day. Nick's winks made me warm and melty.

The person I assumed to be Dante came out from the back room and they did a whole handshake thing while I strolled the room, looking at pictures. After a solid ten minutes of low-talking, I heard Nick say, "What are the odds that you could fit my friend Emilie in this afternoon?"

"Sure." Dante glanced over at me and asked, "Do you know what you want? And have ID?"

I pulled my ID out of my pocket, walked over to him, and ran a hand through my hair. "Yeah. Here. And it's just seven words. I took a screenshot of a font I like."

"What seven words?" Nick put his hands in his pockets and looked at my ID suspiciously.

"None of your business."

"That's four," Dante said.

"Keep in mind that this is on you for life, Hornby," Nick said.

I don't know why, but I really liked it when he called me by my last name. "Er, doy, Stark." But little did he know that I'd wake up tomorrow on another February 14, skin fresh and un-inked.

Dante had to go help someone who walked in after us, and Nick gave me a look. He leaned closer, lowered his voice, and asked, "Why do *you* have a fake ID?"

My face got warm as I stuttered, "I don't—I mean, it's not—"

"I'm not going to tell on you." He nudged me with his elbow, and my stomach went wild with butterflies. His deep voice rumbled out, "I just can't believe bookish Emilie Hornby has a fake. A fake library card, maybe, but a fake driver's license? Not so much."

I felt a little less ridiculous and said, "Chris works with a guy who bought some kind of black-market machine and he practiced on us."

His mouth dropped into an O. "Chris? Ultra-nice Chris from Drama?"

"Yup."

He shook his head, smiling. "You goody-goodies are out here running wild. Who knew?"

"Ready?" Dante was back, and I followed him to a room, grateful Nick was with me; I was actually a little nervous. When I showed Dante what I wanted—one of my favorite lyrics—Nick said, "Are you sure? I mean, I get that you're feeling brave today, but in a few years, or even hours, you might regret having this tattooed on your skin."

I said, "Believe me, I know what I'm doing."

I didn't, or at least with regard to the technicalities of a tattoo I didn't. I started to get nervous as Nick sat down on the chair to my left, and Dante grabbed the stool to my right. After Dante wiped down my forearm, rubbed on the template, and turned on the gun, I quickly learned just how painful getting a tattoo was.

I mean, yeah, it was relative. It wasn't like getting a tooth extracted or getting stabbed in the face with a screwdriver, but it felt like someone was sticking a needle in my arm and then dragging it down my skin.

Because, you know, they *were*.

"So how do you guys know each other?" I felt the need to say something as Dante leaned over my arm and worked me over, even though I knew exactly how they knew each other. "Just from Nick's tattoos?"

Nick said, "You're so nosy."

"He works here." Dante didn't glance up, but said, "Stark's our little bitch; he didn't tell you that?"

I raised an eyebrow and grinned at Nick, and he gave me a head-shake while half smiling. Looking at his face made me think of the almost-kiss, and I don't know if my face changed or not, but his did.

His jaw flexed and his eyes were hot as the moment hung there. It felt like there was an invisible string, pulling me in his direction. An invisible string that had an electrical current that actually felt stronger than the needle dragging through my skin. I swallowed and blinked.

What had Dante just said?

"No, um, he failed to mention that detail."

"What, are you ashamed of us, Nickie?" Dante teased.

Nick said, "She's too nosy and doesn't need to know shit."

That made me snort. "Whatever. Nickie."

Dante thought that was pretty funny, but I couldn't laugh because Nick was looking at me like *that* again. The intensity of his gaze rendered me incapable of all thought and communication as Dante grunted and muttered syllables while finishing my tattoo.

When Dante was finally finished, he showed me the tattoo and I gasped, lightly running my fingers around the newly inked spot on my arm. "Wow—this is incredible."

I had a marvelous time ruining everything

I loved it.

Dante left the room to go get something, and Nick stood. He stepped closer to me and slid his hand under my forearm so he could raise it to his eyes. My breath got stuck in my chest as he moved his thumb just under the tattoo—ever so softly—while he was so close to me that I couldn't remember what the world looked like beyond his face.

"I like it," he said, his thumb still brushing back and forth over my skin. It felt like he was talking about more than the tattoo as his face hovered over mine, an inch away.

"Let me just put this on your arm," Dante said as he charged back into the room, a tube of something in one hand and Saran Wrap in the other, "and you can be on your way."

Nick took a step back, and I was too shocked to do anything other than nod and try to make my heartbeat slow down. Nick walked out of the room and Dante talked to me about how to take care of the tattoo while he put salve on it and covered it in a bandage and plastic wrap. I barely listened, knowing the tattoo would be gone when I woke up to another February 14.

When Dante led me out to the lobby, my DONC partner was standing over by the front door, talking to a guy with spiky black hair and tattoos all over his arms. My cheeks got insta-hot when Nick glanced over at me, and I quickly followed Dante to the counter.

I paid, and when I was signing the receipt, Dante said, "How'd you get the little hermit to come out and play?"

"I actually bullied him into coming." I handed him the piece of paper and he smiled a really nice, really warm smile.

"Well I'm glad. Nickie's grown up too fast since the accident and he needs to have a little fun."

"Accident?" I glanced behind me to make sure Nick didn't hear and think I was being nosy. "Nick was in an accident?"

"Not Nick—Eric."

"Eric . . . ?"

"His brother. Today's the anniversary?"

Nick came over and straightened the look book on the counter. "You ready, Hornby?" He didn't look like he overheard anything, and I couldn't help but feel like I stumbled upon something Nick didn't want me to know.

I nodded and cleared my throat. "Ready, Stark."

Nick said a goodbye to his friends, and I yelled, "Thank you!" as we walked out the front door.

"Jesus, it's cold," Nick grumbled, zipping his jacket.

I hugged my own jacket—no, *his* jacket—tighter to my body. "Have I thanked you for your delightful coat?"

"No problem." He looked at me, and his eyes roamed down

over the big coat before he got a funny expression on his face. He swallowed visibly and his jaw flexed, and he was quiet for a moment before finally clearing his throat and saying, "So where to next?"

I glanced to my left and pointed to the ladder beside us that ran up the side of a squatty brick building. My eyes followed its upward trajectory, and it looked like the building was only a few stories high. All I wanted was to distract Nick from whatever had just made his face look sad, and when you combined that goal with the fact that it was the DONC, climbing onto a rooftop seemed like a great idea.

"Nope," Nick said.

"Because we were already up on a balcony?"

"Because if we're going up on a roof, we're taking something hot to drink." He turned his attention from the ladder to me. "And I know a better spot. Come on." Nick grabbed my hand and pulled me, tugging me closer as he started walking down the sidewalk. His legs were so much longer than mine that he was practically dragging me.

"Slow down," I said, and laughed.

"It's too cold for slow, Em." He brought us to a stop, turned around, and gave me his back. "Get on."

"Again?" I asked, a little breathless over the intimate use of my nickname. "I *can* walk faster—you don't have to carry me like a small child."

He looked at me over his shoulder. "Nah—I like it. Keeps me warm and I get buzzed on your perfume."

We shared a funny smile before I climbed on, like we were

wordlessly acknowledging this attraction. I wrapped my arms around his neck and he said, while grabbing my legs and holding them tighter against his body, "Let's go."

He took off, walking so fast that it was the speed of my run. Luckily there wasn't much pedestrian traffic so it was easy for him to trudge down the street with a passenger clinging to his body.

"You okay back there, Hornby?"

"I'm getting heavy, aren't I?"

"Getting?"

"Shut up."

I could feel the vibration of his laugh through his back and I laughed too, tightening my legs around him and earning another laugh. He went another block, then put me down when we got to a small coffee cart on the corner. THRIVE COFFEE appeared to be a charmingly restored camper that was all shiny wood and contemporary finishes.

The person who was working looked at us through the ordering window and said to Nick, "I saw your parents yesterday, and your mom *still* looks pissed at me."

Nick grinned and said, "You wrecked her car—does this surprise you?"

The guy—his name tag said Tyler and he looked like he was probably in his early twenties—laughed and started telling me a story about the time Nick gave him a ride to work in his mother's car and it got stuck in the snow. Apparently, Tyler was supposed to just give the car a little gas when Nick got behind it and pushed, but

Tyler thought it made more sense to gun it and "blow that bitch out of the snowbank," which resulted in the car shooting forward, swerving and slamming into a parking meter.

Nick was full-on laughing. "Ty got out of the car, looked at the damage, and then seemed genuinely offended by what the parking meter had done."

It was kind of amazing, witnessing Nick looking totally happy. I was almost overcome with the desperate need to do whatever necessary to make him like that all the time.

"This is Emilie, by the way," Nick said to Ty, and we exchanged nice-to-meet-yous.

Then Tyler asked, "Shouldn't you kids be in school right now?"

"We actually should," Nick said, turning his smiling eyes on me. "This criminal convinced me to ditch with her. Now she wants to climb onto a roof in the cold like this is a goddamn movie."

"Nice." Tyler nodded his approval. "Taking her through T.J.'s, then?"

Nick nodded. "Yeah, but we need hot drinks first."

"The usual, Big Man?"

"Make it two."

Tyler disappeared from our line of sight to make our drinks, and I said, "Who *are* you, Nick Stark?"

He narrowed his eyes, and a gust of wind blew between us when he said, "What do you mean?"

"I mean, people our age don't have actual lives. We hang out with school friends and maybe, like, drive to the mall. But here you are," I said, gesturing at the coffee stand and the downtown buildings, "With grown-up friends and, like, a downtown life. Are you a secret agent? Are you actually forty?"

His eyes moved all over my face and he said in a low voice, "I could tell you, but then I'd have to kill you."

"They always say that, but do they *really* have to murder?" I tucked my blowing hair behind my ears and said, "Can't it be 'I could tell you, but then you'd have to promise to keep my secret forever'?"

"Two large mochas, extra chocolate, double whipped cream." Tyler appeared in the window with two huge paper coffee cups.

I looked at Nick, who clearly had a massive sweet tooth, and said, "I have a cavity just from hearing that order."

"Right?" Tyler grabbed Nick's debit card and they started talking about someone I didn't know as he rang up the order, and I just watched. Nick seemed so comfortable—so *warm*—when he was with his friends, and that was a side I hadn't really seen before. At school, he always just seemed like he was trying to get through the day without having to talk to anyone.

This . . . was so different.

After we finished at the coffee stand, Nick led me one block over, where we went inside an unmarked apartment building. He refused to answer any questions, simply walked ahead of me. We took an elevator to the top floor, went down a long hallway and into the maintenance closet, and then Nick gestured to a ladder that sat between two rusty boilers and looked like it led up to a cage. "I'll go first and open the hatch if you'll hold my cup."

I blinked. "Um, what? What hatch?"

He held out his steaming drink and said with his eyes on mine, "Do you trust me?"

I just nodded and held out my free hand.

"Good girl." He gave me his cup, then turned and started going up the ladder to God knows where. I heard his shoes on each metal rung, and then all I could hear was the sound of hardware before a gust of icy wind blew around me and the boiler room was flooded with light.

"I'm coming for my coffee," I heard him say as he climbed back down, "so don't try to start climbing with full hands."

A second later his legs came down in front of me and he grabbed his coffee. "You should probably go up first, so if you slip, I'm here to break your fall. Do you think you can climb one-handed? If not, I'll leave my cup down here and I can carry yours."

"Wow." I looked up at the chute and said, "So chivalrous."

He raised his eyebrows and said, "That, or I really like the looks of those leather pants from behind."

If someone else had said that, I might've wanted to slug them. But his lopsided grin told me he said it on purpose because he knew it would rile me up. I rolled my eyes and started climbing.

Once I got to the top of the ladder and stepped out onto the roof, I was assaulted by freezing-cold winter air. Nick emerged behind me, and before I could even look around, he said, "Close your eyes."

I did, but I said, "This seems like a bad idea on a roof."

"I know, I know," he said, and I felt him grab my free hand and start to lead me. "But I promise not to kill you. I just don't want you to see it up here until you're in the perfect spot."

"I already saw the city from the forty-second floor. How different can this be?"

"You have no idea." I let him maneuver me, leading me around things until finally, he stopped. His breath was warm on my cheek as he leaned in close and said in a quiet voice, "Okay, Emmie—open your eyes."

CONFESSION #15

I went out for basketball in seventh grade because I thought it would make me popular. I wore pink Chuck Taylors and I scored two points over the entire season. It didn't work.

I opened my eyes and was breathless as I took in the beauty. Where the skyscraper had been cool because you could see everything from way above, this view was as if I was surrounded in a hug of my favorite city. We were right in the heart of the Old Market, just above it, so we could see the horse-drawn carriages and the people walking and the huge fountain they'd just installed last summer.

We were *in* the Old Market, as opposed to above it, but we were invisible.

It was breathtaking. I whispered, "This is magical."

"Right?" he said, looking out at something on the horizon. "This is my favorite spot in the city."

"Again, who *are* you?" I took a sip of the rich, decadent hot chocolate coffee and looked at his strong jaw. "How do you know about this?"

"My brother used to live in this building," he said, still looking at something far away. "So every time I came over, we always hung out up here."

"Lucky. My siblings are tiny and not really my *real* siblings. Where does he live now?"

I was staring out at the fountain but when Nick didn't answer, I turned to him. Fidgeting with the cuffs of his sleeves, he sighed and said, "Yeah, this is awkward. He doesn't."

Oh no. THE accident. "Um, Nick, I—"

"He died in an ATV accident."

"Nick, I am *so* sorry."

He shrugged. "It's okay; it's not like it just happened. I mean, it's been, like, a year."

"A *year*? That's not a very long time at all." A year was like it happened yesterday.

"It's fine." He didn't look devastated, like there was fresh grief. He looked . . . weighed down with it. Exhausted by it. Drained by it as he gave me a tired smile. "I didn't mean to drop that on you. It's so weird to talk about."

"Well—"

"It's actually a year today." He swallowed and looked like he was trying to sound casual when he said, "He died last Valentine's Day."

"Seriously?"

He gave me a half-smile and said, "How's that for a Hallmark holiday, right?"

"I would want to drop-kick everyone talking about flowers and candy, if I were you." It felt sick, the idea of someone dying on a day where people sent balloon bouquets and heart-shaped pizzas. I also felt like a total baby for feeling sorry for myself about my parents' breakup anniversary when Nick was dealing with *this.* "Like, who gives a crap?"

That made his smile grow just a little. "Right?"

It totally made sense now, the way he lived his adult-in-a-high-school-body kind of life. How would things like prom and parties and basketball games seem like anything other than pointlessness after experiencing a loss like that?

"I totally get it if you don't want to DONC with me, Nick." I set my cup on the railing beside where he'd set his, shoved my hands in my pockets, and felt guilty for dragging him along on my adventures. "Maybe you'd rather—"

"Hang out with my parents and listen to how quiet the house is? Nah—this is way better."

I followed him over to a bench that sat next to a dead plant on the roof's corner. He sat down, and when I sat beside him, he grabbed my sleeve and pulled me closer. Slid me into him so my back was leaning against his front. He wrapped his arm around my shoulders and rested his chin on top of my head.

"This okay?" he murmured, and his voice vibrated through every follicle of hair on my head.

"Mm-hmm," I replied.

We sat there like that, quietly watching the world all laid out in front of us, for what felt like a very long time. It wasn't uncomfortable, though—just silent.

"Y'know, the weirdest thing about it is the disconnect in my brain between life and death." Nick's voice was nonchalant when he said, "I can spend an hour thinking about the fact that he's dead, but then five minutes later if I hear a noise down the hall, I'll think bizarre shit like, *E must be taking a shower.* It's like my brain knows but my memory forgets or something."

"Um—that's so incredibly awful."

"In a way." His voice was quiet, and the sun made my cheeks marginally less cold as he said, "But part of me likes that confusion because for that half-second, it feels like things are normal. Weird, right?"

"Not at all." My heart hurt for him, and I set my hand on top of his. "But the half-second after that half-second has to be awful."

"The worst." He made a half-laugh, half-groan noise and said, "How did you know that?"

"I don't know how it couldn't be." I ran my finger over his knuckle and asked him, "Were you two close?"

"Yeah. I mean, close the way brothers three years apart are close. We spent most of our childhood fighting, but we were always together."

"You must be so lonely now." I knew there were things far worse than loneliness, but I also knew firsthand that the empty achiness of feeling alone could be utterly suffocating. I turned around on the bench and set my hands on his cheeks, stricken by the sad in his eyes.

I had no idea what I was doing, but I kissed the tip of his nose. Because this wasn't about boys and girls and love and attraction, this was about a human soul needing to feel seen. I knew that because even though it wasn't comparable in scale to what he must be feeling, I felt that loneliness often. Every time my mom forgot it was her weekend or my dad left me a note telling me to just order a pizza because he and Lisa and the boys already had dinner, I felt like I was all alone in the world.

"Stop that." Nick's hands covered mine, trapping them on his face. "Stop wearing that heartbreaking look on your face. Were you just thinking about Sutton?"

"What?" That made me snort. And I realized that I felt nothing at the mention of my ex-boyfriend. "You know, I actually forgot that he existed."

"Then what was that?" His thumb stroked over my hand as he removed it from his face and then wrapped his fingers around mine. "What made your face so sad?"

I rubbed my lips together. I never—ever—talked about my parents to anyone. But as Nick looked at me as if he actually wanted to know, I found myself telling him everything. Our fingers ended up linked together, caught in between us as I got lost in rambling away about infighting and shiny new families.

I didn't realize the level of share I was at until I saw the bubble of tears blurring my vision.

No, no, no, you dork—don't cry in front of Nick Stark, the one person who should be crying.

"Sorry." I blinked fast and said, "That was weird—I never talk about that stuff. It's probably the last thing you need to hear about today, my pathetically mundane family life."

"You're wrong." He swallowed. "Somehow knowing I'm not the only, um . . . fuck . . . lonely one? Yeah, somehow I think that helps."

I forced my mouth up into a smile. "So you're happy I'm crying. *Such* a dick."

That made him grin and squeeze my hand. "Little bit."

We both laughed, and I said, "I actually do know what you mean. Nothing makes you feel alone quite like thinking you're the only one who is alone."

Nick smiled and said, "Tell me more about you. It's a good distraction."

I told him a million little stories, but he seemed fascinated by each and every one. He joked and teased, but it was warm and sweet and everything my lonely heart needed.

"You sociopathic little deviant," he laughed, tugging on a piece of my hair after I told him about my secret box of lifetime confessions. "Hazelwood's valedictorian is not at all what she seems."

"For the record, I haven't added any confessions in quite some time," I clarified.

"Bullshit," he coughed, and we both laughed.

"Oh! This is a good one," I said. "All I wanted for my ninth birthday was this purple unicorn cake from Miller's Bakery. It was majestic, Nick, for real. It had glitter *in* the frosting, so it looked like it was dusted with a thousand tiny diamonds. Every Saturday, when my grandma took me to get doughnuts, I would gaze at that glittery, beautiful cake. I loved it for like a year, and I wanted it as my present. No toys, no clothes; it was the only thing I wanted, and I talked about it nonstop."

"Sounds like an ugly cake," he teased, his fingers gently rubbing against mine. "But carry on."

"So my birthday comes and I am beside myself with excitement, right? My mom and her boyfriend drive me to the roller-skating rink, and I am bouncing off the walls. I skate with my friends for a bit, and then it comes time for the cake."

"I feel like I'm going to hate this part," he said.

"Oh, absolutely." I smiled at the warmth in his eyes and said, "Because my mom looks at my dad and goes, 'Tom? Cake . . . ?'"

I shook my head at the memory. "And he says, 'Beth? Cake . . . ?'"

"No," Nick groaned.

"*Yes.* So then they morph into their whole fake-smile-but-homicidal way of conversing, arguing because since the party is on my mom's day, he thinks it's her responsibility. But she thinks since I saw the cake when I was with *his* mother, it's his responsibility."

"Meanwhile you're just hearing the word 'responsibility' and feeling like a piece of shit, right?"

"Exactly. Like, if they cared about me and my birthday, shouldn't they have wanted me to have that purple unicorn cake, no matter what?" I rolled my eyes. "Then they said 'Oh well' and just stuck a bunch of candles in the pepperoni pizza that kids had already started stealing pieces from."

"There was no cake at all?" he said, looking outraged.

"Nope." I kind of wanted to laugh at how offended he looked. "Did you and Eric ever have any cheesy roller-skating birthday parties?"

"Hell no—we went with laser tag."

"Studs."

He started talking about his brother, sharing memories that made his voice crack while his eyes smiled, and I couldn't get enough. He told story after story of the two of them, running around after Eric moved downtown, doing obnoxious things and texting each other immature memes. I was crying again, but this time it was because I was laughing so hard.

"So." I sat up straighter. "Is your tattoo about Eric?"

"Yeah." He looked down at my—his—jacket and put his hands on the front, pulling the top together a little more. It was a nurturing gesture that made me warmer than the coat itself. "It's the exact match of what he had."

"Exactly?"

"Yep."

"That's actually really cool. Did Dante do it?"

"Yep. He did Eric's, and then he did mine."

"Can I see it?"

He smiled a dirty smile. "I'd have to take off my shirt."

"Oh, well, I'm sure you don't want to," I teased, pretending my cheeks weren't suddenly on fire. "You're probably ashamed of your marshmallow body, anyway."

His eyes crinkled. "You really want to see my chest, don't you, Hornby."

"Don't flatter yourself." I gestured to my forearm and said, "I'm just super into tattoos. Obviously."

"Yes, that's right, you badass."

"Just forget it." I rolled my eyes dramatically and said, "I don't want to see it anymore."

He gave me a grin and stood. He had that ornery-little-boy look in his eyes—the one I imagined he'd worn every time he screwed around with his older brother—as he took off his coat and dropped it on the bench.

"It's freezing, Nick—maybe—"

"If Emilie Hornby wants you to show her your tattoo," he said, casually pulling the back of his sweater over his head like he was changing alone in his room and it wasn't freaking freezing outside in the middle of the city, "you show her."

I got up, laughing as he stood there with his sweater in his hand.

Stepping closer, I forced my eyes to stay trained on his tattoo, which was some kind of Celtic pattern that wound up his bicep and twisted around his shoulder.

I set my fingers on his skin and let them glide over the inked lines, my eyes never daring to look up at him. He was all lean muscles under tight skin, and it felt more like we were alone in the dark than exposed on the roof as my hands moved over him.

He groaned. "Okay—stop. This was a terrible idea."

I looked up at his face and his eyes were hot. I managed to nod and take back my hands, and I watched as he put his sweater back on, and then his jacket. I started to wonder if I should feel awkward for feeling him up as he zipped his coat, but then he said, "I gotta hand it to you, Hornby—the DONC was one hell of a good idea."

That dissolved any tension that might've been building, and I grinned. I said, "Okay. I have an idea of what we can do next, and it's either great or terrible."

"So probably terrible."

"Probably." I took a few steps away from him, pacing as I tried pitching it in a way that would make him see its merit. "But since it's the one-year anniversary of Eric's death and he's obviously on your mind, what if we, like, pay him tribute?"

"Emilie."

"No—hear me out." I kept walking, taking steps back and forth to keep warm. "It sounds like you guys always had a blast in the city, like it was the setting for a lot of your best memories. So, what if we revisit some of those activities?"

He opened his mouth to speak, but I ran over and set my hand on top of it. "Let me finish, Stark."

He tilted his head and his eyes crinkled at the corners, so I let go and started walking again, happy that he was smirking. Any time that I could be responsible for *that* look on his face, I was thrilled. "What if we, um, zip the scooters over to the Joslyn like you guys did on the Fourth of July? Or maybe we could ride bikes to the park and go down the big slides. Feed the ducks the way you guys did when your mom brought you down here in grade school. I don't want to overstep, but it'd be kind of cool if you were able to feel like Eric is somehow with us on the DONC."

"Hornby."

"Please don't be mad that I'm butting my—"

"Emilie."

"—nose in. I just want—"

"For the love of God, Em, stop talking." He stepped over to me, grinning, and put *his* hand over *my* mouth. "If you don't shut up, I can't tell you that I think it's a great idea. Christ."

I looked up at him, giving me teasing eyes from such close proximity, and I realized that I was actually feeling kind of big things for him. I mean, yes, we hadn't known each other long, but I felt like I knew more about him than so many people who were important parts of my life.

I felt like he knew me.

And I rarely felt that from anyone.

He lifted his hand from my face and said, "Shall we embark upon the next part of our journey, then?"

CONFESSION #16

When I was little and my mother made me apologize, I silently added, ". . . though I really am not" to the end of every single apology.

"So that's why you don't date?" I stopped chewing my pizza and gave Nick the most screwed-up face I could come up with. "You don't have *time* for it?"

It was starting to get dark outside, so Nick and I had wandered into Zio's Pizza for a few slices to fill our bellies and warm us up. After hanging on the rooftop, we'd ridden scooters to the Joslyn Museum (Nick still had Eric's admin code from his brief stint working as a "scooter-jockey," so he'd been able to override the Bluetooth so we could leave the zone), where he'd taught me five things I'd never known about Van Gogh as we'd explored the art museum.

Some people theorize that the artist Gauguin was actually the one who cut Van Gogh's ear and it wasn't self-inflicted at all.

Van Gogh painted a portrait of himself with a bandaged ear after the cutting.

He only sold one painting in his lifetime.

He shot himself in the chest in a field where he was painting, but managed to walk back to his house afterward and didn't die until two days later.

His last words were "The sadness will last forever."

I might've been depressed, because that was wildly depressing information, but then Nick taught me two more things about Van Gogh that were obviously untrue and made me feel much better:

His friends actually called him Van, and when he stuck around too long and became annoying, they tormented him with their cries of, "Van, go!"

The woman who received Van Gogh's ear sold it on eBay and made so much money that she started lopping off her own body parts and selling them. One of her toes went for a million dollars so she lived happily ever after and named all seven of her sons Vinnie.

After that, we ditched the scooters and rented bikes, which we rode over snowbanks (very difficult) and through slushy puddles (very messy) until we reached the big slides in the park. Nick with the great ideas ran into a convenience store and bought wax paper to slide upon, so we shot down the slides so fast that our only option had been to get big air and then land in a huge drift of snow.

While, of course, screaming at the top of our lungs.

After that we fed birdseed to the ducks—Nick had purchased that, as well—until our toes were too frozen to do anything else outside. I was a little afraid that after sitting in the heated pizzeria for well over an hour, we were going to freeze to death when we finally had to leave.

"Don't say it like that—it's smart." He picked up his soda with one hand and pointed at me with the other. "I don't have time for all of the emotional bullshit a person has to put out in order to make another person happy. It'd be worse if I dated people and then just pissed them off by being a cold, distant asshole, wouldn't it?"

I rolled my eyes and set down my pizza. "There's a backward logic to what you're saying, I suppose, but I really think you're overestimating the actual number of minutes required to emote your feelings properly. A text that says 'I love the sound of your laugh' takes, like, fifteen seconds to send, and it'd mean everything to someone who really cared about you."

He said, "You're being obtuse on purpose."

"No, *you're* being obtuse on purpose. Your excuses are vague and overgeneralized and quite frankly—pathetic."

"So I'm pathetic now." His face was serious and intense and I was infatuated with the way he teased.

I nodded. "Little bit."

"Give me your crust. Now."

He reached over and grabbed my crust. I was on my third piece of pizza, and we'd already established that my least-favorite part was his favorite, making him my cleanup crew. He lifted it toward his mouth and asked, "Is it so wrong that I like being single?"

"It's not, but you don't."

He took a bite of the crust and said, "How do you know?"

"Because I *know.*" I wasn't being delusional, convincing myself of what I wanted to believe. I wasn't even talking about me in this scenario, to be honest. I was absolutely just talking about him. Nick Stark was warm and funny and caring, and his face lit up when he was with his friends and remembering his brother.

The Nick he was forcing himself to be at school, though, distant because he couldn't work up the strength to take on any additional emotional lifting, was work for him. I think he truly believed that happiness was elusive and fluid because of what'd happened to Eric, and instead of reaching for it and risking being shattered, he was just no longer interested in reaching.

For love, or even for friendship.

"Well, let me ask you this, then," he said, grabbing a napkin from the dispenser and wiping his hands. "If you *know*, how come you thought you were madly in love with someone this morning, and now you 'forgot that he existed'?"

"Let's not talk about that," I said in a teasing voice, but I really *didn't* want to talk about it. I was way more interested in Nick. "How about we move on."

"Okay. But." He narrowed his eyes. "First, tell me the thing he does that works on your last nerve."

"Oh my Lord," I laughed, "It has to be his ringtones."

"Please explain."

I lifted my cup and poured an ice cube into my mouth before saying, "He still thinks ringtones are hilarious. Y'know, like we all did in middle school? He actually takes the time to save a different one for every single person he knows, and he finds it funny to sneak into my phone and add them when I'm not paying attention."

"He gets in your phone?" He shook his head.

"I don't care about that—I have nothing to hide. But he assigned a neighing horse to his name in my contacts. He thinks it's hilarious that every time he texts, I hear the sound of a stallion."

"What a tool," Nick said.

Nick looked a little jealous, and I wanted him to be. I said, "The funny thing is that it just bugs me. The sound of that horse makes me want to throw my phone through a window."

"I bet."

"But he thought he was being nice by adding it for me." I grinned and said, "He beams every time he hears that stupid whinny."

"So you pretend to love it?" he asked.

I just nodded, which made him make a face and shake his head like I was pathetic.

"Can we stop talking about relationships now?" He pushed his plate and cup into the center of the table before checking his phone. "We should probably head back to the truck, actually."

After we bundled back up and went outside, Nick gave me another piggyback ride. I couldn't stop laughing as he decided it would be funny to loudly hum "our theme music," which sounded a *lot* like the "Thong Song" even though he denied it. My stomach hurt from laughing as I snuggled my face deep into the side of his neck for body heat.

"Jesus, your nose is cold," he said, sounding like his teeth were close to chattering.

"Sorry," I said, but I wasn't. I full-on let my face absorb his warmth.

He coughed out a breathy laugh. "I'm not complaining."

I realized that Nick was incredible. He was fun and beautiful and I'd never felt more comfortable around a boy. Like, ever (except for Chris).

Weird, right?

Because this no-holds-barred Em that I was being on the DONC wasn't me at all, so my lovesick musings didn't even make sense. The real Emilie Hornby would never get this close to someone she barely knew before today, so this person he was seeing wasn't actually real at all.

Right?

Or was this actually maybe sort of me . . . ?

As we walked by an apartment with the blinds wide-open, we saw it at the same time. On the TV in that stranger's living room, Rose and Jack were standing on deck, watching steerage passengers kick around a ball of ice that had fallen from the iceberg the ship had hit.

Titanic was playing.

Nick didn't believe in fate, and neither did I, but how *weird* was it that *Titanic* was playing at the exact moment we were walking by?

"Wow, you were so right, Hornby," he said sarcastically, stopping in front of the window. "Playing soccer with iceberg chunks? That is obviously the best. Movie. Ever."

"You're a ghoul, Stark," I replied, climbing off his back. "An absolute ghoul."

We stood there for a minute, just watching the movie in the window, and when I glanced over at him, I was terrified at the thought of going home. Of ending the day.

He'd agreed to take me to my dad's when we were done so I could sneak in and grab a key to my grandma's house (wherein he could make fun of the boy-band posters that he *knew* adorned my bedroom walls) and then he was going to drop me at her place where I could sleep in peace with no parental third degree.

But he wasn't going to remember it.

Not any of it.

The day had been unbelievably wonderful, yet when I woke up tomorrow morning, it wouldn't have existed for anyone but me. For some reason, I had to clear my throat and blink fast to recover from the emotion that came with the realization.

He looked over at me. "You okay?"

I tried to sound light as I said, "I don't want the DONC to end, Nicholas Stark."

"Same." He stepped closer, so his face was all I could see, and his voice went deeper and quieter. "And I've thought about it, and I really want my DONC to include kissing you, Em."

"You do?" My voice was embarrassingly breathy.

"Yes." He put his hands on my waist, one on each side, and leaned even closer. I could feel a hint of his breath on my ear as he said, "But I don't want to if you're still tied up about Sutton."

My voice barely had sound when I said, "I meant it when I said I forgot that he existed."

"So it's okay, then?"

On a normal day, I probably would've given him a shaky *Okay* or maybe even a *Yes, please.* But it was the DONC. The second half of the DONC, to be exact.

I nodded and in one move, lifted onto my tiptoes, put my hands on his chest and my mouth on his.

His lips were warm, and he kissed me like he'd been dying to kiss me for the whole of his life. My fingers curled into the soft fabric of his jacket as he opened my mouth with his, making me a little dizzy while he wrapped his arms all the way around my waist and pulled me closer.

Just like that, I could feel every inch of his solid body against mine, knees to chest to lips, and it made me weak as I slid up my hands and grabbed on to his shoulders for support. It was heady, heady stuff, being kissed by Nick Stark. He kissed me like he was trying to prove something.

Everything disappeared except the feel of his stubble against my skin, his fingers flexing on my back. He finally lifted his head and pushed a piece of my hair behind my ear.

I felt almost shy as we looked at each other. I ran my tongue over my bottom lip and said, "Don't you think it's weird that before today—"

"We didn't really know each other, and now it feels like we've known each other for years?"

I nodded. "Yes. I mean, it's kind of . . ."

"Bizarre? For sure." His eyes moved over my face and I could feel the vibration of his voice in his chest against my chest when he said, "I didn't know you this morning, and now I know the feel of your hand in mine, the sound of your voice when you're trying not to cry, and the taste of your mouth. I know that you hate potato salad and love that video with the cat that dings the dinner bell."

I grinned, feeling swept off my feet by his words. I said, "And I know that the scar above your eyebrow was from the time Eric chased you into a heating vent; I know that you scream obscenities when a cool girl is beating you in a scooter race; and I know that you kiss with teeth. In a good way."

His lips turned up. "It's really only been one day?"

"Hard to believe." I was happy he hadn't stepped back; I liked being pressed against his body, held there by his arms. I grinned up at him and said, "I have a confession, by the way."

"Let me guess—you cheated. You had those answers written on your hand."

I held up my hands. "Nope."

"Then . . ."

"Then, um, I have to confess that I think I'm obsessed with you. With this." I swallowed and said, "With us."

A crease formed between his eyebrows. "Emilie."

"Oh my gosh, don't ruin it, Stark. I don't care about anything but today, okay?" I rolled my eyes and poked him in the chest.

"I'm talking about being obsessed with us *on the DONC.* I'm talking about being obsessed with the day we just had. I don't care about the future, so quit looking like *that.*"

I leaned my face closer, like I was going in for another kiss, but I reached into his coat pocket instead, and wrapped my hand around his keys.

He groaned, and the sound of his disappointment made me feel victorious.

"Looks like Emmie's driving home." I pulled them out and held his keys over my head, giving them a quick shake before I turned and started running in the direction of the lot where we'd left Betty.

"Give me the keys, Hornby," he called calmly, following me, still leisurely walking.

I looked over my shoulder as I jogged. "I don't think so. I'm going to cruise in Betty and you're going to ride bitch."

His eyebrows went up and he said around a laugh, "You better give me the keys."

"These?" I started giggling and jingled them again. "You want these keys?"

His face broke into a grin and he said, "That's it."

I screamed and started running faster, and I could hear him sprinting behind me.

"You're gonna regret this."

"I don't think so—"

He caught me, wrapping his arms tightly around my body and lifting me off the ground. I screamed, and then I screamed again when he lowered his shoulder, lifted me higher, and then threw me over his shoulder.

"Nick!" I couldn't stop laughing. "Put me down!"

He easily got the keys from my hand, and then he swatted my backside. "I don't think so."

"Come on!" I cried, laughing hysterically as we walked by an older couple taking their dog out.

"Not a chance." He tightened his grip on me and said, "If you behave like a wild person, young lady, I'm going to treat you like one."

"Good evening," the parking attendant said as we passed the ticket booth.

"Good evening," Nick said in a booming voice, as if he were the friendliest woman-toting person on the planet.

"Are we almost to the car?" I asked, staring down at his very-perfect butt.

"I can see her," he said.

"So put me down—I'll be good."

"I think that's impossible for you," he said, but then a minute later he set me down beside his truck.

"Thank you," I said, pushing back my hair and straightening my shirt. "For the ride to the car. It's actually what I wanted when I stole your keys. Walking is for suckers."

Nick's entire face changed into a smile and he slowly shook his head as he looked down at me. "I like knowing you, Emilie Hornby."

I swallowed and thought again as he grinned down at me that

he wasn't going to remember this. Any of this. He was going to wake up tomorrow and not know me again.

I hated that so much that I felt a pinch behind my eyes, but managed to sound casual when I said, "Same, Nick Stark. I had the best day with you today."

His face grew serious, but he didn't say anything. The moment just hung there, strung in between both of our gazes. His eyes roamed over my cheeks and forehead and chin, and it occurred to me that the two of us were seeing that moment in entirely different ways. I was desperately hopeful that he would remember it all the next day, and he was memorizing every moment to look back upon fondly.

Because the DONC, for him, meant forgetting today once the sun came up tomorrow.

"Ready to go home?" he asked, his voice quiet and a little gruff.

I nodded, incapable of speaking through the disappointment.

"Em. Wake up."

"Hmm?" My eyes fluttered open and there was Nick, smiling at me as I awoke from the nap I'd apparently just taken while my head was resting on his shoulder.

That face—damn. He looked sweet and amused and hot, and I really wanted to go back to sleep. On him. Forever. He said, "We're at your dad's house."

I looked through the windshield, a little disoriented, and was relieved when I realized he'd parked by the back of my house, instead of in the driveway.

"Oh. Yeah." *Please don't let me be drooling.* I sat up and reached for the door handle, a little sleep-drunk from the smell of Nick and the warmth of his truck. I stepped out, and he was right there beside me in the cold darkness.

"You sure you want to sneak in?" he asked, walking beside me after I closed the door and headed for the back of the house where my window was. "Seems risky."

"It's not." I opened the gate and went into the backyard. The moon was high and bright as our feet crunched over the snow, and I was a little surprised he was coming with me and not waiting in the warm truck. "My room is in the basement, so my dad and Lisa sleep two floors above me. And he snores like a freight train."

"Spoken like a criminal," he said, and my laugh made a cloud in front of my face.

I unlocked the basement door and pushed it open, and I could feel Nick's warmth as he followed me inside. He didn't say anything as I opened the door to my bedroom, but as soon as I closed it behind us and we felt a little safe from getting caught, he full-on grinned in the dark—thank God for the bright moonlight shining through the window—and whispered, "You *are* a sociopath."

I followed his gaze to my bookshelves, which were color-coded without a single book out of place, and I had to admit that my room looked a little . . . sterile. Even without the lights on. I just shrugged and smiled as I opened my nightstand drawer and grabbed the keys.

"Is that . . . ?" He pointed to my closet with his eyebrows raised. "*The* closet? Where the infamous confession box lives?"

Something about the fact that he remembered made my heart flutter. I felt like Nick saw me—saw all of me—and it caused a warm pinch in my chest. I nodded, giving him an embarrassed smile, and then I said, "Wanna see?"

"Stop trying to get me to play 'five minutes in the closet' with you," he whispered, his eyes playful. "And *of course* I want to see."

I opened the door, flipped on the light, and pointed.

He stepped inside the walk-in closet, and I went in behind him. My mind immediately raced to intimate places as I quietly closed the door; we were so, so alone together in the quiet of my basement bedroom closet. Thankfully, before I could overthink too much and die of a heart attack, he gave me an open-mouthed grin of surprise and said, "Wow, your closet is color-coded, too. *Are* you a deviant?"

"No, I just like to know where everything is, and this system makes it simple."

He whispered, "I might be a little afraid of you right now."

"Then maybe we shouldn't pull out the confession box."

"Please show me." He crisscrossed his hand over his chest and said, "I'll be good."

A quiet giggle escaped as I reached behind him for the shoe box. He poked me in the ribs as I stood on my tiptoes, and I was so ticklish that I nearly fell on top of him as I grabbed it. I heard his deep, quiet chuckle in my ear—he was so close—and it occurred to me that my closet was a really nice place to be.

Especially when he said into my neck, "Your perfume is making me dizzy, swear to God. We need to hurry."

That made me breathless as I spun around and held out the box. "This is it."

He narrowed his eyes. "Just a shoebox? Really? I pictured something much more interesting."

"It's undercover. Hiding in plain sight, and all that."

He took the box in one hand and set the other hand on the lid. "Can I . . . ?"

I rolled my eyes and nodded, nervous to let someone see all those past vulnerabilities but confident that Nick was safe to share it with.

He opened it and picked up a paper strip. Read the words, then raised his eyes to me. "You threw potatoes in your neighbor's pool?"

"They were out of town and I was bored. I wanted to see if I could make it into their pool from our deck."

"And?" He was looking at me like I was about to confess to murder.

"And I did. Chucked fifteen spuds in a row."

His grin returned with a vengeance. "Did you get caught?"

"No one ever even suspected me."

He reached into the box and grabbed another strip. He immediately started cracking up when he read it and I had to shush him as I laughed, too, and waited to see what he'd read.

He was still laughing as he asked, "You have a performance video on YouTube with a hundred thousand views?"

I nodded and bit my lip, trying to quiet my giggles. "I was

in seventh grade at the time. It's not under my name and I was wearing a disguise, so you'll never find it."

"But you'll show me, right?"

"Maybe someday." I shrugged, trying to be light and flirty but the awareness of his impending amnesia about all of this almost made it impossible. I said, "You have to *earn* that privilege."

"Is that right?"

The way he said it, his voice quiet and his eyes hot, made breathing difficult.

I just nodded.

"At least tell me what song." He put the strip back in the box and asked around a smile, "What song did the little bookworm deviant sing?"

I cleared my throat before whispering, "'Lose Yourself' by Eminem."

He didn't even blink. "You're joking."

I raised my chin and met his gaze, which made him smirk and shake his head.

We went through a few more confessions, but had to stop when Nick cracked up upon learning I'd used my dad's credit card to send flowers to Justin Bieber's hotel room, and we were afraid of waking up my dad. And just as I was tucking away the box, we heard footsteps upstairs and we both froze.

Waited.

Whoever was up there seemed to be pacing, or walking in circles, and finally after a few minutes I whispered, "Let's just go."

"You sure?" he whispered back.

I shrugged, remembering it was the DONC. There had been times that day when all I'd been focused on was the Day of No Consequences, yet at other times, I'd forgotten about it entirely.

But the bottom line was that tomorrow wouldn't count, so tonight was all I had.

Tonight was my everything.

He grabbed my hand and we made it out of the house undetected. By the time we got to Grandma Max's, I was glad I'd stopped for the key because the lights were all off like she was already asleep.

Nick looked down at me under the yellowy glow of the porch light as I stuck my keys in the lock. He opened his mouth and got out "Well" before I covered it with my hand for the second time that day. If he was never going to remember this, I was going to tell him how I felt.

"I love you, Nick Stark." I blinked fast and was surprised by how emotional I felt. My throat was tight as I said, "It won't count tomorrow and it'll be like I never said it, but on *this* Valentine's Day, I fell in love with you."

His jaw clenched, flexing and unflexing, and I watched his throat move as he swallowed.

I whispered, "But only for today, I promise. Tomorrow it's all gone."

He looked at me like he was frustrated and confused and also completely into me in spite of himself, and I felt the gravitational pull of him leaning closer.

And then he looked down at his watch. Pressed a button.

"Come on," he said, grabbing my hand and leading me off the porch. He was nearly running as he pulled me over to the dark side of my grandma's house where there were no porch or street lights shining. His feet crunching in the snow, he walked toward me until my back was against the cold siding of the house.

We were face-to-face. With a shaky breath, I said, "What are you doing?"

"There's only seven more minutes."

I felt dizzy as he looked down at me through the most intense gaze. "So?"

His body leaned into mine as he cupped my cheeks and breathed against my lips, "You only love me for seven more minutes."

I raised my hands and set them on his jawline. He lowered his face, and I whispered, "Let's make it a good seven, then."

He couldn't know that tomorrow none of this will have happened, but he kissed me like we had seven minutes before the world ended. I felt his fingers on my back and against my skin as they slipped under my sweater. This was Nick Stark—those were his confident hands—and my heart was absolutely his at that moment.

His heart was pounding under my fingers, and our bodies strained against each other. And then, in the blink of an eye, it changed. Our kiss didn't get slower, but suddenly felt deeper. Or maybe that was just me, because I was hyperaware of how this moment would disappear with the morning, but things became rich, every movement meaningful and infused with emotion.

Nick kept kissing me lightly, but his eyes opened. I felt lightheaded as we watched each other, his blue eyes making me dizzy with their intensity. His hands were still on my back, but his fingertips were softly stroking along my spine. He lifted his mouth the tiniest amount and whispered my name against my lips, and then—

"Dammit."

He stepped back and his hands fell to his sides. It took me a second to hear the beeping and understand.

Our seven minutes were over.

The DONC was done.

He scrubbed his hands over his cheeks, looked down at my face like he was disoriented, and then he said, "Christ. I don't want this, Hornby."

"What?" I swallowed and shook my head. "Oh. I know. It was nothing."

"Emilie!" My grandma's voice rang out from the front yard. "Are you out here? Your keys are in the door and there's a truck in my driveway. I'm calling the cops if I don't hear—"

"I'm here, Grandma," I yelled. Nick and I put even more space between ourselves and straightened our clothes.

"Listen, Nick—"

"Come on, before your grandmother calls the cops," he said, cutting me off. He grabbed my hand, leading me around to the front yard. I followed, still processing what had happened, and when we reached the porch, my grandma looked a little ferocious as she scowled at us.

"Grandma, this is Nick Stark," I said, hoping my lips weren't swollen from the kissing. "Nick, this is my grandma Max."

"Nice to meet you," he said.

"Please get off my porch," she replied.

He nodded and smiled like he appreciated her bluntness before he walked to his truck and drove away. I just stood there, watching, as my mind replayed every little thing we'd done on that incredible day.

"I'm going to kill you in the morning, dear," my grandma said, opening the door and stepping inside. "But I need some sleep first."

I stayed on the porch, wishing the night would never end. "I love you—g'night, Grandma."

"G'night to you, you little pain in the ass."

It wasn't until I went inside and slid off my shoes that I realized I was still wearing Nick's jacket.

CONFESSION #17

I went through a phase in sixth grade where I wore the same T-shirt every day, just to see if anyone noticed. They didn't, so I gave up after sixteen days in a row.

"Wake up, Emilie!"

My dad's voice woke me up with a start. My heart was pounding as I squinted up into the bright light and tried to see him. He was standing beside the bed with his hands on his hips, looking furious. I said, "What time is it?"

"That is a great question, Em." His voice boomed. "It is one fifteen in the morning."

"What?" I sat up, pushed my hair out of my face and grabbed my glasses from the nightstand. "What's wrong?"

"What's *wrong*?" His face was beet red and his voice got even louder. "What's wrong is that my daughter never came home last night. What's wrong is that you ignored my texts and stayed out without telling me where you were. We called all of your friends and were just about to call the goddamn police because we thought you might be dead!"

Wait. *One fifteen?* "It's not Valentine's Day anymore?"

He huffed. "Did you not hear me say it's one fifteen? Get your stuff and let's go. *Now.*"

"Thomas, you need to settle dow—"

"No, I don't, Mom. She didn't come home last night and I was worried sick." My dad literally spat the words at my grandma, his voice louder than I'd ever heard it. "I should've known she'd be here."

Or in the basement closet—under your feet in your house—with Nick Stark.

"Oh, now, that's helpful." My grandma crossed her arms over her chest. "I assumed you knew she was here. The poor thing always comes here because she's invisible to you and Beth."

"Spare me." My dad turned back to me. "Get your stuff and get dressed now."

I scrambled out of bed, grabbed my stuff, and ran into the bathroom. I closed the door behind me and quietly dug my phone out of my bag.

"Where's my car?" My dad yelled through the door. "Out on the street where it can get dinged, I'm assuming?"

"Um, not exactly." I set down the phone, opened the door, and wished there were a way to make this seem less bad. I gnawed on my lip and looked at my grandma when I said, "I got pulled over for speeding, and they impounded the car. I've got the information about how to get it—"

"They *impounded* the car?" Okay, now *that* was the loudest I'd ever heard his voice as he stacked his hands on top of his head and stared at me as if I'd just confessed to murder. "How fast were you going?"

I swallowed. "Um—"

"Go change, Emilie." My grandma stepped between me and my dad and stared at me with huge eyes. "Now."

I closed the door and let out a breath as my grandma argued with my dad and led him down the stairs. I picked up my phone off the counter and my hands shook as I powered it on and waited for calendar confirmation. Because—um—was it actually the fifteenth?

I could feel my heart beating in my neck as the apple lit up my phone just before I saw my home screen.

Holy shit. It *was* February 15.

I quickly changed out of the pajama pants that I kept at my grandma's and pulled on the leather pants from the day before, absolutely freaking out as reality hit me square in the face. Flashes of things I'd done the day before started rushing over me.

Stealing the Porsche, telling off Lallie, Lauren, and Nicole, breaking up with Josh via the intercom, quitting my job, tagging the aforementioned people when I posted a picture of my tattoo to social media . . .

I was going to be sick.

Then I glanced down at my arm. Oh no. *No, no, no*. I pulled back the bandage and gasped.

I had a marvelous time ruining everything

Dear God, I had a tattoo. That said *that.*

"Oh my God." I looked into the mirror and stared at my own face.

What have I done?

CONFESSION #18

I've gotten three flat tires in the past year. All three were because I wasn't paying attention and drilled a curb.

"Your mother is here—that's awesome."

We pulled into my dad's driveway and I felt queasy when I saw my mom's car, parked a little off-kilter next to the curb as if she'd squealed onto the block and sprinted to the house from her vehicle.

Inside, she was standing in the kitchen with her arms crossed, and the second we entered, her long index finger pointed directly at me. Her teeth were gritted and she said, "Emilie Elizabeth, go get whatever you need from your room. You are coming home with me. Now!"

"For God's sake, Beth, can you settle down for a minute?" My dad dumped his keys on the counter and looked exhausted. I felt guilty for making him worry, especially since he'd refused to talk to me in the car.

The minute we'd walked out of my grandma's I'd managed to get out the word "I'm" before he barked, "Don't talk to me right now, Em."

I'd spent the rest of the three-minute drive thinking of all the things I'd done on the DONC. It seemed fuzzy after the multiple Valentine's Days, and I wasn't 100 percent sure it all had really and truly happened.

Because it couldn't all have happened, right? I mean, repeating days didn't exist in real life. Surely there was some other explanation. Maybe it'd been a dream on top of a dream, like a dream *about* repeating days.

"Are you kidding me? Settle *down*?" My mom's eyes were narrowed and she was ready to fight. She was wearing tartan plaid flannel Ralph Lauren pajamas, and her hair was pulled back in a tight ponytail. The faint smell of her moisturizer cream wafted across the kitchen and hit me with a one-two punch of nervous dread and homesick longing. "I have a hard time settling down when your lax parenting led to our daughter misbehaving at school and not coming home last night."

"Shh." Lisa, who was sitting in a chair at the table, moved her hands like she was patting the air to remind everyone that the boys were sleeping.

"Oh, come on, you know I'm not a lax parent." My dad lowered his voice and dragged a hand through his messy hair. "Emilie is a teenager. Teenagers make stupid decisions sometimes. Just because she did does *not* mean that—"

"Yes, it does!"

"You guys—shhh!" Lisa pointed upstairs, where the twins slept.

"No, it goddamn doesn't," he whisper-yelled. "I know you're perfect, Beth, but the rest of us—including our daughter—are not. Can you just be reasonable—"

"Don't you *dare* call me unreasonable when you couldn't find her!"

"Shhh!"

"*You* shh, Lisa—Christ!" My mom gave up on volume control and barked at me, "Go get your things *now*; tomorrow—*today*—is my day, regardless of this bullshit."

I was still just standing right inside the door, paralyzed by their fighting. I glanced at my dad and he gave a terse nod, so I ran up to my room. I blinked fast and tried not to cry as I jammed clothes into my backpack; I was way too old to cry about parents fighting, right?

It was just that it'd been a while since they'd had a big fight. And I *hated* when I was the cause and they talked about me like I wasn't there. Like I was an object they were arguing over instead of the kid they were supposed to love.

Thankfully, I discovered early on that I had the power to extinguish many of their Em-related disagreements. By bending over backward to please whichever one of them was aggressively upset, I was often able to curtail the fight.

My superpower, if you will.

Unfortunately, that wasn't going to help me—at all. Not this time.

I ran down the stairs, and the second I walked into the kitchen my mom said—

"I will be at my lawyer's the second his office opens, Tom. I'm filing to amend our custody arrangement because there's no way in *hell* I'm letting her visit you in Texas after this."

"I haven't even had a chance to tell her—"

"Good."

"Beth." His breath hissed through his teeth. "You are out of your mind if you think Em forgetting to text me is grounds for an amendment."

From upstairs, and through the monitor on the kitchen table, Logan's sleepy wail rang out. Lisa glared at both of my parents for a second but then swung her gaze to me, accusing me of once again screwing everything up before she stood and marched up the stairs.

Logan's cry got louder through the monitor, and the three of us kind of just stared at it for a second, listening.

"Come on, Emilie." My mom had her keys in her hand. "We're leaving."

"Um." I cleared my throat. "I'll be right out. I just need to grab one more thing."

"You have one minute."

She went out the door, and I turned to my dad. "I'll talk to her. I'll make her—"

He held up a hand. "Just go before she comes back in."

I swallowed. "I'm sorry, Dad."

He finally looked me in the eyes, and there was so much disappointment on his face that tears blurred my vision. He swallowed and his mouth was sad when he said, "You have no idea what you just did, kid."

As soon as we got to my mom's house, she launched into a forty-five-minute tirade about how irresponsible I was. Apparently *she* wasn't concerned about her husband or puggle sleeping, because she yelled the house down.

She took my phone and told me I was more grounded than anyone had ever been. No friends, no phone, no library, no car—I was essentially under house arrest. I could walk to school and back and that was it.

She grounded me from reading.

Seriously.

"I removed all the books from your bedroom, and don't even think about checking anything out from the library." She'd crossed her arms and looked disgusted by me when she said, "It's a bizarre thing for a parent to have to do, but I think you'd be happy in solitary confinement if you had a book to read."

She changed the Wi-Fi password so I couldn't go online at all, and she told me she'd called Boystown to get all the details on how to send a "troubled" child to live there for a while. I knew she was just blowing smoke, but when my mom got in a rage you just never knew what she'd do.

And I couldn't blame her for being mad. I mean, I *had* crashed at grandma's without telling anyone, making them freak out and worry and spend hours calling everyone I knew.

I went to bed, but sleep was elusive. There was so much pinging around in my brain that the power button was totally stuck in the on position.

First of all, I couldn't stop wondering *why*. Why had I experienced that cosmic anomaly, that it-isn't-possible movie-plot repeating of days? Because as much as I wanted to sweep it under the rug as a blip, the reality was that it had happened.

It had.

Whether it was an altered state of consciousness—like a drug interaction or some bizarrely long dream—or the real thing, I had experienced multiple Valentine's Days.

I wasn't delusional.

So . . . *why?*

I tossed and turned for a while, but worrying over what had caused my bizarre experience was ultimately overshadowed by the enormous sense of impending doom. Because with every passing minute, I remembered something else—something awful—that I'd done on the DONC. Things I'd done, words I'd spoken, people I'd surely pissed off.

How was I going to go to school in the morning?

Was there a way to change my appearance so no one would recognize me? Could I switch schools before tomorrow morning? I buried my face in my pillow and groaned because, short of a violent accident, there was no way my mother would give me a break on school.

And that wasn't an exaggeration.

I could be projectile vomiting in the morning and she'd tell me that I should just grab a Ziploc to spew into during my classes. *Every time you hurl, Emilie, think about how you could've avoided this situation. It'll be a good lesson.*

There was no way of getting out of it. I was going to have to go to school and be destroyed by the entire student body of Hazelwood High School. Lauren, Lallie, and Nicole were going to annihilate me in some sort of public spectacle, and no one in the entire school was foolish enough to jeopardize their own social status by going against those girls to support me.

Everyone else would pile on to save their own asses. And who could blame them?

And I had no idea what to expect with Nick.

Just thinking about him on the side of the house made me lightheaded. It'd been a perfect day with him, ending on a perfectly hot seven-minute make-out, but every second of it had been framed with a DONC expiration date.

What was going to happen the day after? Would he pretend it'd never happened, or would he be the same with me as he was on the roof of his brother's old apartment building?

I don't know what time I finally fell asleep, but at three fifteen I was still lying there, rotating between swoony recollections of Nick Stark and nightmarish imaginings of what was awaiting me at school.

When I woke up at six, I got out of bed and went straight downstairs without consulting my planner. Screw the planner.

The house was quiet and deserted, and I immediately started practicing my argument because I had to be brave. After school I had to find a way to get my mom to listen. I wanted my dad to be right about her not having enough to warrant an amendment, but my stomach clenched as I worried about what they didn't yet know.

Would she have grounds if she found out about my reckless-driving ticket?

I couldn't bear the thought of not being able to go to my dad's; his house felt more like *home* than my mom's. Even if he moved and left me behind, I knew he'd send plane tickets so I could visit all the time. But if my mom convinced the judge that he was a bad influence, God only knew how often—if ever—I'd be able to see him until I was eighteen.

I unloaded the dishwasher, put in a load of laundry, and got ready for school. I'd be lying if I said I didn't spend extra time on hair and makeup that morning. I wanted Nick to give me *that* look when I walked into Chemistry, and if mascara and lip gloss could make it happen, I was all about it.

Unfortunately, I didn't realize until it was time to leave that since I didn't have my phone, I couldn't ask Roxane or Chris for a ride. I was going to have to walk to school, and that sounded positively awful.

I looked at the thermometer outside of the kitchen window. Thirteen degrees.

Awesome.

CONFESSION #19

I almost drowned in the Platte River last summer
on a day where my parents hadn't even noticed I was gone.
Thank God Rox was a good swimmer.

The second I walked through the front door of Hazelwood High, all hope of no one remembering the previous day disappeared.

I unzipped my coat and pulled off my hat and gloves, frozen to the core and missing my Astro van in a desperate way. I glanced at two people standing by the office, two random girls I didn't know, and they whispered and watched me walk by.

In front of me was a group of four guys—they were dressed like burners but I didn't actually know them—and they turned around and all smiled and chuckled at me, but in a supportive way. Like I'd done something funny they approved of.

My face got instantly hot and my vision focused sharply on the fact that everyone was looking at me. Like, every-freaking-one. That girl by the snack store, those dudes by the trophy case, the mathletes by the counselor's office; every eye in the building was on me.

I pretended not to notice and headed for the safety of my locker.

"Holy crap, Em, you are my hero!" Chris came up behind

me and I'd never been so happy to see him in my entire life. "I seriously cannot believe you. Even though the tattoo is over-the-top nutjob, the fact that you had the guts to do it—and tag Josh in your post about it—is blowing my mind."

"I can't believe it myself." I looked around and no one seemed to be paying attention to us, thank God. Chris was beaming, which made me ask, "So what happened with Alex?"

"Em—listen to this. We had the *perfect* night. He came over, and it felt like we'd hung out a hundred times. Like, *so* chill, just talking and watching movies. And then," he said, lowering his voice and glancing over my shoulder, his eyes wide with wild-happiness, "when I walked him to his car, he pressed me against the side of that silver CRV and kissed me like . . . like . . . "

"Like he was starving and you were the only thing that could nourish him?"

His mouth dropped open and he squealed. "It sounds like something out of *Twilight*, but you nailed it—that's it exactly!"

"Shut up!"

"I cannot!" He was jumping up and down a little, and I joined him in his celebration, because nothing was better than Chris finding love. He deserved all the movie moments. "And he already texted to tell me he can't stop thinking about me."

"Of course he can't; you kiss like a dream."

"You wish you knew."

"I don't need to wish when you've told me that, like, a hundred times."

"I do, though." He leaned closer and said, "It's my special gift."

"We all have special gifts."

He rolled his eyes. "Don't quote *Pretty Woman* at me when I'm having my great-date freak-out."

"Carry on, then."

"Did I tell you he's going with me to Village Pointe after school to shop for jeans?"

That made me snort. "Seriously? I mean, jeans-shopping is the worst, right?"

"Focus, Em. He wants to go." He beamed and looked totally love-drunk when he asked, "Is it too soon for the L-word?"

I love you today, Nick. I shook my head and said, "Not at all."

He looked at his phone and said, "I've got to go."

"Hey, can I get a ride home?"

"Of course." He started walking away and said over his shoulder, "Meet me at my locker after school."

I made it through my first few classes by pretending not to notice that the eyes of the world were upon me. I ignored everything and replayed in my head the moments with Nick the day before, choosing to concentrate on the swoon instead of the actual dumpster fire of the day's reality. I overheard people saying my name in the halls during passing periods, but I pretended not to as I counted down the minutes until Mr. Bong's class.

On the way to third hour I saw *those* girls walking in my direction. Lallie was talking and the other two were walking beside her, listening to what was certain to be a riveting conversation. The halls were jam-packed with students because it was a passing period, and it felt like time was moving in slow motion as Lauren turned her head and looked directly at me.

Oh no, they were going to destroy me.

I did what anyone would do in my situation. I turned to my right and pulled open the door to the auditorium. It was mostly dark inside, with just a couple of stage lights shining, and I crept to the right as the door closed behind me.

Would they follow me in? I heard the bell ring as I ran down the last row of theater seats and crawled behind the big box that they used for props storage. My heart was pounding as I squatted and waited, and I wondered if this was rock-bottom.

I heard a few random voices as I crouched behind the container—clearly there was a music class about to start—and my heart pounded as I literally had no idea what to do. *Crap, crap, crap.* This was not normal behavior, right? People didn't just hide during the course of the school day.

"All right, all right, settle down," I heard someone say, a woman whose voice sounded very teacher-y as it boomed through the auditorium. "I know you're excited, so if everyone's ready, let's just try it from the top and see where we're at."

My squatting legs felt wobbly as music started playing over the sound system. The noise made me think it might be safe to come out and sneak toward the door, but as soon as I peeked around the corner, I knew I was screwed.

Because at that exact moment, fifteen or so pop choir students on the stage burst into "Summer Nights" as they began rehearsing. Every single one of those superstars would see me if I came out now.

Dammit.

Not only was I going to get in trouble for ditching the class I was supposed to be in, but now I was going to have Danny and Sandy's meet-cute song stuck in my head all day.

I sat down behind my box and got comfortable.

As it turned out, they weren't too bad. Their loud rendition of the songs from *Grease* kind of made me forget my trainwreck of a life for a little while as I hummed along. "Hopelessly Devoted to You" was still kind of catchy—who knew? When the bell finally rang and the auditorium started emptying enough for me to be able to leave my hiding spot without being noticed, I straightened my cramped legs and hightailed it out of there.

Unfortunately, the second I opened the auditorium door I ran right into Josh.

"Gah!" I jumped back, my body feeling the collision even after the split-second bump passed.

"Emilie." Josh's nostrils flared and his eyes moved over my face before he said, "What were you doing in the auditorium?"

"I, um—"

"You know what? I don't care." He touched my arm and said "C'mere" as he led me over to the enclave of hallway trophy cases and away from passing students. He moved closer to me and asked in a quiet-but-angry voice, "What in the hell *was* yesterday, Em?"

I cleared my throat. What to say? *Um, I didn't know the fifteenth would actually ever come? I saw you kissing someone but I don't even know anymore if it was real or not?* Yeah, like that wasn't bonkers. "I thought—"

"Things were fine with us in the morning at my locker, and then you just walked away from me to go humiliate me over the intercom? And then the tattoo? Who does that?"

His face was a little flushed and he looked hurt. Sad, actually, as he looked at my face like he genuinely needed an answer. I took a deep breath and said, "Listen, Josh, I know it seems—"

"Like you're an asshole?"

Wow. That was the first time that a guy I'd loved had ever called me a name, and it was a jarring, nasty feeling. I said, "Maybe I wouldn't have acted like one if you weren't still involved with your ex."

His eyes widened a little, like he was surprised. But it wasn't just surprise that I saw—there was something else as his head tilted the tiniest bit. Almost a satisfaction that I was jealous . . . ? He said, "Macy and I are just—"

"Just what? Friends who kiss?"

He blinked, a slow blink that somehow made him look pretty and accentuated his ridiculously long eyelashes. "We didn't kiss."

I tilted my head. "Don't lie to me."

"I have no idea what you're talking about." His eyebrows were all scrunched together. "You think I kissed Macy?"

Man, he sure looked like he was telling the truth. "Didn't you take her with you on a coffee run yesterday?"

His eyebrows unscrunched. "Yeah . . . ?"

"You didn't share a moment in the parking lot? In your car?"

He narrowed his eyes and opened his mouth to speak but then closed it again. Swallowed before saying, "I'll admit that things are a little, um, complicated with Macy. But I swear to God, I didn't kiss her."

"Really." I looked at him, really looked, squinting my eyes to try to find my hurt. The first couple of times I'd seen him kiss her, it'd felt like my insides were being twisted. But now I looked at him and just saw . . . a guy. A guy who was a relatively attractive person but had absolutely no emotional hold over me. "Well, I guess I uncomplicated it for you. Later, Sutton."

I turned away from him and very nearly sprinted to Chemistry, head down, desperate to avoid more conversation. I didn't want to be decimated by the mean girls, and I didn't want to be talked about like I was some sort of urban legend for being an asshole.

I took a deep breath and walked into the classroom. It didn't look like Nick was there yet, and I was glad to have a minute to get myself together before seeing him. I sat down and got out my book, more nervous than I'd been all day.

Because I had no idea what to expect.

Would Nick be funny and warm like he'd been the night before? Would he be the surly lab partner I'd had all year? Was he going to ask me out—and maybe kiss me again—or was he regretting all of his choices from yesterday?

My heart was pounding as I waited for him to show up.

But when the bell rang, he still wasn't there. Bong marked him absent and started talking about our upcoming projects as my brain kicked into paranoid hyperdrive.

Where was he? Was he sick? Absent? Ditching class?

And was it because of me? I mean, I *knew*, logically, that it wasn't the case, but my insecure heart had a bad feeling about Nick Stark's absence.

Mr. Bong spoke for a solid five minutes before he turned his attention directly to me.

"Are you recovered from yesterday's misbehaviors, Ms. Hornby?" Bong looked down his glasses at my face. "I'm assuming the office spoke with you regarding punishment?"

"Um, yes," I said, dying of mortification.

"Good." He looked back at the class. "We've got a lot to cover, so let's get right to work, folks."

He started lecturing and I started taking notes, face aflame, but the burning ball in the pit of my stomach didn't go away. It got worse with every passing minute.

Was Nick avoiding me?

Twelve hours ago he'd been kissing me, but now he was nowhere to be found.

The rest of the day went by in a blur. Between my lack of sleep, Nick's absence, and the fact that all eyes were on me all the time, I was basically numb. I went through the motions of the afternoon, shuffling from class to class and trying to be invisible, and when I finally got home, I went straight to my room and shut the door.

Hopefully, I could avoid parental confrontation. I knew my mom was probably champing at the bit to give me a little more hell, but I didn't have the energy.

Apparently my closed-door plan worked—incredibly well—because I stress-ate Cheetos and watched reruns of *Gilmore Girls* until I fell sound asleep in my clothes.

Didn't talk to my mother or Todd at all.

Didn't wake up until the next morning, in fact.

As someone who'd always taken great pride in self-discipline, waking up in the previous day's clothing with Cheeto residue on my fingertips wasn't a great sign. And yet, for some reason, I didn't hate the way it felt.

I took a deep breath and walked into the classroom. I could see the back of Nick's head as he looked at the book on the table in front of him, and just like that, I had a stomach full of butterflies.

When I got to our table, he was texting and didn't look up. I sat down and got out my book.

Nick looked up and our eyes met, and all the memories of the DONC came rushing at me.

He gave me a closed-mouth smile, like he didn't know me, and then he went back to his phone.

I felt the heat flood my cheeks and I swear to God I lost the ability to hear for a second.

I looked at him, but Nick was still just staring at his phone.

Why wouldn't he look at me?

I opened my mouth to tell him I had his jacket in my locker when Bong walked in and said, "Put your books away—it's test time, kiddos."

Ugh—I'd forgotten all about the test. I'd forgotten to study. I put away my stuff and moved to the other table, but the knot of dread in my stomach kept growing.

And it had nothing to do with my lack of preparation. For the first time in my life, I didn't give a shit about my grades.

All I cared about was the fact that Nick was ignoring me.

Avoiding me.

Two days before, he'd been making out with me in the dark on the side of my grandma's house, but now he couldn't even smile or say hi or just acknowledge my existence?

I spent the entire class period working on my test, struggling to keep my thoughts at bay while I grasped for answers. When the bell finally rang, I packed up my stuff, and when I grabbed my backpack, Nick was already walking away. I wasn't about to beg or chase him down, but I did walk a little faster than usual, desperately hoping to see him waiting for me.

He wasn't.

I spent the next hour being sad, feeling absolutely destroyed by his rejection.

But then I realized something.

The old Em might just accept his brush-off and deal with it, but the DONC had changed me. It might've been a wild time and an absolutely ridiculous day, but living my life for myself had felt *good.* I'd always lived to please everyone else, but who would ever do what I really wanted, if not me?

It felt a little bit like fate when I was about to enter the library at lunch and Nick came out the very same door. He looked serious and in his own head and didn't even see me until I said, "Hey, you."

I turned around so I was walking beside him in his direction. "So did you get detention, too?"

His eyebrows went down just a little, like he was processing my words and sudden appearance, but he didn't smile. He said, "Not yet."

"Lucky." I lightly bumped into his side. "I'm going to have detention for two weeks, but a big part of that is my intercom thing. Apparently I used the A/V equipment to 'bully another student.' Can you believe that?"

"Yeah, um, wild." He stopped walking. "Listen, I've got to go that way." He pointed down the hall to our left. "So, see you later?"

"Sure, later," I said, but as he walked away, I pushed through people to catch up with him again.

"Nick!"

He looked back at me but kept moving. "Yeah?"

"Are we okay?"

"Um . . . sure?" His eyebrows went down and he looked at me like I was out of my mind. "I'm kind of in a hurry, so I'll see you in Chem tomorrow."

People went around me, bumping and jostling as I just stood there, unmoving. I watched until his head disappeared in the crowd, my heart breaking into a thousand tiny pieces.

"And it didn't hurt?" Rox was talking about my tattoo as we exited the side door after school. "Man, my mom would *kill* me if I did what you did."

"I mean, it did, but it wasn't too bad." I pictured Nick in the chair to my left, keeping me company while Dante tattooed me.

"Did Nick Stark hold your hand?" she teased, waggling her eyebrows.

"Shut it," I joked, but for some reason, I hadn't told my two best friends about everything that happened. No one but Nick and I could ever understand how one day could be so huge; I wouldn't have believed it myself before it'd happened, and I wasn't ready to open it up for discussion.

"She's so mum about the whole thing." Chris put on his sunglasses and said, "Part of me thinks something major happened."

I rolled my eyes but couldn't find a smile. "Not everyone has a perfect Valentine's Day with a hottie, Chris."

Rox said to me, "Can you believe he kissed *Alex*?"

Chris said, "It was like movie-level shit."

I was jealous of Chris's love hangover as I said, "So romantic."

"Shotgun." Rox opened the front door of Chris's car and got in, and I was about to pile in the back when I heard Chris say, "Looks like Em's tattoo buddy is having car problems."

I stopped and turned around. The hood to Nick's truck was up and he was leaning over the side with a can of starter fluid in his hand.

"Screw this."

"What?" Chris looked at me over his shades.

"Oh—I didn't mean to say that out loud." I blinked. "But I deserve a conversation, at least."

"Em. Um, what?"

Chris and Rox exchanged an is-she-okay look while I unzipped my backpack, pulled out Nick's big jacket, then dropped the bag onto the ground. "I'll be right back."

I walked over to Nick's truck. "Need me to get in and turn her over?"

He looked up. Swallowed. Said, "Nah, I'm good, but thanks."

I rolled my eyes. "But if I start it while you hoosh it with fluid, isn't that way easier?"

"I got it, Emilie." His voice was clipped, like when I'd asked him about his family after the coffee shop.

"Why are you acting like this? Are you mad at me or something?"

He sighed and shook his head with pursed lips. "No. It's just—I mean, I told you the other night that I don't have time for this."

"For what? I'm not asking you for anything. I offered to help with your—"

"Emilie." He bit out my name. "It was really fun. It was. A fun day. But it's a different day now, okay?"

I closed my mouth, mortified. I was about to walk away, but then I changed my mind and said, "So I had an epiphany the other night, after both of my parents screamed at me, grounded me, and vowed to fight to the death in court over who I should live with. Do you know what it was?"

"I don't—"

"It was that no matter how it turns out—good or bad—I'm going to start living for me and what *I* want, instead of for other people and what I think they want me to do. Because if I don't, who will?"

He straightened and put his hands in the pockets of his coat, his face unreadable.

"That day, with you, was incredible. I know you don't 'have time' or want a relationship, and I'm cool with waiting or just being friends. But the DONC was—"

"A fantasy," Nick said. "It was a mirage, Emilie."

"So . . . what? You're going to avoid happiness completely because it might float away?"

He looked at me for moment before he turned away and said, "I'm just not interested in you that way, okay?"

My brain immediately went to *I must have misunderstood—I'm so sorry.*

My mouth actually opened to say it.

But I hadn't misunderstood.

And I wasn't sorry.

"You can insist on that, Nick," I said, angry and disappointed that he would rather be a dick to me than be honest with himself. "But I'm not imagining what that day was. Days like that don't happen, Nick—they don't. I get why you're scared to put yourself out there after Eric, but—"

"Please don't bring my brother into this."

I pressed my lips together and looked away, frustrated.

He dragged a hand over the top of his head and said, "You don't know shit about my brother, and you're using what I told you to convince me—and yourself—that there was more to our skip day than there actually was. I'm sorry to break it to you, Emilie, but the DONC was just a playdate. A day where two people blew off school and screwed around downtown. That's it."

"Um, okay, then." I blinked back big, fat tears of humiliation.

"I don't want to hurt your feelings, Em, but that's all it wa—"

"Got it." I thrust his jacket at him and went back to the car, where Chris and Rox were sitting inside with the windows down, witnessing the entire mortifying rejection. I squeezed into the front seat, and my friends didn't ask me a single question. Rox put her arm around me, and Chris handed me one of the Kleenex pouches he always kept in his center console.

Just a playdate.

CONFESSION #20

In sixth grade, when I ding-dong-ditched Finn Parker across the street, I fell down his steps and broke my wrist. To this day, my parents think I broke it roller-skating.

After I got home, I finally let myself cry. I felt an aching emptiness where Nick had been, which was weird when I'd only ever known him on February 14. But I felt like he somehow saw me—all of me—and understood me. None of it would ever make sense, but I felt a huge sense of loss over Nick.

I heard my mom come home, and I did *not* want to deal with her anger. I was certain she was probably still pissed, especially since I'd hidden in my room last night, but I just didn't feel emotionally equipped to deal with any more conflict.

I started on my homework—I didn't know what else to do with myself—and my stomach dropped when I heard her yell, "Em! Dinner!"

I took a deep breath and ran downstairs. I could smell spaghetti and meatballs—my favorite meal—but something about the scent added to my melancholy. It brought back memories of spaghetti at the old house, when it was just my mom, my dad, and me in that old yellow dining room. Then it made me think of meals in my dad's tiny apartment, when it'd just been the two of us, and it brought back sneaky memories of both of them feeding me spaghetti and introducing me to the new loves of their lives.

I knew Nick had made me soft when spaghetti was making me sad.

I sat down, and I could feel my mom looking at me. I steeled myself for a lecture.

"Are you okay, Emilie?"

Todd, my mom's husband, was nice, a harmless salesman who always seemed like he had an opinion to share on everything, including things that had nothing to do with him and everything to do with me and my dad.

So his question made me nervous.

"I'm fine." I looked down at my spaghetti and put my napkin on my lap. "Why?"

"You just look . . ." He gestured toward my face with his fork.

"Like she was out too late the other night?"

Thanks, Mom.

"Like she's sad." Todd tilted his head and said it like it was extremely impossible. "Like she's been crying. You sure you're okay, kid?"

I nodded. Something about the unexpected concern in his voice made me feel more shattered than I already felt.

"Em?" Now my mother tilted *her* head. "Everything all right?"

I nodded again, but my vision blurred with tears, my eyes too full to keep them all inside.

"Emilie." My mom sounded truly bewildered by the sight of my tears. "Honey?"

The endearment did it. I crumpled into a sobbing mess at the kitchen table, blubbering into my spaghetti and meatballs while my baby "brother," Potassium, stared at me like I'd lost it.

"You're shitting me."

"I'm here, aren't I?" I took a sip of my Americano and said to Rox, "My mother, the woman who gave away my guinea pig when I was seven because I forgot to clean his cage, actually ungrounded me."

"Aw, I forgot about Dre."

I sighed. "RIP to Dre, the guinea pig my mother gave to the Finklebaums next door, who proceeded to immediately lose him in their backyard the very next day."

"So, I don't get it." Rox took off her glasses and looked at them, wiping something off one of the lenses. She was one of those people who looked good in and out of glasses. Her skin always looked perfect, whether she wore makeup or not, and she looked good in any hairstyle. Since I'd known her she'd had braids, dreads, short hair, long hair, blond hair, pink hair, and an Afro, and she looked good in them all.

I ran a finger over the logo on the cup and wondered if perhaps it was time for me to change *my* hair, too. All of a sudden, my usual aesthetic felt wrong for me.

Rox said, "You actually deserved to be grounded this time—no offense—and *now* she's being lenient?"

"Well, no." I sat back and felt a little shaky, still. "It's more like she decided to be a human mom. I had a bawling meltdown at dinner last night that started because of Nick but then morphed into the latest situation with my parents."

"Which is?"

I told her about my dad's promotion and my parents' fight. "The good thing about my meltdown was that I was already so blubbery that I blurted out my honest feelings about who I want to live with."

She asked, "And that is . . . ?"

I groaned. "Both of them."

But for once, my mom had actually listened. She'd hugged me and then we called my dad on speakerphone. I didn't know if ultimately it would change anything, but he'd promised to talk to Lisa and explore all possible options.

And that mattered a lot.

Rox said, "I'm glad it happened, then, because you needed to tell them. It's about damn time."

I swirled the drink in my cup and said, "Agreed."

The pathetic part was that I'd wanted to tell Nick about it. He'd been so amazing when I told him about my parents when we were on the rooftop downtown that my heart thought he would appreciate it. I mean, he'd had empathetic tears when I'd cried about it, for God's sake.

It was just a playdate, I reminded myself, the memory still stinging.

Rox looked at her phone—probably a message from Trey—

and said, "Did Chris tell you that Alex took him to dinner after they went shopping last night?"

"No." Chris's dreamy love story was the only thing getting me through all of this. "Was it good?"

"That boy called me at one a.m. and talked for an hour about Alex. It's the cutest thing I've ever seen."

I watched over Rox's shoulder as the barista yelled *"Carl!"* for the third time and I said, "I want them to never break up."

"He told me that Alex said he didn't want to freak him out, but he thought he was already in love with Chris."

"What?" That brought my eyes back to her. "Seriously? Wow."

She nodded and looked curious. "Are you ever going to tell me what happened with Stark on Valentine's Day?"

I thought about it for a second. "Um. Basically we had an amazing day together and now he wants to pretend I don't exist."

Rox shook her head. "What a dick."

"Yeah. But that's what makes it so shitty—he's not."

And then I did what I promised myself I wasn't going to. I sat there, at our favorite Starbucks window table, and told her everything. Not about the repeating days—I was pretty sure I could never tell anyone about those—but every little detail about what happened on the DONC.

When I was done, I don't know what kind of reaction I expected, but I was met with her pitying face. She took a deep breath and said, "He told you all day that he didn't want anything more than that day, and what do you do? You assume he's hurt or wounded. Afraid to put himself out there. I love you and I think he's a ginormous prick, but he called his shot, sweetie."

"Yeah, but—"

"And you got your phone back, right?" She gave me a look that was 100 percent a reality check. "Were there any messages waiting for you from him? Did he even apologize for making you cry after school?"

My eyes itched again, because *of course* I'd checked the second my phone had been given back to me by my mother. "No."

"No." She lifted her cup to her mouth and said, "But I'm glad. Now you know, so you can get on with it and not look back."

Because she was an amazing friend, she slid right into listing off fifteen reasons why he was not nearly good enough for me, followed by ten amazing things she loved about me. I was still super bummed about Nick, but she'd made it marginally less awful.

On Monday, I wore jeans, a T-shirt, Chuck Taylors, my glasses, and a messy bun. I was serious about the whole living-for-myself thing, and I didn't feel like making an effort.

I didn't even know where my planner *was.*

I breezed through the first couple of hours of school, and then before third period, I turned a corner in the hallway and walked right into Lauren, Lallie, and Nicole. How were they *always* together? Their gazes met mine and I knew I was dead.

"You guys." I took a deep breath and blurted out, "I'm sorry for being a bitch last week. I shouldn't have freaked, but I felt bad for Isla when you were talking crap on her."

Lally blinked and said, "Oh."

Lauren said, "Were we talking crap on Isla?"

And Nicole said, "It's whatever."

She gave me the brush-off, like I wasn't worth her time, but they didn't destroy me.

I couldn't believe it.

Then, on the way to my following class, I saw Josh. He spotted me from the other side of the commons and headed straight for me.

"Em!"

I grasped the books in my hand and said, "Yeah?"

"Can you talk after school?"

"What?"

"I need to talk to you. Will you meet me after school?"

"Um—"

"Please?"

"I—maybe. Let me think about it."

I walked away, wondering what he could possibly want to talk about. And I was still wondering about it when I went to Chemistry. But then anxiety took over, and I swallowed down my nervous dread and went to my spot. Nick was already there, but we behaved the way we always had.

Like we didn't know each other.

I felt him look over at me when I was scrolling through my news feed, but I just kept scrolling until my phone whinnied because I got a text from Josh. I glanced up to make sure Mr. Bong hadn't heard, but he wasn't even in the room. I put it on vibrate and read the message.

Josh: Hi.

I stared at it for a second.

Me: Hey.

Josh: Have you decided?

Me: Decided what?

Josh: If you'll talk to me.

Me: NO.

Josh: No, you won't?

Me: No, I haven't decided. Honestly, what do you want?

Josh: Ouch.

"Tell me you aren't texting the guy who cheated on you."

I raised my eyes and Nick was looking at me. There was annoyance in his voice when he said, "You're smarter than that."

I wanted to go *off* on him, but then he'd think I was still into him. I calmly said, "I'm sorry, but I don't think it's any of your business."

"I know it's not." He looked . . . frustrated. He scratched his eyebrow and said, "But I'd hate to see you trust a guy who's only going to cheat again."

"I will take that under advisement, thank you."

My phone vibrated on the table at that moment, and I'd never been happier to ignore someone and look at my phone. I picked it up.

Josh: I need to explain something.

I could feel Nick's gaze on me as I started typing out a response.

Me: Let's just move past everything. You're forgiven. It's water under the bridge.

Josh: Seriously?

Me: Yeah.

"Are you doing this on purpose?"

I looked at him out of the corner of my eyes. "Doing what?"

"Texting him."

I shook my head. "First of all, no. Believe it or not, I text *lots* of people and it has nothing to do with you. Second of all, I can't understand why you're inserting yourself in this situation."

"I just don't want to see you get—"

"Hurt?" I looked him square in the eyes. It felt like my heart skipped a beat when I said, "You are the last person who could protect me from that."

He swallowed. "That's not fair."

He was looking at me with those eyes and it hurt to look at him at all. I glanced down at my phone and said, "Okay."

Thankfully, Mr. Bong walked in, shutting down the chance for any more painfully awkward conversation. But I was bothered by our exchange for the rest of the class. Because he didn't have the right to be jealous when he didn't want me. Why would he care if I was talking to Josh?

I texted Josh: Can you give me a ride home after school?

Josh: You got it.

When class ended, I packed up and left as fast as I could. I needed to forget all about the surly one, even if it was hard to focus when the smell of his Irish Spring found its way to my olfactory senses and tormented me with memories of the seven minutes we were in love on the side of my grandma's house.

"Em!"

I heard Chris's voice in the hall, and when I turned around, there he was, walking my way while holding hands with Alex.

"Hey."

"Your look?" Chris raised his eyebrows and said, "Did you have to clean out a basement before school today?"

Alex pressed his lips together, too polite to laugh at Chris's snark.

I said, "New Emilie didn't feel like glamming it up today."

"New Emilie doesn't look like she's ever heard of glam," he replied.

"Why don't you leave me alone and figure out how to fix your own cowlick?"

He was obsessed with the one tiny imperfection in his thick, curly, gorgeous hair.

"Oh, God help us," he teased. "New Emilie is evil."

"The new Emilie," Alex said, grinning at me, "looks adorable. Just like your cowlick."

Alex and Chris shared a glance that made me envious, so I rolled my eyes and said, "You're giving me cavities with the sweet. Knock it off."

I took a step in the other direction, then turned back and said, "Oh, yeah—I don't need a ride home."

"'Kay," he said, and I knew he would text me next hour to see why.

It only took five minutes.

Chris: Who is driving you home? Is it Stark?

Me: Josh.

Chris: Omigod what in the actual?

Me: No idea. Said he wants to talk to me. Can't hurt to listen, right?

Chris: I guess not. But don't let him back in.

Me: Trust me—I won't.

After school, Josh was waiting for me at my locker. My heart didn't flutter when I saw him there; in fact, my first thought was, *Does he even own a pair of jeans?*

"Hey." I opened my locker. "Care if I stop by the office on the way out?"

"Sure."

I dropped to a squat and grabbed my Chem book out of the bottom of my locker, adding it to my already bulging backpack. "It should only take a sec."

I straightened, shut my locker, and we started walking toward the office. It should've felt like something, walking with him after the turmoil, but I felt really detached from the whole thing.

"What do you have to do at the office?" he asked.

"Well," I said, giving him a half-smile, "I have to schedule my detention for bullying you."

He gave his head a confused shake and said, "You're kidding, right?"

"Nope. Apparently I violated the student bill of rights *and* did it over the intercom." I smiled at Mr. Bong as we passed him and he didn't smile back. "And then I have to pick up my deposit for the Northwestern summer program."

He looked stunned. "Why?"

"Well, for starters, I found out that the applications were scored incorrectly and I didn't actually get accepted."

He looked super stunned. "For real?"

"For real." I gave a *hey* smile to a girl from my Government class as she walked by. "But I'm actually kind of glad. After I thought about it for a while, I realized that I'd really like to just chill out and relax this summer."

His eyebrows went down. "Relax?"

I'm sure he couldn't fathom that sentiment. I said, "I know—I can hardly believe it myself.

Josh waited outside of the office when I went in, and things went fairly smoothly, for what it was worth. I apologized to the principal and scheduled the days for my detention, which he was surprisingly cool about, and then I popped over to Mr. Kessler's office.

He looked nervous to see me after my outburst the day before, but once I apologized and said I was no longer interested in joining the program, he turned into the guy who was once again wildly enthusiastic about my future plans.

When I came out of the office, Josh was still standing where I'd left him.

"Thanks for waiting," I said, hitching up my backpack.

"Yeah," he replied, giving me a weird look like he was trying to figure something out. He didn't say anything else as we walked to his car, but as soon as he started it and buckled his seat belt, he said, "So here's the thing, Em."

I was a little distracted looking at his car, because the last time I'd been in there, I'd been wedged between him and Macy and my boots had smelled like garbage.

"The reason I wanted to talk is because I owe you a huge apology for Macy."

Wow—*that* wasn't what I'd expected. No denial? No blame? "Really?"

"I care about you, Em; you're seriously one of my favorite people and I hate that I hurt you. She asked to go along on the coffee run and I knew she liked me—I was wrong to take her."

I looked at his face and felt . . . unfazed.

"But you have to believe me that nothing happened."

I thought about what he was saying, and the weird thing? I genuinely believed him. Even though I'd seen him kiss her on other cosmic days, I believed him that he hadn't on *that* day. And really, he *wasn't* the kind of guy who cheated.

That being said, if I still wanted him, his words probably wouldn't have mattered.

I would've been too hurt to forgive him.

Like I'd been on the first Valentine's Day.

But now—meh.

He wasn't finished explaining, though.

He said, "I don't expect you to forgive me—I was totally in the wrong and you have every right to hate me. But I just want you to know that you're amazing. I was totally happy with you."

"Um." I didn't really know what to even say to that. "Sorry. I just—I'm stunned you're being so nice after the intercom thing."

He glanced over. "I mean, I didn't love that, but I probably had it coming."

"Wow, Sutton—you sound so mature."

That made him look at me again, I think checking to make sure I was teasing. When he saw my grin, he smiled. "We'll call it personal growth."

"So." I tucked my hair behind my ears as my brain filtered through information. "You said it's complicated. Are you going to ask Macy out now? Reconnect with her?"

He crinkled his nose. "I doubt it."

"What?" *He was crinkling his nose about Macy?* "I mean, it's none of my business, but why not?"

He downshifted and glanced over at me. "Besides the fact that I just got out of a relationship?"

I gave him an eye roll.

"Well," he said around a sigh as he turned his eyes back to the road, "I'm just not really into Macy anymore."

That answer irritated me. "But you two have chemistry." I saw it. More times than I wanted to.

"We have *history*."

"That's a pointless distinction."

"It's not." He swallowed. "I mean, of course it is. But do you know what popped into my head when we were alone in my car?"

"'WWJD'?"

"Hilarious." He reached out and adjusted one of the heat

vents. "What popped into my head, smart-ass, was the realization that you've never been like that with me."

"Like what?"

"Buzzing." He shook his head, his eyes staying on the road, and he said, "Nervous. I've always known that you like me—as a person—but I've never felt like you were into me."

I squirmed a little in my seat. "What is this, couples' therapy? Are you filing a complaint that I wasn't attentive enough so you had to go elsewhere?"

"That's not at all what I'm saying." He turned onto my street and said, "It was more that I had this moment where I wondered if you'd ever been into me at all."

"That's not fair," I said, even as I doubted.

"I'm not directing this at you, Em. My point is that I wondered, when I went back to class after the near-kiss with Macy and tried to figure out what in the hell had just happened, why we were dating at all."

I looked down at my lap; I couldn't meet his eyes. The words "because you were on my checklist" hovered on my lips, but I held them back.

Josh was the perfect boyfriend for me on paper: smart, motivated, and charming. But I didn't realize until I watched him kiss Macy that the paper didn't always translate.

Josh was the guy that the girl I wanted to be should want.

My throat felt tight as I thought about how wrong I'd been, how wrong I still was. If planning didn't root out true love, and fate didn't either, was it even a tangible thing one could hope for?

"We like each other *so much.*" He cleared his throat and downshifted. "We have since the beginning—we're, like, the perfect match. And we have a blast together. But can you honestly say that you have feelings for me?"

I raised my eyes to his face, and he was giving me a patient smile. But then Nick's face popped into my head, the face that weakened my knees every time he looked at me. The boy *I* had instigated a downtown kiss with.

"That's what I thought." He looked at me and slowly shook his head, but it wasn't mean. It was a little bit sweet, like a gaze of fondness. "I think the idea of us together was so good that we both might've forced it."

I took in the fact that Josh knew how I was feeling before I did. "So you never—"

"I think you're hot, Em—don't worry." Like always, he kind of understood the way my brain worked. "I just think that maybe we're meant to be the best of friends."

"Stop saying things that make it sound like you're dumping me. Remember the intercom."

"Oh, I remember." He coughed out a laugh and said, "I'll be ninety-five years old at the home, and I'll *still* remember you slamming me and the Bards."

That made me laugh. "Gah—is this weird? That everything feels just as comfortable, even though we aren't a thing anymore?"

He shook his head. "It feels right, I think."

"Can I torture you a little, though?" I crossed my arms. "Kind of like my own special goodbye to us?"

He slowed as a car tried miserably to parallel park on the street. "I'm scared but okay."

I looked out the window at the late-day winter sun and I said, "I got you the Coach watchband for Valentine's Day. If we hadn't broken up, you'd have a stunning chocolate leather band on your wrist."

He lifted his hand off the shifter to cover his heart as if I had mortally wounded him. "You know how to deliver quite the parting blow."

"Right?" I said, grinning at him as he smiled at me.

"I know this is absolutely unheard of in real life, but do you think we can still hang out? And not, like, just say it?" He swallowed and said, "Because I really don't want to lose you."

"Let's play it by ear." I pulled out my phone and checked for messages. *Nothing*. "But I could theoretically continue to kick your ass at Scrabble if you don't piss me off."

"Good." He turned into my driveway. "Because if you desert me, who will call me out on my contrarian shit?"

"Ooh—I do enjoy doing that."

He gave a little laugh. "Thank you for hearing me out, by the way."

"Ditto." I opened the door. "Thanks for the ride."

"Anytime. Seriously."

I got out and slammed the door, and was almost to the porch when he yelled, "Em—wait."

I looked back and his window was down. He was waving me over. I dropped my bag and jogged to his window. "I'm not going to kiss you goodbye, Sutton."

"Ha, ha." He put the car in reverse and looked at me intently. "So . . . what's the deal with you and Nick Stark?"

I felt my face flush. "'Deal'?"

"When I was waiting for you to come out of the office, we had a little talk."

Wait. "What? You talked to *Nick*?"

His brown eyes were full of humor when he said, "The second you went inside the office, he walked up to me. Honestly, he looked mad and he's kind of tall, so I was a little intimidated."

My lips were tingly and I felt breathless. "What did he say?"

"He said, 'I don't really know you, Josh'—and he totally said my name like he thinks I'm a douche."

"Well, I might've—"

"I figured." He gave me a look and said, "But then he goes, 'Emilie's too good for you. If she takes you back, don't screw it up this time.'"

I couldn't believe what I was hearing. "What? He said that?"

"The thing is, and I can't believe I'm saying this, the guy seems really into you." Josh rested his elbow on the open window and said, "So if you like him—"

"I don't." I shook my head and felt sick to my stomach. My body was all aflutter at the thought of Nick pining over me or giving a shit, but it wasn't enough. "Thanks for telling me all that, but Nick likes me enough to want me not with you, but not enough to actually do something about it."

"Oh." He looked surprised. "Well."

"Yeah," I said, trying to force my lips into a smile as my heart ached inside my chest.

That made him get out of the car. "Come here."

Josh wrapped his arms around me and pulled me close. It wasn't a casual hug, but a tight, all-encompassing embrace that felt like a goodbye to us, to Josh and Emilie. The smell of his familiar cologne comforted me, but in a friend way.

"You okay?" he said into my hair, and I just nodded and swallowed.

Somehow, over the course of many February fourteenths, one DONC, and multiple days of fallout, everything had changed.

I was emotional, yet again, by the time I got inside. As someone who rarely got feelsy, it was beginning to get ridiculous. I threw my keys on the table just inside the door, but stopped short when I looked to my left and saw that my mom and Todd were already home.

"Hey." I slipped off my shoes. "How come you're home already?"

"I want to talk to you," my mom said. "Sit down, Em."

I went into the room and sat down on the love seat across from them. "Time for an impromptu family meeting?"

Todd said, "In a way."

"Your dad and I had lunch today," my mom said, steepling her fingers together like she was in a boardroom, not a living room. "To discuss our situation."

I glanced at Todd, and he gave me a reassuring closed-mouth smile.

"He is still taking the job in Houston, but his company is allowing him to work remotely until August. That way you can finish your junior year, and then decide if you want to move with him or stay here."

I blinked. Did she mean—

"After much discussion, we've decided that as long as your grades stay up and you stay out of trouble, you can make the call on whether you want to finish with your friends at Hazelwood, or start over with your dad in Texas." She gave me a smile and said, "We will respect your wishes, no hard feelings."

"Are you serious?"

My mom nodded but her brow was wrinkled, like she was unsure about the whole niceness thing. I looked at Todd and he smiled.

"Oh, thank you!" I got up and ran over to my mom, hugging her even though we didn't really do that very often. I breathed in Chanel and hairspray as I said, "Thank you so much!"

My mom smiled when I pulled back and she pushed my hair off my face. "It was Todd's idea, and your dad was the one who had to renegotiate his new job."

"Still," I said, my heart nearly bursting with love for the

confusing woman whom I both loved and was terrified of, "I know how hard it is for you to, um—"

"Give in?" Todd laughed and said, "Yeah, she's growing."

My mom smiled at him like he was her whole world, and for once, it didn't piss me off. Then I hugged him, too, feeling guilty for the thousands of unkind thoughts I'd had about him over the years.

Maybe he wasn't so bad after all.

CONFESSION #21

I knocked down a mailbox with my car
last month and didn't even stop.

"You guys are ridiculous." I pushed the pile of balloons into my locker before slamming it shut. "This is horrifying."

"Horrifyingly fantastic." Chris laughed and Rox straightened one of the streamers on the outside of my locker. It was March 4, my birthday, and instead of being subtle, they'd decorated my locker and filled it with balloons.

Which, I had to admit, was nice. I'd been bummed for the past couple of weeks, but now I was able to make it through an entire period of Chemistry without looking at Nick Stark once.

I was a damn hero.

Things were feeling better, so this celebration was like a little punctuation mark on my life's refresh. I'd worn an adorable new black-and-white dotted dress that made me feel like Audrey Hepburn, and the ruffled cardigan I paired with it made me feel a little Taylor Swift, as well.

"I've got to get to class," I said, pulling my bag over my shoulder. "Meet you here after school?"

"You got it," Chris said, grinning at Rox like they were hilarious before walking away with her.

I had Lit after that, then—ugh—Chemistry.

I went straight to my stool, pulled out my book, opened it to the correct page, and then immediately started scrolling on my phone. Like I'd done every day for the last couple of weeks.

I'd just opened Instagram when Nick said, "Emilie."

I stopped scrolling but didn't look up. "Yeah?" Did he need a pen or something?

"Happy birthday."

I raised my eyes and said, "Gee, thanks."

But in that half-second before I looked back at my phone, my brain archived his serious blue eyes, clenched jaw, black hoodie, and the gravel in his deep voice.

"Is it—"

"Please don't." I slow-blinked and managed, "You've said all you've needed to say, okay? We're good."

He didn't say anything, but just swallowed and gave me a nod.

Bong came in and started lecturing, and I forced myself to forget about Nick and think about how much fun I was going to have with Chris, Alex, Rox, and Trey after school. We were going downtown for a birthday dinner at Spaghetti Works—my favorite restaurant—followed by ice cream at Ted and Wally's.

I couldn't wait.

When class ended, I gathered my things and got out quickly, just in case Nick tried to make himself feel better again. The day dragged by so slowly—probably because I was beyond excited for it to end—but eventually the final bell rang.

"Finally," I said, smiling as I saw them waiting at my locker. Alex was quickly becoming part of our little friend group, mostly because he and Chris were inseparable, and I felt lucky that we'd found him.

"Let's go, Birthday Girl."

They let me select all the songs on the radio as we drove through the streets, which was my favorite thing in the world. We had a blast singing at the top of our lungs, but I swallowed hard when we got downtown.

Because my favorite place was now stained with memories of him.

I looked out my window and there was the bank building, hovering above us with the vivid recollections of Nick doing the awful Cupid Shuffle, giving me a piggyback ride, almost kissing me in the elevator, and racing me up the stairs.

It'd been the best day.

I forced myself to put those events out of my head and focus on fun with my friends.

We rummaged through antique stores, vinyl shops, and expensive boutiques before finally going into the restaurant.

"I'm starving," I said, breathing deeply as my favorite smells in the world found their way to my nose.

"You're always starving when carbs are involved," Chris said, and he wasn't wrong. He actually attempted to eat healthy and had always been disgustedly amused by my utter lack of caring.

"Have you ever had their chicken strips?" Alex asked as we followed the hostess to a table.

"You're in *Spaghetti Works,*" I said, rolling my eyes and making a face at him. "Please do not embarrass me and order chicken."

"I wouldn't test her," Rox said, holding hands with Trey as they followed behind us. "She's absurdly loyal to this place."

"Noted," Alex said.

When the hostess led us to a big table that overlooked the salad bar car, Chris said, "I'm sorry—can we get a window seat?"

I looked at him and smiled, and he threw one right back at me. Chris and I used to play a game at the window seats, where we'd guess the backstory of every person who walked by. I was kind of touched that he was still sentimental about it.

"No problem," she said, and gestured toward the table in front of the big bay window that overlooked the sidewalk.

"Thanks," I said, and we all sat down at the window table.

We lost ourselves in laughter and conversation after that. Rox and Trey and Chris—and, as it turned out, Alex as well—were the funniest people I knew. There was nothing as fun as having multiple hours to just hang with them without things like jobs, homework, and boyfriends getting in the way.

They made fun of me—rightfully so—when I finished my second helping of spaghetti before Alex had even finished his first, and I cackled when Rox and Chris got super into the backstory game.

"The couple walking the dog have been together for fifteen years, but only married for one," Chris said. "It's been their worst year, and they both know they ruined it by taking those vows."

"Dark," I laughed.

"Right?" said Alex.

"She finally caved because she could tell her annual refusals hurt him," Rox said, "but now she is the one hurting. They both want to end it, but neither of them can work up the energy to say it."

"He works sixty hours a week just to avoid going home," Trey added.

"Actually," Chris added, pointing toward the dog, "that dog is their glue right now. Neither of them can bear the thought of giving up custody of . . ."

"Meatball."

"Yes, Meatball," Chris said, acknowledging Alex's addition with a nod of the head. "Neither of them can bear losing Meatball, so they walk that beast together every night after dinner, each of them dreaming about being anywhere other than where they are."

I took a sip of my soda and said, "You just took the game and made it depressing. Fix it with this lady."

We all looked out the window, and a tall woman in a jumpsuit and a beret was walking by, talking into her phone.

Chris said, "This is Claire. She used to be a model, but quit her jet-setting lifestyle to come home and take care of her uncle Billy."

"Who lost his memory in a microwave oven accident." Alex beamed, getting into the game. "Now he can only talk about NASCAR and the women from *The View*."

We all started laughing.

Rox said, "She takes care of that guy during the day, but at night she likes to put on her supermodel clothes and search the

Old Market for men who might be interested in taking her swing dancing."

"Does that mean sex?"

"Of course it means sex." Trey rolled his eyes and added, "She dances with them, and when they fall asleep, she kills them and sells their organs on the black market."

"Brutal."

"But lucrative."

I giggled and reached for Chris's garlic bread. "Okay, Alex—you do this guy."

Alex glanced at me, then looked out the window. "Everyone who knows this guy thinks he's a jerk because he never smiles."

I glanced up from my bread and saw a guy in a black jacket walking by with a box under his arm.

"But he's actually a nice guy who is wracked with regret for being a jerk to someone he truly cares about."

The guy glanced up at the window and—

It was Nick.

"He had a perfect day with the perfect girl," Rox said, "but his cynical heart refused to believe it could last, so he pushed her away."

I looked at Rox and could barely find my voice to say, "What are you doing?"

"It wasn't until he cleaned out his truck and could still smell her perfume on his brother's jacket," Trey said, "that he was almost suffocated by how much he missed her."

"What is this?" I sniffled and blinked fast as Nick stopped walking and looked directly up at us.

At me.

Alex continued as if I hadn't spoken. "He knows he screwed up his chance, but he just wants to give her a present for her birthday. Then he'll go."

I looked down at his face, handsome, and the only face in the world that made me want to cry. As I watched him, he swallowed and gave me the intense stare that I could feel from the top of my head to the tips of my toes.

I shook my head and looked away from the window and into the faces of my friends. "I don't think my heart can take this game anymore."

Chris said, "Just go hear him out."

I took a deep breath. Then I stood and walked across the restaurant and over to the front door, throwing it open and stepping outside. I was about to walk in the direction of where we'd seen him through the window when I heard, "Em."

I looked to my right and there he was, standing beside the door, waiting for me.

It wasn't fair how handsome he was. He was still wearing the black hoodie, and I hated how the sight of him negated every little bit of fun I'd been having with my friends. Looking at Nick just made me want to go home and cry.

I crossed my arms and said, "I'm trying to have dinner with my friends. What do you need, Nick?"

He gestured with his head for me to follow him over to one of the outdoor seating tables that was vacant because it was too cold for anyone to eat outside. I rolled my eyes and walked behind him, irritated that he was somehow managing to be bossy on my birthday.

"Open it." He set the box on the table, looked at me with those eyes that'd haunted me in my daydreams, and he said, "Please."

He seemed so . . . intense. His jaw was clenched, his eyes laser-focused on me. I took a deep breath and told myself that I didn't know why my stomach was full of butterflies. I reached out and pulled the edge of the red ribbon that was tied into a perfect bow, but when I pulled the lid off of the white box and looked inside, I couldn't believe what I was seeing.

I glanced at him and the only word I could come up with was, "How?"

He shrugged as I put my hands in the box and pulled out the cake.

The purple unicorn cake with the sparkly frosting.

The one I'd wanted on my ninth birthday.

I couldn't believe my eyes as I lifted it all the way out and set it on the table. The shiny golden horn, the glittery unicorn, the sparkly purple frosting. It said *Happy Birthday, Em*, the way I'd desperately wanted it to when I was in the fourth grade.

But . . . Nick had never seen the cake before.

"How on earth did you do this, Nick?"

He gave a little shrug of his shoulders. "I got help."

"You're going to have to do better than that," I said, putting my shaking hands on my hips and trying to figure out this guy who might've just gotten me the most thoughtful gift I'd ever received.

He said, "Max knows the bakery owner."

"Max?"

"Your grandma."

My brain wasn't firing fast enough for me to keep up. I squinted at him and said, "My grandma helped you?"

He nodded.

"Um, as far as I'm aware, the one time you met her she asked you to get off her porch." I searched his face for an answer, but his mouth slid into his tiny smirk, the one that made him look pleased with himself but not quite friendly. I said, "Please explain yourself, Nick Stark."

"I went over to your grandma's and asked what she knew about the purple unicorn cake." His eyes moved over my face, making my heart pound, and he said, "As it turns out, she's been having a fling with the bakery owner for years, so she called him and asked him to make one for you."

I blinked. "My grandma's dating Old Man Miller?"

"I don't know if it's technically dating since she said they just have sleepovers—"

"Ew."

"But they're close."

I stared at the cake, unable to slow down my thoughts. *Nick went over to my grandma's just to see if she knew about the cake?*

I managed to say, "I can't believe you remembered the cake."

"I remember everything about you, Em."

The crack in his voice brought my eyes back to his face.

"I do." His voice was raspy when he said, "I remember the 'Thong Song,' the breathy sound of your voice after I kiss you, and the way you kissed my *nose* when you thought I was sad."

A train whistle blew in the distance, its sound almost haunting in the cold darkness.

"I messed up," he said as he stared down at me, "and I've regretted it every minute since you walked away in the school parking lot."

I swallowed and my eyes traveled all over him, drinking in the one person I hadn't allowed myself to really look at since he'd broken my heart.

"I fell in love with you on Valentine's Day, Emilie, but I need more than just seven minutes."

"You do?" Warmth started sliding through every molecule inside of me. I wanted to be closer to him, but first I had to ask, "What about everything you said after Valentine's Day, though? What about the mirage?"

Nick lifted his hand like he wanted to touch my face but stopped himself and said, "You were right. About me being stupid because of Eric."

I cringed. "I didn't say that."

"You implied I was holding back because of him, and it's come to my attention since then that it's probably true."

"It has? Really?"

"Yeah." He made a face like *It's all so dramatic* and he said, "As it turns out, when your parents have a yard sale and you lose your ever-loving shit because they're giving away your dead brother's baseball hat the day after the one-year anniversary, you have issues."

"Oh no." I take a step toward him, reaching out my hand to touch the sleeve of his hoodie. "That sucks. I'm sorry."

"It's okay." He cleared his throat and said, "Believe it or not, I'm glad. I've actually started seeing a therapist. I don't know, it's really weird, talking to a stranger, but also kind of like a relief."

"Nick, that's so grea—"

"Stop." He looked at me out of the corner of his eye and said around a smirk, "The last thing I want is the girl I'm obsessed with to tell me she's proud of me for going to therapy. I've got a mother for that, thank you."

That made me laugh. "I knew you were obsessed."

"Yes, Emilie Hornby, I'm here to tell you that I'm a little obsessed with you. With this." He raised his hands and cupped my face. "With us." His eyes crinkled at the corners and his mouth slid into the full-on smile that made me weak in the knees.

"Don't get all clingy on me now, Stark," I said, but the "k" sound got cut off when his mouth covered mine. Electricity and liquid warmth drizzled through my body as Nick kissed me like only Nick could.

Somewhere in the distance I heard my friends clapping, but nothing could've pulled me away from the one person in the world who knew it took a sparkly purple unicorn cake to sweep me off my feet.

Nick stayed for the celebration, holding my hand as we all walked around the Old Market together after dinner. And when it was time to call it a night, he asked me quietly, so no one else could hear, "Can I drive you home?"

Of course I said yes.

He looked over at me as I held my hands in front of his truck's heater vents on the way home, and he said, "Do you ever dress warm enough?"

"I don't like to cover up a good outfit with a bulky coat," I said, grinning as he looked at me like I was a silly child.

"Well, here," he said, reaching a hand into the back seat while he drove. "You can wear E's jacket again. It still smells like your perfume from the DONC."

He held out the coat to me, and it was like looking at an old friend. "I didn't know this was your brother's coat." I took it gently and laid it over my lap, running my hands over the fabric.

"That's because you acted like it belonged to you," he teased.

"True," I agreed, thinking about all the times I'd worn it that he didn't even know about. So many crashes on repeat, so many wearings of that jacket.

Although.

I looked down at the army-green coat. Now that I was thinking about it, I'd worn it on the very first Valentine's Day. The one that'd started it all.

Valentine's Day.

The anniversary of his brother's death.

But I never fell asleep in it—until the DONC. The last Valentine's Day.

Dragging me out of my thoughts, Nick found my hand and interlaced it with his. He gave me a look that made butterflies go wild inside me, and then he said, "By the way, I never thanked you for making me go along with your DONC day. I had a great time with you—"

"Of course you did," I teased, which made him give me a funny grin.

"But the stuff in the afternoon?" He looked over at me with superserious eyes. "E would've loved it."

"Yeah?" I looked down at the jacket.

"Yeah," he said, merging onto the freeway. "I'm not going to act all trippy-universe-hippie shit, but swear to God, if you knew him, he would've thought it was the perfect day."

Whoa. I leaned back against the seat and buried my hands in the pockets of that coat. Eric's idea of a perfect day—the day I forgot to give back the coat—was the day the time loop ended.

"Why are you smiling like that?"

I hadn't even realized I was smiling. I glanced over at Nick and asked, "Like what?"

He kind of laughed, his eyes crinkling in the happy way that I adored, and said, "You're scary-grinning."

"I'm not scary-grinning."

"You seriously were." He shook his head and said through a big smile, "Like some creeper who likes watching televised parades and dressing cats in sweaters."

He was quoting himself, from one of the forgotten Valentine's Days, and he had no idea. I fell hard into his teasing laughter, the warm rumble of happiness that should've always been his sound, and I felt incredibly grateful.

Thank you, Eric.

"I'm not a creeper." I scooted closer to him on that old truck's bench seat. "I'm just a girl who is incandescently happy at the moment."

His eyes met mine, his grin mischievous, and he said, "Any girl willing to rip off Austen to express her happiness is totally my kind of creeper."

And I was.

I was absolutely Nick Stark's kind of creeper.

I glanced down at my arm and smiled. I couldn't see the tattoo through the sweater and jacket, but I could almost feel it buzzing. Its words were like an electrical current burned into my skin.

Everything in my life *had* changed, but I had zero regrets.

I had a marvelous time ruining everything

PLAYLIST

1. Lover (Remix) [feat. Shawn Mendes] | Taylor Swift, Shawn Mendes
2. Let's Fall in Love for the Night | FINNEAS
3. coney island (feat. The National) | Taylor Swift, The National
4. New Romantics | Taylor Swift
5. betty | Taylor Swift
6. Play with Fire (feat. Yacht Money) | Sam Tinnesz, Yacht Money
7. ...Ready For It? | Taylor Swift
8. The Passenger | Volbeat
9. Street Lightning | The Summer Set
10. Sabotage | Beastie Boys
11. Nervous | Shawn Mendes
12. the last great american dynasty | Taylor Swift
13. Ghost Of You | 5 Seconds of Summer
14. fuck, I'm lonely (with Anne-Marie) | Lauv, Anne-Marie
15. Lose Yourself | Eminem

16. Amnesia | 5 Seconds of Summer

17. fOol fOr YoU | ZAYN

18. So Damn Into You | Vlad Holiday

19. I Don't Miss You at All | FINNEAS

20. Forgot About Dre | Dr. Dre, Eminem

21. gold rush | Taylor Swift

22. Everything Has Changed (feat. Ed Sheeran) (Taylor's Version) | Taylor Swift, Ed Sheeran

23. Driving in the City | Brandon Mig

24. The Joker And The Queen (feat. Taylor Swift) | Ed Sheeran, Taylor Swift

https://open.spotify.com/playlist/4gex4YF0tYiPSuhID55dEY

ACKNOWLEDGMENTS

Thank YOU, delightful reader, for picking up this book. You've affected my life in an incredible way, playing an integral part in my dream come true, and I'm eternally grateful.

Thanks to Kim Lionetti, my incredible agent, for giving me a dream career that you constantly make better. You are more than I ever knew I needed.

Jessi Smith, my editor—the vision you have for books is nothing short of remarkable, and I'm so lucky to have worked with you. You make my thoughts and words SO. MUCH. BETTER, and I'm BEYOND thankful for your expertise.

To all the talented folks at SSBFYR and S&S Canada—Marketing and Digital Marketing, Publicity, Sales, Education & Library, Subsidiary Rights, Production, Supply Chain—thank you so much for the incredible work you've done on this book. Liz Casal and Sarah Creech—thank you for another swoony cover that I love so much. Morgan York and Sara Berko—thank you for overseeing the nuts and bolts of the process and making sure the story became an actual book!

Thank you to my Berklete friends for letting me join your gang and hang out with you all the time (aka group chat). You've made the highs higher and the lows less low, and I don't know what I'd do without you.

Thanks to all the Bookstagrammers, TikTokkers, YouTubers, and bloggers; you're out here doing incredible work for zero compensation, and I'm really not sure what we've done to deserve you. You are talented, amazing creators, and I cannot thank you enough for every single thing that you do in the name of books. Haley Pham, I adore you and your delightful followers.

Lori Anderjaska—you're the coolest badass in SW Omaha; thank you for being my 402 editor and for lending me your children's names.

Also—thanks to Taylor Swift, for writing songs that feel like books.

And the fam:

Mom—you're amazing and I love you more than words. I wouldn't have THIS without you.

Dad—I miss you every day.

Cass, Ty, Matt, Joey and Kate—thank you for being incredible human beings who make me proud and crack me up. I think you're all super cool, but that's probably just because I built you.

AND KEVIN:

Thank you for accepting that my happy place is often alone in a room with my computer. Thank you for accepting that I suck at the domestic arts, and that I only bring six recipes to this relationship

(I still can't believe that number). Every love interest I write is inspired by you, because every love interest should be thoughtful, respectful, sarcastic, kind, and really freaking hilarious. You are by far my favorite human, and I don't deserve you.

ABOUT THE AUTHOR

Lynn Painter writes romantic comedies for both teens and adults. She is the author of *Better Than the Movies* and *Mr. Wrong Number*, and she is a regular contributor to the *Omaha World-Herald*. She lives in Nebraska with her husband and pack of wild children, and when she isn't reading or writing, odds are good she's guzzling energy drinks and watching rom-coms. You can find her at LynnPainter.com, on Instagram @LynnPainterKirkle, or on Twitter @LAPainter.